FLOATING SHORE

BOOKS BY SALLY ITO

Floating Shore

Frogs in the Rain Barrel

FLOATING SHORE

Sally Ito

THE MERCURY PRESS

The publisher gratefully acknowledges the financial assistance of the Canada Council for the Arts and the Ontario Arts Council, and further acknowledges the financial support of the Government of Canada through the Book Publishing Industry Development Program for our publishing activities.
The publisher gratefully acknowledges the assistance of the Multiculturalism Directorate of the Department of Canadian Heritage in the publication of this book.

THE AUTHOR IS GRATEFUL FOR THE ASSISTANCE OF

COMMITTED TO THE DEVELOPMENT OF CULTURE AND THE ARTS

Edited by Beverley Daurio
Cover design by Gordon Robertson
Composition and page design by TASK

Printed and bound in Canada
Printed on acid-free paper

1 2 3 4 5   02 01 00 99 98

Canadian Cataloguing in Publication Data
Ito, Sally, 1964-
Floating shore
ISBN 1-55128-063-9
I. Title.
PS8567.T63F56 1998   C813'.54   C98-932204-1
PR9199.3.I86F56 1998

The Mercury Press
Toronto, Canada   M6P 2A7

TABLE OF CONTENTS

I

II

Acknowledgements

I would like to thank the many people who assisted me in writing this book. In particular I would like to acknowledge Greg Hollingshead who assisted in the development of this collection at its earliest stage. Thanks must also go to Sandra Birdsell and Alistair MacLeod, who provided guidance on individual stories. For editorial assistance, thank you, Beverley Daurio. Your dedication and patience is much appreciated. For financial assistance, I would like to thank the Alberta Foundation for the Arts and the Banff Centre, both of whom provided me with the time and money to write this book. Above all I would like to thank my family: my husband, Paul Dyck, for his constant support and patience; my mother, Akiko Ito, for all the stories; my sister and brother, Daniel and Cathy, for their abiding interest in the things that I do. Thanks also to my father Kunitaro John Ito (now deceased), a provider of stories in his own quiet way. Thanks also to my in-laws, Peter and Kathie Dyck, for all the child care that allowed me the time and energy to concentrate on writing. Last but not least, thank you, Kenji Dyck, for being yourself, my son.

Some of the stories in this collection have appeared previously in slightly altered forms. "Foreigners" was published in *Dandelion,* "A Child of the Age," "Black Water Angel" and "Teruko" were published in *Grain.* "Japonisme" was published in *Prism.* "Shrine Maiden" was published in *The Capilano Review,* and was given honourable mention in the 1997 National Magazine Awards.

Section I

Between us lies the floating shore
Who can bridge it?
Neither you nor I
but only the winged bird
whose cry echoes
above the distant tide.

— Seizan, *Songs of the Shorebird*

MISSIONARY

For the hundredth anniversary of the Kyowadan Christian Mission Board of Japan, it was decided that a book containing various reminiscences and reflections of past missionaries would be compiled and published. A call went out to all former missionaries to submit stories of their experiences.

The early Kyowadan missionaries— many of them young university graduates from the cities— were sent out to remote, rural areas of the country. They were to cover these areas by bicycle, evangelizing to the villagers using large picture cards known as kami-shibai. When a missionary arrived in a certain village, he would set up his cards in a conspicuous place and do a show on the life of Jesus. This was the only way a missionary could reach the illiterate villagers.

The following account was submitted by the widow of Takamura Shinkichi. Takamura, a literature graduate, served the Board for only two years. This account was the only available piece written on Takamura's work. It was not included in the book because of various theological inconsistencies and literary digressions. However, it remains a compelling account of the time in which these dedicated missionaries lived and worked.

When I think now of what happened, I can see the workings of His grace in it all. But it would not have been prudent of me to have reported things the way I saw them to the Mission Board. They simply would not have understood. Even for an educated man such as myself, things are often not what they seem. A villager once told me I was too intellectual, a creature of the city, and therefore able to perceive only what I had read and not what I had truly seen.

I had just graduated from university in the city when the Board sent me out to a small area in the south full of poor but hardy farming folk. I was given the bare necessities— a sturdy and reliable bicycle, one good suit, and a set of picture cards. I had a room in a mid-sized town, rented to me by a kindly who was not Christian but who was sympathetic to church people, and from there I ventured out daily to the surrounding villages.

Little information was given to me about the people of the area. I assumed, not incorrectly, as I later found out, that the people there believed in spirits— spirits of the dead, spirits of animals, spirits of trees and other such natural phenomena. It was not easy to bring them the story of yet another spirit, the Holy Spirit, Who, in Jesus Christ, was God with us.

I began with great hope to tell the story of the gospel using my beautiful picture cards. They were given to me by the Board. The story of Christ was drawn with such beauty and excellence that I handled the cards with care, taking great pains to make sure they were never soiled or bent out of shape. When I first presented the story, the villagers were curious and drew near with great interest, but as soon as they discovered that I was telling a story of a great spiritual truth, they laughed at me. "You're just another story-teller like the rest," they said. "What makes your story so special?" Soon afterwards, they began taunting me, calling me the Yaso, after the name Yesu, our Lord Jesus. "Yaso! Yaso!" they cried out. "Here he comes to save us with his dead god!"

It was most disheartening: I would have soon given up if not for my sheer belief that in Christ I would prevail. I knew *I* must prove His truth to the people. The Lord, whom I knew sensed my hardship, provided me with a friend, Jimbo, who lived in the same town. Jimbo had come also from the city and was now teaching high school. Together, we often prayed for the many souls we met daily.

"It is hard to reach these people," Jimbo told me one night after prayer. "They believe in their truth as much as we believe in ours."

"There can only be one truth," I said, "and that is the truth of Jesus Christ."

"Yes, but Jesus is all-powerful. Do you not think there are other ways for His truth to be revealed?"

It was a perplexing question, one I could not immediately answer.

Indeed. It is not for us to know the mysterious workings of His grace. No one knows the hour, the moment of His coming. When I first set out on that strange day of my encounter, it seemed like any other day. I had no portent, no sign or omen of things to come. I arose at dawn, as usual, and after packing the lunch the old woman had given me, I set out on the road towards the villages.

It was a fine day. The sun was climbing up into the sky above the hills. The farmers were already out planting their seedlings. Slowing down, I pulled up to a paddy belonging to an old woman known as the village gossip. She came occasionally to my shows, but only to observe me and, perhaps, report my behaviour to the others. She was quick to call me Yaso, but ever inquisitive and curious, she was never one to turn down an opportunity to talk.

"Obasan!" I called out to her.

A small bevy of straw hats turned up towards my voice.

"Obasan!" I called out again.

The old woman pretended to ignore me. She continued working, her face rigidly fixed to the ground. Her legs moved like stumps through the mud as she planted seedling after seedling. *Why did she not respond?* I thought indignantly. *Please Lord*, I prayed. When I opened my mouth, my voice rang out with the robust words of a hymn:

All for Jesus! All for Jesus!
All my being's ransomed pow'rs;
All my thoughts and words and doings,

All my days and all my hours!

I sang loudly and with great feeling. The old woman immediately looked up at me.

"Shush!" she hissed, waving her hands at me in annoyance. But I continued:

Since my eyes were fixed on Jesus
I've lost sight of all beside;

So enchained my Spirit's vision,
Looking at the Crucified!

The hymn filled me with wonderful strength. And now the others were beginning to notice. They stopped their work to look at me.

The old woman angrily strode up to me.

"Be quiet, you!" She waved her hand at my face.

I paused and looked down at the woman.

"But Obasan," I said, "do you know what I am singing? A song about the wonderful love of Jesus."

"Cheh!" the woman spat. "I don't want to hear any of your Yaso talk."

"Yesu," I corrected.

"Yaso," she spat again. Her eyes grew into dark, suspicious slits. "Your Yaso is an evil spirit. Bad things are happening in the village because of him."

"Bad things?" I said. "What bad things?"

The woman's voice grew low. "Stealing," she hissed. "That's what. Saké, potatoes, rice— stolen."

"Really!" I was shocked. Then I thought for a moment. "But Obasan, what does Jesus have to do with all this? You must report this stealing to the authorities."

The old woman fiercely shook her head. "No, no. You don't understand," she said, "no one can do anything about this thief. He's too small, too smart. And now he's getting bold. Wanting things he shouldn't have. Wanting things we haven't given him."

"Well, if you know who he is," I said, "why have you not reported him?"

The old woman cackled loudly and slapped her thigh. "Yah, Yaso, you make me laugh, you are so blind. No one can catch this thief."

The old woman shook her head again. She abruptly turned away from me and strode off. But after a moment's pause, she came scuttling back. Without speaking a word, she took her wrinkled fingers and traced a line over her eyes and up over her nose as if shaping an imaginary snout. Then she squinted, her eyes narrowing to dark slits. She put her two fingers upright against her temples in the form of ears, and bobbed. She was performing a little dance in the paddy, cackling most hideously the whole while.

"I do not understand," I said flatly. It was uncomfortable watching her; I could not imagine what this rather silly dance had to do with this grave matter of stealing. I tried to steer the conversation back to that topic again.

"This stealing— are you sure it is not someone from the village?"

The old woman suddenly stopped. She looked indignant.

"Of course not," she said coldly. "No one from this village!" she added adamantly. Then she drew back. "Go away!"

"Wait!" I called out, but it was too late. The woman had hastily removed herself over to the farthest corner of her paddy and was now planting out of sequence to avoid me.

I struck out a few bars of another hymn, but my voice wavered. It was apparent no one was listening. They had all gone back to their planting. Dejected, I got onto my bicycle and pedalled away.

Why could I not speak the right words? I wondered. Words that could move the heart, as Christ had moved mine? What was preventing me from communicating His glorious message? I remembered an old man who had asked me questions once— suspiciously, but with curiosity.

— *How could a god become a man? He wouldn't be a god, then, would he?*

— *This God I believe in became a man to know what it was to be one of us.*

— *I would rather stay a god. It is hard to be human.*

— *But this god, Jesus, wanted to know what it was like to be human. He became one of us to know us.*

— *Ah, then he has come to play tricks with us, has he? To torment us?*

— *No, no. We tormented Him and killed Him. We blamed Him for all our suffering. We did not know who He was.*

— *Then this god died at a human's hand?*

— *Yes.*

— *Then I say what I said before. This is not a god.*

Lord, I prayed, remembering this conversation as I pedalled uphill, *please give me words that I may move those who hear Your message.* When I finally reached the crest of the hill, I stopped to wipe my sweaty brow. Down below, in the valley, I could see the next village I was to visit. I was not eager to go there. The people were hostile and suspicious. Weeks before, someone had thrown a rotten vegetable at the picture card I was showing the children. The unsightly stain from the splatter remained on Christ's image despite my attempts to clean it off.

Thinking about that village made my stomach form knots. I turned away from the sight of it and looked towards the mountain. For the first time, I noticed a trail snaking upward. It looked like a tunnel—deep and green, cool and inviting. *Come away*, it appeared to say. I glanced nervously back at the village. It was still there, an ugly huddle of brown buildings brooding on the edge of the shimmering paddies that surrounded it. A cool rush of air blew across my cheek. The breeze was coming from the trail. I suddenly wanted to know where it led. It was a most curious and spontaneous desire.

Pushing my bicycle off the road, I determined I would climb the trail. But then I caught a glimpse of the cards. They lay upwards, Christ's figure on top. I realized I could not leave the cards there. The old woman had spoken of thieves. If the cards were stolen, I could never forgive myself. It would be a betrayal of everything I had come here to do for Christ. With firm resolve, I took the cards off my bike, strapped them to my back, and set off on the path.

The cards soon proved to be burdensome and unwieldy as the trail grew steeper. Thick heavy branches kept snagging on them and scratching their surfaces. Afraid of damaging the pictures, I stopped to turn the story inside out. Then I resumed my struggle up the trail as it wound its way upwards. This trail must have been for pilgrims or woodcutters, I thought. No one could possibly live at the top! Far up ahead, I noticed a faint light. As I approached, the light grew brighter. I emerged into a large, sunny meadow. The grass was thick and deep, tinged with the gold hue of the sun. Insects hummed over the meadow, the dull beating of their wings vibrating in the air.

Where am I? I wondered, wading into the thick grass as if into water. In the distance, I perceived the winged tips of a wooden rooftop. I headed towards it at once. As I neared it, I could see that it was the abandoned shell of an old shrine. In front of it were two nubbly and worn statues of foxes. A chipped dish with crusted grains of rice lay at the foot of one statue. I recognized it at once as an offering dish. It was empty, and looked as if it had not been used for a long time. *How curious*, I thought, recalling a conversation I had recently had with a villager.

— *We have our gods to whom we give offerings already. Why should we worship yet another god?*

— *This god does not need your offerings! He Himself has made the offering for you*— *the offering of His Son once and for all. Think how weak your gods are, needing your food and drink! The God of all gods does not need such things from men.*

— *Then what does he want of us?*

— *Our repentance, our love.*

— *Love? Pah! What would our love get us? More hardship and suffering? We have enough already.*

I picked up the dish, pondering the villager's bitter words. If, indeed, they were still offering food to the gods, why then were these dishes empty? I looked around me. The place was clearly abandoned. When had the villagers stopped their pilgrimages, stopped giving offerings? I had not heard of any drought or famine in the area and usually at such times, people were more observant than less. Could it be that these villagers were neglecting their own gods? This was to me a strange sign of a most perverse evil. Had not one man cried out to Christ— help thou my unbelief?

My stomach rumbled loudly, startling me. I glanced up at the sun and noticed by its position that it was noon. The hike up the hill had me hungry, and now my body was reminding me of its want of nourishment. Perhaps the empty offering dish had triggered such a response. I set down the cards that were on my back and took out my lunch box. When I opened it, I saw the usual three riceballs, but beside them was a special treat— a thin slice of fish! How appetizing it looked! I started first with a riceball, quickly stuffing it into my mouth. Its sweet stickiness was as refreshing as a drink of cold water. Now for the fish! I had eagerly picked up the thin slice of smoked cod with my chopsticks when I realized I had forgotten to pray. The riceball in my throat went down like a lump of clay. *Oh, Lord! Please forgive me! How gluttonous I must look!*

I set aside my lunchbox, and closed my eyes.

Dear Father in Heaven, forgive me my haste in eating. I thank You for Thy provision. Lord, be with me this day as I witness to those who do not yet know Thee. Help me reach but even one soul, Lord, so that he may taste of Your Love through Thy Son, Lord Jesus, in Whose name I give this prayer. Amen.

I opened my eyes and was about to reach for my lunchbox when I was startled to see a man squatting in front of me. He was dressed in tattered skins, looking dirty and squalid. His eyes, yellow with dark centres, were shaped like bright hard moons. In his hand was my empty lunchbox.

"Hey!" I cried out.

The man drew back, but he grinned widely, exposing a black cavern of rotting teeth. Rice stuck to his beard and throat. He scratched off the sticky grains and thrust his fingers into his mouth, making loud smacking noises.

"You have eaten my lunch!" I said, feeling terribly disappointed, for I had been very hungry. The man did not respond to my words. He only clutched the lunchbox tighter, his fingers curling around the edges like sharp claws. His chest heaved with breathing, although he did not make a sound.

"Who are you?" I said, leaning forward. Slowly, I extended my hand in a gesture of good will. The movement startled the man. He hastily withdrew. The nauseous stench of sweat like the odour of rotting fish filled the air. I held back a choke.

The man lingered away and then tentatively returned. He dropped the lunchbox and began poking at the picture cards.

"Don't touch!" I said abruptly.

The man cowered. Instantly, I felt regret.

"I'm sorry," I said, changing the tone of my voice. "Don't be frightened. I don't mean any harm."

Slowly, I stepped towards the man. He hissed and drew back. But he did not run away. He stood behind the statue, his hands curled around the stone body of the fox.

"You like these cards, do you?" I called out, waving one.

The man drew near.

"Would you like to hear a story?" I said slowly and soothingly. "The greatest story on earth?" I took the cards. "Now this is the God, Jesus Christ, who became man to redeem us from our sins. To bring light into the darkness." The man drew closer; his eyes were fixed on Christ. He followed my hand as it pointed at the man in the pool with the dove over his head— at the same man walking alone in the desert— talking on the mountain to a great crowd— with a woman bent down pouring oil over his feet— eating with a group of men— clasping his hands in a garden— carrying a wooden cross— dying on that cross— being put into a tomb— suddenly alive again. The man's yellow eyes followed after the other man's into his journeys, into his days and nights, into his moments with men, into his moments alone. "Now this is the God, Jesus Christ, who became man to redeem us from our sins. To bring light into the darkness."

I was repeating myself. The rolled-away tombstone picture brought out an urgent grunt from the man to begin again. And so I did. Once more. Twice. Thrice.

The afternoon was slipping away. I thought of the other waiting village. I must stop this repeated telling. I will pray for him, I thought. *Poor soul— he must be a crazy mountain hermit.* But there was little I could do for him.

The man reached out for the cards.

"No, no," I said softly, "I cannot give these to you. I need them to tell the others. You must understand. I need them."

The man began to whimper.

What a pitiful creature! I shook my head sadly. I made exaggerated motions of prayer, clasping my hands, bowing my head and closing my eyes.

"Lord," I said loudly. "This man seeks out Thy truth. May Thy Son, the Lord Jesus Christ, touch his heart and cause him to repent and bring forth Your blessing and forgiveness. Amen."

When I opened my eyes, the man had vanished.

A cool breeze rustled through the trees as I headed down the mountain. At the bottom of the trail, I could see my bicycle. I felt a sudden urge to make haste, as if I had lost a great deal of time up that mountain. Quickly, I strapped the cards back on and then hurriedly pedalled to the next village. My mind was strangely numb, though at the same time I felt agitated, as if wanting to get things over quickly. Just as I entered the village, I was suddenly confronted with an angry crowd of villagers barring the road with upturned hoes and sickles in hand. Before I'd even had a chance to speak, they formed a tight circle around me.

"Get out, Yaso, and don't come back here!" growled one stocky man. He thrust his hoe at me threateningly.

"What is going on?" I said in complete bewilderment.

"You're bad luck. That's what. Get out!" the man said again, this time louder.

The crowd hissed. A baby began crying.

"I-I do not understand," I stuttered.

"There's a thief underfoot," the man said, "— a thief, y'hear me?"

From the side, an old man whimpered, "He's not afraid of us any more, he steals and he steals because the gods are not happy with us, that's why he steals— "

"What are you talking about?" I said, shaken. "I have not stolen anything! Look, you can check my bicycle, my bag."

I offered myself to them but they stood back, aloof.

The old man whined. "No, no— we don't want your god here. He makes our gods angry, he makes our friend steal, he does, he does, we didn't have that stealing before, no, because we gave him things, we did, always. Please, please go away."

The old man bowed deeply. He was pleading, his trembling, clasped hands raised high to the heavens. For a moment, I had a glimpse of belief— a ray of faith that hadn't been there before. With sudden clarity, I understood the meaning of the words *sore afraid*.

The stocky man stepped in front of the old one.

"Get out, Yaso!" he said to me again, waving his hoe. "And don't you ever come back!"

"But you d-don't understand, I-I am sure it is someone else," I said, my voice trembling. "You must report this to the police."

"Report this?" the man laughed in loud disbelief. The crowd laughed with him.

"Someone is stealing your things," I said. "You must stop him. Make a plan, trap him."

The crowd fell silent.

"I think you are all mistaken. This thief can be caught, *should* be caught." I tried to speak with authority. "I will go to town right now and tell the police commissioner."

I got onto my bicycle and looked at the faces of the villagers, each one etched with suspicion and doubt, as if drawn by a devilish hand. Penetrating their souls was no more possible than reaching into a painting and touching its subject.

"I'm sure this can all be settled," I said bravely.

I pedalled off, truly shaken and disturbed by their animosity. How could they think *me* a thief? I had been amongst them daily, preaching and telling my stories openly in their sight! And now, they thought I was a criminal! Quickly, I pedalled towards town, my mind racing. The pebbled surface of the road spun below me like a wheel. Who *were* they talking about? Why were they not doing something themselves? Why were they blaming me? It was all so perplexing, and yet I knew without a doubt that I *must* prove to them it was not me! I *must* absolve myself or they would never listen to the gospel. A nagging doubt that had plagued me when I first began my mission work began troubling me once more.

Was it a mistake for me to come here, to try and convert these people?

"No!" I answered myself aloud. "My Lord, I am doing the best I can!"

I spoke to the wind as it sighed through the trees. The leaves rustled loudly. I could feel a chill in the air. The sun was setting quickly and it was growing dark. Something pressed against my mind as if against water, a memory of something persistent, aching almost. *What is happening to me?* I thought. *What am I trying to remember?*

I stopped at the crest of the hill. My eyes wandered to an opening in the trees. A path, I thought distractedly. It looked vaguely familiar. I paused to think, and then I began to vividly recall what had happened only hours before— the climbing of the trail, the sweating with effort, reaching the meadow, seeing the old shrine. But there was something more... I closed my eyes.

A cool sensation as if of stone filled my mind, followed by a foul, fishy smell. *Stone. The rolling away of the tomb. Stone. Statues of animals. Foul, the smell of animals. Foul, too, the smell of...* I suddenly blinked open my eyes... *the smell of* that *man*! I remembered him now in great detail— the hair in long, stringy locks; arms blackened with dirt; breath the stench of dead fish. It was not a dream. No, the man had been quite real, standing there that bright afternoon in that grassy meadow by the shrine.

Now it dawned on me of whom the villagers had spoken. I began my descent down the hill in a mad rush towards town. *The sooner I get to town the better,* I thought. *The sooner this foolishness can be reported the better. The sooner, the sooner sense can come...*

And then, suddenly, in the gloom of twilight, two bright eyes distinct as moons appeared in the road right in front of me, as if waiting. Two eyes huddled in the darkness, in the cover of fur and hair. *What in God's name—* but it was too late. I drove sharply off the road, headlong into the woods. The bicycle struck a rock and I flew over the handlebars, landing with a hard thump on the ground. My head smacked against a tree. A sudden, nauseous surge of black filled my eyes.

Then silence.

A roaring wind began to blow down from above, thrusting past the trees, parting the branches like water. A great voice spoke.

"O SON OF MAN, WHY HAST THOU FORSAKEN ME?"

"Oh Lord," I cried out, "I have not forsaken thee!"

I groped for the voice, but touched only darkness.

"I have been Thy faithful servant. I have done for Thee what Thou hast asked. Let me show Thee…" I stretched out my hand. *The cards, I must show Him the cards. Where are they? Must be on the road, must go out there, yes, farther and farther— must reach for them, ah, there they are, but what is this? Double moons? Eyes! Horrid yellow eyes!* "Get off those cards, get off, I say! Those are mine!" *Your claws, your filthy dirty claws on my Sav— Oh, no! Now standing, oh, Lord, so big! Don't come to me; I am not worthy. Your footsteps, so heavy the ground is shaking. Quickly, must sit up, but this throbbing—* DON DON DON*— footsteps now louder—* DON DON DON. *Here he is— utter, utter darkness— now bending, such sharp round light— what is it? Ah, the moon! What is he doing now?* "Away from me, away!" *Ohhh, such pain, my leg pierced with many prickling nails. But what's this smell? Fish, the stench of dead fish. Now something trickling down my face. I can taste it. Salt. Ye are the salt of the earth. But if the salt loses its saltiness, how can it be made salty again? Up, up, I must get up and fight this darkness! Must get the cards! Lunge! Ah, there he is, My Lord. Dost Thou attend me? Dost Thou witness the work of Thy servant?*

Must lean towards him, for he cannot hear me. Oh, oh, the darkness! Wetness down my face. Salt, more salt. No, but this is blood, my blood that has been shed for many. Trickling, licking, lapping, rough gritty warmth against my broken body, pressing. Light is fading quickly. Head getting heavier, down, down, it goes. It is finished, I hear. And darkness came over the land.

When I awoke, it was morning. I was lying in bed in the old woman's home. Jimbo was at my bedside.

"Oi!" he said when my eyes fluttered open. His large ruddy face filled up my sight. "You're awake, thank God!"

I tried to sit up. A white patch slipped down my forehead, obscuring my vision momentarily. Jimbo gently pushed it aside before slipping his arm under my back to sit me up.

"I sure was worried about you," he said. "The old woman told me you hadn't come home last night. I got on my bicycle right away and went out looking for you. When I saw the wreck, I knew something terrible had happened. Then I saw you in the woods, lying on the ground, all bloody and wet. I don't know when the accident happened, but you must have been waiting a long time. You'd already bandaged yourself."

"Bandaged myself?"

Jimbo pointed to a dirty skin of orange fur by the bed. It was stained with blood.

"That was on your leg," he said.

I picked up the skin. It felt prickly and smelled smoky and wet, like charred fish. I pushed the blanket off me and noticed a fresh white bandage on my leg; I could feel the pain of the gash underneath. Then, with sudden clarity, I remembered the yellow half-mooned eyes, the crouching, the licking. A strange shudder went up my spine.

"The cards!" I said, sitting upright at once. "Where are the cards?"

"Cards?" Jimbo said perplexed.

"The picture cards!"

"There were no cards anywhere," Jimbo said, shaking his head.

I dropped my head into my hands.

"The cards!" I wailed. "They must be—"

Blackness lunged into my eyes.

"Whoa, there!" I heard Jimbo's voice. I felt his broad arm like a plank against my falling chest. "You're not better yet. You must rest."

Jimbo laid me down.

"Those cards don't matter," he said to me softly, "only their message does."

Only their message does. In a distant part of my memory, I could hear my voice speaking as if through a deep tunnel. *Now this is the God, Jesus Christ, Who became man to redeem us from our sins. To bring light into the darkness.* And I could see, through the tunnel, a dim light in the shape of a man descending the hills and taking his place among the villagers, so no one could speak any more evil of a god who knew at last what it was to be man, to suffer, and to die.

Shortly thereafter, I was recalled to the city by the Mission Board. Nothing was mentioned about what had happened to me, although I heard rumours that I had been recalled because of complaints. When the Board asked me for the cards, I told them I had given them away. This was my only deception, and as I said at the beginning, I did not feel at that time that it was prudent of me to speak truthfully of what had occurred. The cards were never recovered.

I leave these words now only as a written memory. I do not mean to justify myself through them in any way whatsoever. However the Lord may reveal Himself, I will ever remain His faithful servant. Amen.

KARAFUTO

Tane Tsuruta feels the hard clamp of clear plastic against her cheeks. A rush of cool oxygen fills her nose and mouth. She sneezes violently, then grabs at the mask and tears it off. "Mitsu!" she cries out for her son, but the ambulance attendant has grabbed her arms and is strapping them down. Tane writhes and wriggles.

"A feisty old one, isn't she?" the attendant says loudly to his partner.

"Please!" Tane hears the timid voice of her son interrupt. "She's never been to hospital." His face appears moon-like from behind the large attendant.

"Mitsu!" Tane's eyes dart toward him. "Washi doko ni tsure te iku no? Where are they taking me?"

"Daijobu, Mama," he says soothingly in Japanese, although his eyes look frightened. "I'm coming with you."

He clambers into the ambulance behind her. *Where are they taking me?* Tane wonders again. *Where?* No one will answer her. Desperate, Tane wriggles her arm out from one of the straps and tries to sit up. *I must get away now before it is too late. Before they come.* Pain shoots through her leg, forcing her down. Her whole body feels numb, like a large cumbersome log. She cannot control her movements although she can hear insistent, urgent voices. *Run! Run away!* The words pound, a steady throbbing from the bump of her head hitting the floor at the foot of the stairs. Suddenly the siren starts up— a low wail growing into a blare, too late a warning for anything, the shelling already starting, the guns exploding in the harbour. *Ta-ta-ta Ta-ta-ta Ta-ta-ta.* Tane squirms and twists; she feels the pebbled alleyway beneath her feet. *Which way now? Which way?* She twitches her head back and forth. *This lane or that one? Where does this labyrinth of streets lead? I must get out of the city; I must hurry.* Tane looks down at her feet. They have not moved an inch! She stretches out her arms again. "Help me," she cries, "help me escape!"

"Mama!" It is Mitsu. "Quit moving— lie still now. Everything will be all right." The ambulance lurches out onto the freeway. Tane's head jerks violently against the pillow; a hard lump of phlegm shoots up her throat. The hot light above her burns round and round like the morning sun, the same sun she woke up to long ago when she was pregnant. She is feeling it again, that same morning nausea and dizziness. *Where is that bucket? I need it now!* Quickly, quickly, one hand out to lean against the brothel wall, the other on the—but it is too late. Wetness dribbles out of Tane's mouth. A large freckled hand wipes it away. Who does the hand belong to? Tane rolls her eyes, squints. A face leans over— a red-bearded face, a man in a uniform. Tane recoils, her eyes filling with horror. Her right arm flails wildly in panic.

"Delusional," the paramedic mutters, withdrawing his hand.

Mitsu leans over her, mutters hard, "Mama, you must lie still."

Tane's fearful, rounded eyes take in the familiar broad squareness of her son's cheeks, the milky blue eyes, the natural curl of his brown hair now tapering into grey at the temples. He is her son, she is certain of that, but he does not look like her or his father. No, he does not even look Japanese at all. They noticed and said so. Especially Kenji-san's mother. "That can't be our son's boy," she said to Tane, implying, *Who do you think you are? Showing up at our doorstep, claiming to be our son's wife?* Tane's eyes dart to the red-haired man. Then back again to her son. She feels bewildered; things are blurred, layered like silt over the dense landscape from which her first memories emerged.

Karafuto— the place was cold and wet, the thickly forested mountains covered in a dense mist. Tane remembers the bracing wind on her bare arms, the harsh nubbled clods of dirt underneath her straw-sandalled feet. Behind her was the farmhouse, a crudely built shack pieced together by her father, one of the pioneers who had taken on the dream of Japan's unfolding destiny, its empire ever expanding, ever northward, even to this remote place, this raw land whose resources were like gold to those who could fashion out of dreams the hard substance of profit. Tane was the first child of the family to be born there; the others, a boy and a girl, had been born on the mainland. Even though a girl, she was named after her father's hopes. Tane— the word meant "seed."

Tane remembered little of those days with her family— only cruel and jarring moments that made her want to forget, but lingered in her memory, persistent as scars. She could still see, like a moving picture, her father chasing her brother around the yard, flailing him with a stalk of bamboo. The movements were jerky and hard, her father's voice harsh, angry. "Taro, you good-for-nothing idiot! You fool! Weakling!" Then Mayu's soft hand would gently come down on Tane's head, shielding her eyes. Her voice was soothing. "Don't look there. Look up! See, Tane, there's a pretty bird!" And suddenly the world was a blue expanse of sky, a yellow flutter of wings.

But even Mayu could not protect her little sister for long, not from those things Tane knew were inevitable. Like the ashes in the clay urn, her mother transformed, but still spoken of as if there, as if with them in the room. "Mother's going home now," Mayu explained to Tane, her voice trembling as she packed the urn into a wooden box, wrapped it in dark furoshiki. She handed the box to the man in the Western-style suit. Their father, standing by the door, did not move an inch. His face, sullen and grey, twitched with anger.

"Bow!" he roared. "Say goodbye to your mother!" He cuffed them all on the backs of their heads. Tane's jerked down from the blow, an involuntary bow. The man in the Western-style suit stiffly returned the gesture, and then walked out the door.

Tane remembered his receding figure growing distant and faraway, as if he had entered a darkened tunnel, the memory of his first visit slowly snuffed out by the second— a visit which was as marked and permanent in Tane's mind as the sun rising in the morning sky. This time, he was different, not morose, but jaunty, his step light and jocular as he walked up the path to the farmhouse. "Oi, beppin-san, pretty one, your father home?" Tane pointed to the house and followed him inside. She watched the two men sit down, and helped Mayu serve them drink. The man had asked for rikyu, the island's strong liquor, although it was only the middle of the day. As the two men drank, their faces grew redder, their voices louder. The man sidled up to Tane's father, leaned on his elbow. "Now look, Tanabe, if you do this you could buy yourself another sack of seed. Start over. They want girls like her. You've got two of them. Give me the younger one. You told me she was useless, didn't you? Give her to me. I'll look after her."

The next day, Tane felt the pinch of the man's fingers curl around her upper arm. "You're coming with me now," he said. He took her away from the farm. Tane remembered the clack of train wheels, the scenery shuddering past, an unfolding screen of mountain wilderness. It all felt oddly freeing, striking out on this adventure she knew nothing about. She had no idea what the destination meant— a big house by the harbour, the man said, would be her new home. He took her inside, where an old woman in a brown kimono awaited them, her eyes narrow and black, scrutinizing Tane's every move. She made Tane turn around, slapping her backside and thighs so hard Tane bit her lip hard not to cry out. The woman ignored her and continued pinching and poking. Finally satisfied, she took Tane roughly by the wrist and led her down the hall. Tane could faintly hear voices, high, bird-like voices growing louder. Sliding a door open, the old woman pushed Tane into a room in disarray, filled with half-clothed women. The voices stopped instantly. The women all stared at Tane, their sullen, moon-shaped faces opaque mirrors of indifference. One of the woman close to the door took Tane's hand.

"Hello, child— you're a pretty one, aren't you?"

"Pretty young is what she is," snapped an older, huskier voice.

The others laughed, tittering like joyless birds.

"Get her ready," the old woman's voice snapped. "We'll need her tonight."

They took her in, clothed her, did her hair— their hands swift but without feeling, curved with nails, powdered and perfumed. She was taken up a rickety wooden staircase and put into a small room with an oily lamp hanging on a string above a white pile of bedding. No one had told her what was going to happen there. Only the old woman had spoken, squeezing Tane's arm hard as they mounted the stairs. "You don't do a thing but lie there," she hissed. "You understand?"

Tane waited, half fearful, on the futon, her body quivering like a sparrow's. There was a thud of footsteps, then the door slid open with a snap. A man stumbled into the room, his breath reeking of rikyu. "Come here," he whispered hoarsely, grabbing Tane's arm, pushing her down on the futon. Tane squirmed. The man's grip tightened. His other hand began to roam over her body, slipping into her dress, pinching and jabbing. Tane wriggled to get away, but then she remembered the old woman's words: *You don't do a thing but lie there.* Tane bit her lip. How could that be? *I'll look at the light*, she thought, and focused her eye on the dangling yellow bulb pulsating over her. The man was on top of her. It was hard to see the light, but Tane twisted her head, stretched her neck. The yellow bulb flickered and flashed, then suddenly narrowed to a searing orange gash, Tane's eyes clenching shut like fists.

When she opened them again, the bulb was whole, pulsating like a star, distant, airy. The man was off her now, snoring loudly beside her. Slowly, without taking her eyes off the bulb, Tane felt between her legs. She drew her hand up to the light. It shimmered— a pale translucent red.

Tane's eyes blink open. She notices her hand, high up in the air. Quickly she lowers it. She has been dreaming again. Her eyes adjust slowly to the pale darkness around her. *Where am I?* she thinks. She can feel the stiffness of a bed beneath her. A thin blue sheet lies over her legs. She reaches down to touch them and feels the hard plaster of casts. *This is the hospital*, she thinks, groping at the wall for a light switch. A pale yellow beam flickers on, filling the curtained space around her.

Where is Mitsu? she wonders absently. She can hear noises through the curtain— other patients shuffling their sheets. Someone beside her is snoring very loudly. Tane wonders what the other patients look like. Were they all old like her?

"We are moving you to a home," Mitsu had announced a few days before, his voice shaking. "I'm sorry, Mama, but things have just become worse and Kana says—"

"Pah!" Tane spat at the sound of Mitsu's wife's name. But he continued nonetheless.

"Kana says you've been saying things to the children, especially Emi-chan, things she shouldn't hear."

Tane frowned. What things? Her granddaughter is thirteen; why shouldn't she know things Tane knew when she was her age? Things about being a woman. Like how to cover up the smell of one's monthly blood or how to ease the pain of a large organ.

But Mitsu was not listening. He talked hurriedly.

"Mama, it will be good for you. You can be with others your own age."

Tane's mouth curls into a shrivelled plum at the memory of his words. Her eyes grow small as seeds. She does not want to go to a home and has said so many times. It is clear they are trying to get rid of her. *How ungrateful of them*, she thinks. This would never happen if they had not left Japan. It was a mistake for the family to have immigrated to Canada. Tane had said so the minute Mitsu had spoken the thought. But he was enthralled by the new country he had visited on the agricultural exchange the college lab he worked for had sponsored. "Wide open spaces," he'd said, spreading out his arms. "So many different people there, I'd never stick out." The comment hurt Tane. She squinted at him then, tried to erase the features of his distinctive face into a blurred memory of his father, Kenji-san.

For years and years, Tane had carefully cultivated Kenji-san's name to mean something to her son. It was hard now to remember who the actual man had been. She had never really loved him, so there was no ache of passion in her memory. She only recalled that he was affable, friendly, a pleasant customer who knew something of the art of conversation and entertainment in spite of the fact that he was a grocer— or so he claimed he was. Tane had noticed his hands, pink and fleshy, softer than those of any of the other rugged regulars who worked the railways and pulp mills. Clearly, he had been raised in some environment more privileged than what was at hand on the island.

Kenji-san had taken a special liking to Tane, always asking for her, bringing her gifts of fruit and vegetables. Soon he grew bold, announcing his affections, his intent. "You're my favourite, my sweet one. I'm going to buy you out of this place so you'll be mine always." Tane didn't believe him at first. Where, after all, could a grocer get such money, especially during war-time? Tane waved her hand at him in dismissal. "No, really, I am!" he said to her again. He lowered his voice. "I'll be getting the money from the mainland. Things are getting dangerous over there. My family's worried. They're sending it all here to me, do you believe it? They think I'm such a prodigal, but when it comes to saving their skins, they come running to me. Don't you worry. There'll be plenty for me to buy you out of this place."

Those were the last words Tane had heard spoken by Kenji-san, and she lived on them those last days, floating airily through the brothel, her mind filled with plans for another life. If there were rumours that Japan was losing the war, Tane was oblivious. The men were always talking politics; things seemed no different than before.

It was early morning in late summer when the thunderous roar of explosions rocked the brothel, jolting the women awake. They ran to the windows. There was a clatter of footsteps on the street below and then a man burst through the door.

"It's an invasion!" he yelled. "They're in the harbour!"

Invasion. The sound of the word was engraved in Tane's memory. She had a mind to flee like all the others screaming in shock and horror, except for one thing. She had nothing. And what was the point of fleeing with nothing? The hard years of working in the brothel had taught her only that having nothing meant being a slave. That was how the old woman kept them under her control. Tane numbly watched the others scramble to get on their clothes and grab whatever they could out of their measly quarters. None of the girls had anything of value. Everything was taken by the old woman— their money, documents, jewellery, even gifts from customers. Instead of running outside with the others, Tane waited a while before slithering down the stairway to the old woman's room. She would get what she could out of this brief unexpected respite. The door, usually tightly closed and locked, was now airily open. Quickly, she slipped in undetected.

The room was in a mess— paper, clothes, boxes had been thrown on the floor. Tane began rifling through the drawers of the desk where she knew the old woman kept her money. *It's all ours anyway*, Tane justified to herself. But there was nothing in any of the drawers, just chits and receipts. *That old hag!* Tane cursed. *I should've known she'd take everything!*

BOOM! Another thunderous roar jolted the building, the glass windows shuddering loudly. Tane desperately took another look around the room. There, by the window, was a dresser that looked untouched. She lunged for its drawers. She would take anything now— clothes, rings, cuff-links, combs, earrings— anything she could sell later on. Tane thrust her hands into one of the drawers. It was full of silken handkerchiefs. Eagerly, she began stuffing them into her pockets. Then her hands closed on something lumpy at the back of the drawer. She pulled whatever it was out. A billfold stuffed with yen! Tane could not believe her luck. Her hands trembled.

Just then, the door slid open with a snap. Startled, Tane raised her head. A soldier loomed in front of her, a big red-bearded man, his body smelling rank and acrid.

The billfold slid out of Tane's hands, the yen fanning onto the floor. She fell backwards to the ground and began scraping herself into the corner. The soldier laughed loudly. He strode up to her, and snaked the tip of his rifle between her legs.

"Please!" Tane's calves snapped shut against the cold metal. Her trembling fingers reached for the large freckled hand on the barrel, began caressing the coarse fingers. "Please, don't kill me, please!" Her eyes flashed pleadingly at the soldier. Slowly, she slipped one arm out of her dress, and exposed her breast.

The gleam in the milky blue eyes was unmistakable. The man threw down his rifle and fell on Tane with all the fury and ache of a soldier's most base desire.

Mitsu finally comes to the hospital, late in the morning. He has brought Shiotani Sensei, the pastor.

"Good morning!" the pastor says cheerfully. "How are you, Tsuruta Obasan?"

Tane looks at the minister and grunts. Then she gives Mitsu a long hard look. Accusatory. She does not like these *yasos*— these Christians. When her son became one, it was as if he had succumbed to a disease— a disease of abandonment that spoke such terrifying words as, "I have come to turn a man against his father, a daughter against her mother." It was a disease that broke the natural order of things.

"Mama, you *must* talk to Sensei. You must confess to him what you did." Mitsu's voice is desperate.

Tane mutters out of the side of her mouth, "I don't need to confess. I know what I did. It's not a sin."

The pastor leans over to Tane. "It's not wrong, you know, to *feel* what you are feeling. But what you *did*— you just shouldn't have—"

"*I* didn't do anything wrong," Tane interrupts sharply. She points at Mitsu. "*He's* doing wrong. He's my son. He is supposed to look after me. It's his duty. After all, I *saved* him."

Shiotani Sensei looks at Mitsu. Mitsu shrugs.

"Saved him—" the pastor turns again to Tane, "from *what?*"

"Wartime," Tane mutters. "It was war-time and I—"

"I know," Mitsu interrupts his mother a little too abruptly. "She saved me from the war. That's what you told me, remember?" Mitsu turns to the pastor, quick to explain. "Mother's from Karafuto. We came over to the mainland after the invasion. Repatriates. Father died on the island."

Tane does not speak. An image lingers on in the fringes of her memory every time she hears her son speak of his father. A strange wash of guilt and shame like water shudders over that image, muddying it, but never quite erasing it. It had been no fault of her own and neither should she have felt sorry about the half-fanciful story she had made up for her son. *He died, killed by enemy soldiers, defending Karafuto.* But the *real* picture of the man was something she had never spoken about to anyone.

Lying wet, dirty and half-naked on the floor in the brothel, Tane was only too thankful the soldier had left her with only a kick in the side. Slowly, she sat up, then crawled painfully towards the scattered money.

"Kenji-san," she sniffled, stuffing the notes back into the billfold. "Kenji-san."

If she were to survive now, she would need the protection of a man. But when she arrived at the grocery, the place was eerily silent, empty.

"Kenji-san?" Tane called out.

There was no answer. Vegetables lay in boxes, dull green globes under muted light.

"Kenji-san?" Tane's shoes clattered on the floor as she made her way back to the kitchen.

He was hanging by a rope, a kicked-away chair underneath him.

Tane squinted. The tubby, friendly grocer's body had grown thin and elongated, like a match with a burnt-out head.

"Kuso!" Tane swore. She flung the billfold at the dangling corpse. "You stupid, stupid man!"

Tears like hard stones formed on the edge of Tane's lids. But there was no time to cry now. What should she do?

She would take his things. He had said he had family on the mainland. Maybe they would help her. Tane headed for the dresser in Kenji-san's bedroom. This time, everything was there, intact, untouched: money, certificates, bank books. Her hands worked swiftly, brisk and deliberate. She yanked out a drawer and shook it upside down. A bulky photo frame clunked onto the floor, a flutter of papers showering onto it. Tane's furious hands suddenly slowed, the fingers curling around the frame. A photo, sepia brown, of two schoolboys with their mother. There was Kenji-san, the short one, his stubby arm draped over his mother's knee, a trace of a smile on his boyish lips. A warm, salty pebble of water curled out of Tane's eyes, slid down her cheek, and dropped onto the glassy frame. *Shameless*, the word suddenly rose up in her mind like a sharp stick. *You are shameless.* A sob choked her throat. She swallowed hard. She couldn't stop now— there was no time for foolish sentiment. But the pebbles formed hard and quick on the cusp of her sight. Everything was marked by the shape of these melted stones, these tears dropping like rainwater onto everything she touched— a blotch of black on a leather purse, a smudge on some inked certificate, a salty, bulbed enlargement of someone's photographed face. Tears, she knew even then, were selfish. Tears that said, brutally, gratefully, *Arigato, Kenji-san. I will survive this, I promise you, shameless though I am. Forgive me.*

A year later, when she arrived on the mainland as a repatriate, she went immediately to the imposing gates of Kenji-san's parents' house with Mitsu in her arms and Kenji-san's documents tucked securely in the front flap of her kimono. She knew every word she would tell his parents: *Kenji-san died valiantly, nobly to protect this*— his only son, the one to whom she had given birth alone in the dark, dirt-floored kitchen of the old brothel; the one whom she had nourished from her small, sagging breasts; the one for whom she had bribed officials with her body for a birth certificate. She knew what she must to do to survive. In front of his parents, she would bow her head deeply, her forehead pressed to the backs of her hands on the tatami; she would be humble, but not grovelling; she would fight hard for her son's life, as she hoped he would one day fight for hers.

"Ahh— Karafuto." The pastor nods his head deeply. "That's an old, old name."

"Only Mama's generation calls it that now," Mitsu says. "It's gone back to what it was— Sakahalin."

"I know." The pastor nods. "It was tragic— all those Japanese overseas, fleeing for their lives at the end of the war."

Tane closes her eyes, remembering those last days of chaos— running down the alleyway from Kenji-san's empty shop, joining the crowd of others who flowed through the streets like dark oil, trying to find a way out of the city. They travelled overland, neither sleeping nor eating, climbing the heavily misted hills, trampling through wet, dank forest, in hopes of finding refuge or passage back to the mainland in another harbour city, but by the time they arrived, it too, was occupied. "Go back," they were told, so back they went, and now the conquest was complete, victorious soldiers clomping up and down the streets, red flags flapping from the flagpoles. Tane had no choice but to return to the brothel, to creep into its abandoned war-torn frame and suffer quietly the indignities of her broken, weary body.

If only it had ended in the shallow darkness of that paper-walled house. If only the nest of her small existence there could have sheltered her for eternity. But soon that sickness was upon her— the one she dreaded most— the one which woke her to the sun, made her crawl outside, one hand wrapped around her bloated belly, the other inching forward on the floor. She would barely make it to the rusted pail by the door, lean one hand on the wall, before her head would lurch into its tinny circle and fill it with the pungent steam and odour of vomit. Again and again she would lunge, until there was nothing but clear spittle dribbling out of the corner of her mouth.

"You're pregnant, aren't you?" Sayuri, one of the other girls who had returned to the brothel, had said to her. Her voice was cold, indifferent. She looked mildly disgusted, inconvenienced almost. For weeks, she had been freely plying her trade as before, gleeful with the results, rubles in hand. Now that they had conquered Karafuto, the soldiers had become civilized and were willing to pay her for her services. And now, there was no more middle-man— the old woman had long before disappeared.

But Tane was not in any shape to work. The sickness was on her, the nausea worse than her monthly blood.

I must get rid of this, she thought. And there was only one way, one place to do it.

"It must have been terrible," Mitsu says. "Wasn't it, Mama?"

There is silence.

"Mama?"

Tane isn't listening. She has turned her head to the window and is looking at the way the morning light filters through the shuttered blinds of the window. There is something familiar about that light— the slanted patterns, shaft after shaft, falling onto the floor, onto the bed, onto her body.

When Tane had stood at the top of the carpeted stairs in Mitsu's four-bedroom suburban house, her two hands braced against the wall, she was prepared to do the unnatural to show Mitsu what duty was, to show him her survival depended on him. *His wife's out*, she thought, *and the children are at school. Now is the time.* She closed her eyes, remembering that other staircase, narrow and rickety, steeply climbing to the upper rooms where she had worked. So many men had clunked up those stairs, their bold, dense bodies aching in hunger for her, and quickly were they sated, their hard limbs collapsing into a muddle of sleep and sweat beside her. Later, they would tumble down those stairs, some so drunk, so careless, they'd injure themselves— cutting their brows, bruising their arms and legs. Now Tane stood like them at the top of those stairs, her trembling hands pressed against the walls. The watery stone swelled in her stomach, pushed itself forward like a threat. Tane wished she could shape the stone out of her body, toss it down the stairs, let it roll harmlessly away. But she was attached to the thing. They must go together.

The first step was into airy darkness, and the rest was the raucous tumble of bone and muscle, heart and head, rattling against the stairs. When Tane opened her eyes, the morning sun streamed through the diamond panes in the hall window, through the tears in the ripped paper doors, dappling light on Tane's crumpled, broken body.

When Mitsu found her, Tane writhed and turned, stretched out her hand to touch her son. Deliriously, she spoke: "Good Mitsu, my son, Mitsu. I didn't mean to hurt you. I didn't know you, then. It was war-time. Everything so bad war-time. I wanted to go back to the mainland. Couldn't. Was stuck. And then you growing, growing in my stomach. Good Mitsu— always growing, no matter what I did, no matter if I didn't eat for days, no matter if they hurt me— soldiers hurting, that's their job— no matter what I did. Good Mitsu, always growing, always growing. Growing up to look after your mother."

SHRINE MAIDEN

Hanako neatly folded the red hakama and placed them on the square, kerchief-like furoshiki. The red trousers contrasted starkly with the drab cotton cloth she used to wrap them in. Taking the ends of the furoshiki, she tied them together to form a neat bundle. She would return the costume to the shrine priest that day. It was the last time she would ever wear it.

Hanako gazed at the mirror in front of her. Now in her city clothes, she looked like any other ordinary Japanese woman, dressed in a white blouse with a lace collar, a tight brown skirt, and taupe stockings with reinforced toes. Only her hair looked slightly odd, its wavy bulk a little too sensuous, too voluptuous for the demure features of her face. At the shrine, Hanako kept it pulled back into a long thick braid that looked like the gnarled straw rope that hung above the offering box. Now that work was finished, Hanako loosened the knot at the end of the braid and shook out her hair. A trembling mass of curls swept over her back. She opened her purse and took out a brush. Languorously, she pulled it through her hair. *Shaaa. Shaaa. Shaaa.*

There was a thud of footsteps down the hall, then a flutter of red hakama rushed through the door, white sleeves flapping like wings into the room. "Hana-chan! Are you leaving already? Hana-chan, we'll miss you! We've got to go, the priest's waiting!" The young women hurried out of the room as quickly as they had entered. Hanako suppressed a smile. *They're all so young!* she thought to herself. Maybe they seemed more so to her, now that she was leaving. She had announced her engagement the previous week. The priest seemed disappointed, although he tried to hide it. "Getting married? That's a shame, it is, I mean, for us. But for you, my goodness, what an occasion."

She was sorry to have to quit. It had been a good part-time job. But the shrine's position on the matter was clear. Only the unmarried could be shrine maidens.

The crunch of Hanako's shoes on the gravel path from the shrine echoed through the trees. The red cedars lining the path were like pillars in a great hall, mute wooden monuments to the primeval source worshipped in the shrine's inner sanctum. Only the head priest was allowed inside; only he could glimpse the secret of the gods. But Hanako was only vaguely curious; whatever the truth was, it was simply out of reach. Her role was to assist the priest— to hand him the sacred wands with the white streamers, pass him the cups of rice wine. She was to be a perfect instrument of ritual, pure and chaste in the performance of her duties.

The wind sighed through the trees; the branches creaked and shuddered. A spray of needles fell to the ground. Hanako paused and turned back to the shrine. She could see in the distance the lone straw rope, thickly braided, hanging down from the roof. It was swaying slightly, as if someone had shaken it to make a prayer, but no one was in sight. A dull but resonant sound, the noise of the bell when the rope was shaken, echoed through the trees: *kah-ran, kah-ran, kah-ran.*

Hanako turned again, this time forward. She took a few steps down the path. Now she could hear the sound of traffic beyond the shrine's gates. The muffled roars, the honking, grew louder, clearer as her feet moved ahead in quick, clipped strides. At the threshold of the gate— the orange pillared torii— she could see the whole city spread out before her. Plunging as if into a dark stream, she let the traffic of passing pedestrians swallow her up and carry her to the centre of the city.

Norihide was waiting at the train station.

"Hana-chan!" he called out, waving to her. "You're late." He grabbed her hand, squeezing it a little too tightly. The smell of his cologne was overpowering. He was wearing his usual date ensemble— a pair of chinos he had bought at a store in San Francisco, a polo shirt with a cardigan tastefully draped over the shoulders, and dark tan loafers. Tucked under his left arm was a square leather pouch.

"It was my last day at the shrine," Hanako said.

"Gan-chan told me a good place for steak." Norihide pulled Hanako through the crowded intersection. "It's around that corner, near the west entrance."

Hanako nodded. Norihide wasn't listening. She followed his back as it wriggled through the crowd, darting in and out of the light. She saw him as an object then, the muscled back moving like a carved plank through a faceless sea of people. *I don't know him very well*, she reflected to herself. They had met at a college function only a few months before and had gotten along rather well. They had exchanged phone numbers and begun dating. He was pleasant. Hanako could say she did not mind him.

The only thing she regretted was losing that shrine job. But she could not blame Norihide for that.

After dinner, they went to a movie. Norihide picked an American one, a romantic comedy. When the couple in the movie finally got together after all their troubles, Norihide squeezed Hanako's hand in the darkness as if in triumph. Later, after they left the theatre, they went for a walk around the station. Although it was not very chilly, Hanako felt obligated to slip her arm through Norihide's and lay her head against his shoulder as she'd seen other women do with their lovers. She was always watching other couples, even on their walks, noticing how they'd slip quietly into a darkened nook where she knew the entrances to the love hotels were hidden. Norihide and she were too timid to go to one. The most adventurous thing they had done was sit on a bench in the park together at night. He had kissed her using his tongue and attempted to touch her breasts. Hanako did not protest, but arched her back and looked at the moon. All around her, she could hear the rustling and grunting of other lovers. It was an oddly soothing sound; it made her feel as if she and Norihide were doing the right thing. They fit in splendidly.

Their walk that night led them back to the station with its bright lights, its bustle of people. Norihide walked Hanako to the platform where her train was waiting. She rode the futsu, a regular train that made all the stops on the line. Her station was a minor one near the end called SAKURANOMICHI. The area had been given its name a long time ago, during the spring, when its narrow streets were covered with fallen cherry petals.

Norihide gave Hanako a swift peck on the cheek. Hanako's head dropped deferentially, properly, as if out of habit. She could see the glint on her engagement ring; it was as bright as a star.

The trainmaster blew his whistle. Quickly, Hanako boarded the crowded train, letting the bustling throng draw her inside. As the train pulled away, she could see Norihide through the cracks between the bodies of those standing in front of her. He stood stiff as a board, waving his right hand.

Hanako took hold of a handstrap as the train speeded up. She felt tired. The day had been long— working at the shrine all afternoon, then meeting Norihide in the evening. She leaned her head on her upright arm. *Norihide will make the perfect husband,* she thought. He came from a good family that was not the meddling type, and he was a graduate of a prestigious university. That was all that really mattered to Hanako. She closed her eyes, remembering the way the temple priest's eyebrows arched approvingly when she told him Norihide was a Keio man. Everyone was *so* pleased. Hanako smiled to herself. Things could be the way one wished.

At the next stop, a rush of people flooded out of the train, leaving it empty. The velvet, wine-coloured length of seating was now plainly visible, a plush invitation to sit down. Hanako sat in the corner at the end of the car. The trainmaster blew his whistle: *peee-eet.* There was a lurch and a rumble as the train pulled out of the station. The stark, harsh light of the platform was engulfed by the gloom of the night sky. Hanako stared straight ahead at the black glass where her face was dimly reflected. She looked pale, ghostly— a silhouette against the passing darkness of the city.

The train picked up speed, rushing ahead to its inevitable terminus. Hanako's gaze fluttered and fell between the glass and the empty red seat in front of her. The reflection dipped and bowed, the head dropping forward onto the chest. The breathing slowed into small, deep *ohs*, the sound of sighs in a row.

She did not hear him getting on. He was just *there* as if he had been in that seat across from her all the time, a relic from the past now visible. He sat upright in his seat, legs set apart, arms crossed over his chest. Black hair, dark and coarse, bristled on his head. His hands, tucked inside the flaps of his sleeves, made dark bulges in the stiff fabric of his kimono.

He did not look like anyone Hanako had ever seen before. But that he was a *man*, she sensed immediately.

He was staring at her. Quickly, Hanako lowered her head. She noticed, to her chagrin, that her knees had spread slightly. She promptly pulled them together. A warm flush crept over her skin, reddening her cheeks.

She could see his feet. They were squarely mounted on a pair of wooden geta. Between the geta's thick black cords was a broad plain of skin, sparsely covered with wiry strands of hair. Two ankles, sharply defined, stood completely parallel, the rest of the legs disappearing into the dark cotton of the kimono trousers. Hanako's eyes lingered on the hem; she could look no higher. Her eyes moved back to her own feet, tucked into white shoes with golden buckles. There was a mud stain on her left shoe. Hanako frowned. Norihide had inadvertently trod on her foot in the movie theatre, and the stain was dark and obvious, the colour of dried blood. Hanako felt for her purse and quickly pulled out a tissue. Carefully bending, she neatly brushed at the stain until it had almost disappeared. Then she folded the soiled tissue into a small bundle so that the stained part would not show. She put the tissue back into her purse.

Feeling somewhat satisfied, Hanako looked up. The man was still staring at her. She looked down again. She felt panicky, but it wasn't an unpleasant feeling; a vague excitement seemed to accompany it. It was similar to the way she felt standing in the wings behind the priest as he waved the mysterious wand that summoned the gods. Everything and yet nothing was about to happen. *Sha-ka, sha-ka, sha-ka.* The sound of the wand. Then silence.

Slowly the priest would turn around, and his transformed presence would become hard and sure as the man's in front of her now was— a dark material being fleshed out of the ether; hair, bone, skin, suddenly there, so

41

that she, too, might taste of transformation, find breath to speak of it. Startled by the thought, Hanako's eyelids snapped open, the eyes jerking down in their sockets into the harsh light of the empty train. There, in the window, was her pale reflection. The night that had shaped things out of the darkness fell back behind the glass and once more became an invisible stream.

"Sakuranomichi— next stop, Sakuranomichi." The trainmaster's tinny voice floated over the intercom. Hanako stood up. As she walked towards the door, she noticed the stain on her shoe. *Didn't I wipe that off?* she thought absently. She raised her head and looked through the glass of the window as the train pulled into the station. A lone man stood on the platform, waiting to get on to the car she was about to leave. When the train stopped, they brushed past each other without a word.

TERUKO

Teruko arrived at the Shimadas' at four o'clock Sunday afternoon. She took the bus from the hospital. The doctor there had looked at her eye and said the bleeding was bad. "Stay lying down for a few days or the blood will clot and possibly damage your vision," he said. Walking out of the hospital with a wad of bandages pressed to her eye, Teruko fished around in her purse for some money. There was only two dollars— not enough for a taxi. Then, luckily, she noticed the bus. It was one that headed straight towards the Shimadas' house. Teruko got on it immediately. She did not want go back to the group home where she worked. Antony was still on shift.

They had fought about the grocery money— it was always something trivial that they fought over. As usual, they had gone downstairs where no one could hear or see them. They always fought in the spare room with the hot water tank. He had pushed her hard this time, so she pushed him back. And then he hit her in the eye.

He had yelled something at her in Chinese. He always slipped into his mother tongue when he got angry. But Teruko never slipped into Japanese when she fought with him. She was better at English than he was.

"You spoil rich Hong Kong boy don't know how to spend money!" she said when she shoved him. "Especially when it's not yours!"

That was when he hit her. Perhaps, she thought to herself, she had deserved it.

Teruko rang the doorbell at the Shimadas'. No one was at home. *They're at church*, Teruko remembered. She went into the garage and fetched the spare key. Then she opened the door and walked in. She headed straight for the bathroom to look at herself. The purple swirl on her puffed eyelid was mesmerizing— the colour of spring irises. She touched it gently, her fingers sinking into the painful bed of swollen colour.

The doctor had given her painkillers. She took a couple and lay down on one of the Shimada children's beds. There was no use alarming the family by lying conspicuously on the couch in the living room. Betty-chan's room was good enough. Teruko curled up against Betty's stuffed panda. Teruko's head throbbed, but despite the pain she fell asleep.

Mrs. Shimada looked at the eye carefully.

"It's terrible, just terrible, what he did," she said. "Can you see?"

"It's blurry," Teruko mumbled. Little Betty had crawled onto the bed and was staring right into her face.

"Well, you sleep here tonight and stay here as long as you need to," Mrs. Shimada said.

Teruko nodded. She had explained to her aunt what had happened.

"Is Teruko sleeping here?" Betty said, looking up at her mother.

"Yes," Mrs. Shimada replied. It was decided. Teruko would sleep with Betty in her bed.

That night Betty woke up crying. Teruko raised her head groggily. She had wrapped her arm around Betty's waist.

"Black! Black thing!" Betty cried.

"Sshh," Teruko said, tightening her grip. But Betty squirmed her way out and ran towards her parents' room. Teruko fell back into a deep sleep, unaware that Betty had left.

Mrs. Shimada made Teruko move to Betty's sister's room the next day.

"You sleep on the floor in Sharon's room," she said.

Teruko nodded. She took her knapsack full of clothes and carried them down to the basement where Sharon had her room. It was cooler there. There was a poster of an English garden on one wall. On the other wall was Sharon's Japanese fan collection. She had meticulously pinned each one up to form a pattern.

Mrs. Shimada pulled out an extra mattress and laid it on the floor by Sharon's desk.

"Teruko, what are you going to do?" she said as she made up the bed.

"I don't know," Teruko said.

"Well, are you going back there?"

"I don't know," Teruko said again.

"What did they say to you?"

"Who?"

"The group home people."

"They said I could go to the police if I wanted."

"What did you say?"

"No, I said, no."

Mrs. Shimada stopped making the bed. She stood upright and looked at Teruko.

"You and Antony, are you—"

"No!" Teruko said sharply. "That's what they say to me, too."

Mrs. Shimada resumed making the bed. She sat on it and motioned to Teruko to sit beside her. Taking her hand, she said, "If you want to talk, tell me, I am listening."

Teruko nodded, but she had nothing to say.

Sharon came home from school and found Teruko in her room. She had been asleep for a couple of hours, but was now awake reading Sharon's old magazines. Sharon sat beside her on the bed.

"Oh, you're staying with me? That's nice. Betty-chan has nightmares and then wakes everybody up. That's probably why Mom moved you here. You can help me with my sewing project," Sharon pulled out a pattern packet from her bag.

Teruko sat up and looked at the packet. It was for a blouse. There was a fuzzy black hole in the middle of her sight. She shifted the packet to her left and stared at it from the corner of her eye.

"Which one?" she said, pointing to the two blouses on the front.

"That one— I've got to pick the fabric tomorrow."

"Yes, that's a nice one. I like that one, especially the sleeves."

"Yeah, the sleeves are going to be the hard part."

"I can help you."

"Really?"

"Sure." Teruko opened the packet and took out the pattern sheet, laying it on the bed. The black dot persisted like the darting of a fly, jumping from one pattern shape to the other as Teruko arranged the sheet on the bed.

"Hey, is your eye all right?" Sharon said. She lowered her head and looked straight at Teruko's down-turned face.

"It's fine, just fine," Teruko answered. She flicked her head to the side. It was the only way she could see Sharon's face.

Mr. and Mrs. Shimada sat with Teruko late that night after the children had gone to bed. The table had been wiped clean. There were three cups filled with green tea. For a long time no one spoke. Finally, Mr. Shimada shrugged his shoulders. "I'm sorry, Teruko, I can't do anything. My English is so poor, anyway. And who's going to listen to a sushi chef?"

He took a long sip from his cup and then remarked, "Who made this tea? It's bitter."

Teruko nodded meekly. She got up to fetch the hot water from the kitchen.

"There's nothing we can do really, neh? Shikata ga nai, neh?" Mrs. Shimada said, turning to her husband.

"I don't want you to do anything," Teruko called out from the kitchen. She came back and poured hot water into Mr. Shimada's cup. "I never asked you, did I? Besides, I don't really care."

"Still, we feel we have some responsibility..." Mrs. Shimada said.

"People hit each other, so, it's a fact of life," Mr. Shimada said. He shrugged again.

"A fact of life," Mrs. Shimada echoed.

"Are you going to talk to the fellow in charge?" Mr. Shimada asked. "That director fellow?"

Teruko looked down into her teacup and did not answer.

"Well?"

"I don't like him. He won't believe me or anything I tell him. He'll just believe whatever Antony says."

Mrs. Shimada sighed and said, "English is so hard. People never understand what you say to them. They already have their own ideas in their head and have made up their minds before they listen."

The director's office was spare. There was an old wooden desk with scratches on it. In front were two chairs for clients. Hanging on the wall above the director's chair was a large wooden crucifix. Teruko fixed her gaze on it when the director walked in.

"Teruko," he said. "How's your eye?"

He bent over to look at it. The swoop of the director's face into Teruko's vision made her blink.

"It okay," Teruko said.

"So," the director began, "we have a problem here— I know we shouldn't have let you stay at Grace House. Christina had told me you were unhappy there."

"I ask move three times," Teruko said sullenly. "You no listen."

The director did not speak. He drew his hands together on the empty desk. Clenched them as if in prayer. Finally, after a long silence, he spoke.

"You can call the police, press charges, you know. We have let Antony go."

"Go where? He no go any place. He must back Hong Kong."

"Yes, we know that."

"Where he go? He got no money. What about visa?"

"Teruko, don't worry about Antony. We have to talk about you."

Teruko closed her eyes. She didn't want to talk.

"I forgive Antony," she said. "I forgive him."

The director cocked his head. "You do, do you?"

"Oh, yes," Teruko said. She found it hard to look at the director. The black dot in her sight blotted out his face.

"Perhaps you should go into counselling," the director said.

Counselling? Teruko thought. *For what?*

"You have to talk to someone about this experience. You want me to make an appointment at the Catholic Counselling Centre for you?"

"No," Teruko said. "I don't want it."

She stood up to leave.

"Someone told me you were beaten as a child," the director said.

"Who say that?" Teruko said sharply.

"Someone. Is it true? It might explain your reaction to this problem—why you're not facing it as you should."

Teruko looked at him blankly. Who had told the director such a thing? Was it Christina? Angela? Frederick? Had she ever told anyone that her father had beaten her? Once, maybe. They were talking about books and it must have slipped out how her father had hit her because she read too many books instead of being useful. But what did that have to do with what happened with Antony?

"Perhaps you think this is normal— that it's your fault."

Teruko looked at the director.

"Not my fault! You understand? Not my fault!"

The black dot in her eye bounced fitfully in front of her. Teruko suddenly hated the director.

"You don't understand what I am saying. I'm telling you that if you've experienced this before, your attitude might be part of the reason why Antony hit you."

Part of the reason? Was this true? Teruko knew better. She had seen the signs. Antony's short-temperedness. The way he threatened. The way he threw things. That's why she had asked to be moved. Asked three times. She knew, too, the way she talked, how sharp her words, and how even though she knew better, she said things to his face he didn't want to hear. She knew it was coming and yet she had to say the thing. Was she so stupid and stubborn to have ignored the obvious? What was wrong with her?

Sudden, angry tears formed in Teruko's eyes.

The director went over to comfort her.

"There, yes, now cry, let it out."

"Please," Teruko said. "Leave me. I want alone. Go away."

The director left the room.

Teruko let herself cry for a few minutes longer. What was she crying for? Nothing could be done. The director just wanted her to cry and now she had done it. She stopped and looked up at the wall. There was the crucifix and, right in the middle, the black hole.

Sharon took out the fabric she had bought and showed it to Teruko, who was lying on the mattress. She had been there all afternoon, since she had seen the director that morning. She sat up.

"Oh, very pretty. It will match nicely with that skirt you wore to church Sunday."

"You think so? Will you help me?"

"Sure."

Sharon pulled out the pattern packet and handed it to Teruko.

"You have to take the pattern and lay it on the fabric," Sharon said.

Teruko opened the packet and began pulling out the beige pattern sheet.

"You cut the pattern out," Sharon explained, pointing to the outlined squares and curved shapes etched in blue on the beige sheet.

"Oh?" Teruko said. The black dot in her eye became a point tracing the pattern line on the beige paper.

Sharon got a pair of scissors. Teruko took them and began cutting out the pattern. The shapes and lines were different from the ones she knew in Japan. The shapes seemed all so symmetrical here. A triangle for the sleeve. A diamond for the front bodice. Teruko worked slowly, meticulously cutting along the edges of each shape. The black dot moved smoothly down the lines she was cutting. Teruko knew she shouldn't be straining her eye, but she could not help but concentrate on the task at hand. She needed to concentrate on something.

The next day Sharon came home upset. Teruko had laid out the pattern all wrong on the fabric. She had pinned the pattern shapes every which way, without design or plan, closely packed to one another. Sharon had not realized this was wrong. Now the teacher wanted her to do it again.

Teruko was puzzled. She had only done it the way she had always done it in Japan.

"Let me try again," Teruko said. She looked at the picture on the back of the packet and saw how it was supposed to be done.

"No!" Sharon grabbed the packet from Teruko's hand. "I got to do it. It's *my* project. I got to do it myself. That's what the teacher said."

"I'm sorry," Teruko said. She did not know what else to say. What was she going to do? She had hoped to help Sharon sew the shirt, but Sharon was going to do everything herself.

For the next several days, Teruko lay in bed. In the evenings, she would get up and help Mrs. Shimada prepare dinner for the children. After dinner, Mrs. Shimada would help the children with their homework and then go to bed early so that she could be up before the children to make their lunches. Teruko would stay awake until Mr. Shimada came home late at night. While she waited, she made barley tea, mugi-cha, getting out the large brass teapot, pouring the barley seeds into the water and boiling it till it frothed and bubbled. She would wait for it to cool, and then pour the mugi-cha into a large glass pitcher that Mrs. Shimada had received as a wedding gift. Mr. Shimada liked mugi-cha and would drink it after his bath. Teruko would read magazines until she heard the back door open and then she would get up, run the hot water for Mr. Shimada's bath and get a glass of mugi-cha ready for him.

"Teruko," Mr. Shimada said one night. "Have you gone to the doctor yet?"

"No." Teruko handed Mr. Shimada his mugi-cha.

"You better go, neh. You still have that black dot in your eye?"

Teruko nodded. She would make an appointment tomorrow.

"Teruko, did Maki-chan talk to you?"

Maki-chan was the name Mr. Shimada called his wife. But he never called Teruko, Teru-chan, like Mrs. Shimada and the children did. Not even Teruko-san. Just Teruko. The way the people at the group home called her.

"No," Teruko lied. Mrs. Shimada had talked to Teruko many times about God. She assumed that was what Mr. Shimada was referring to.

"God—" Mr. Shimada began, "God knows everything. He knows your suffering. He knows your heart, Teruko."

Teruko hung her head. She knew about God. She heard about Him all the time in the group home. How He loved the children and the poor and the suffering. That was what the home was for— the children. The grown-up children who had trouble speaking, their hands and wrists curled up to their bodies, their tongues hanging out of their mouths and their eyes looking everywhere but at you. You looked after them because God loved them. Died for them.

Teruko remembered the crucifix in the director's office. The slim, emaciated figure of Christ pinned onto the cross, his head hanging down to his chest. How unlike the Buddha on his lotus, transcendent and peaceful. If she could choose gods, whom would she choose?

"Kami-sama wa subarashii. God is wonderful," Mr. Shimada said. "Sometimes, when my life is hard and difficult, I remember that God is love and that comforts me."

Teruko nodded. The Shimadas had become Christians after they came to Canada. Life was hard in Canada. People turned to religion when things were hard.

The doctor shook his head.

"I don't know about that black dot. It might just be permanent. It should have healed up by now."

"Thank you," Teruko said. *Permanent.* The word echoed in her mind.

"Do you have someone to take you home?" The doctor said, worried.

"Yes," Teruko lied. She was going to meet a friend for lunch at a noodle house in Chinatown. That was good enough. She would tell Sachie what the doctor had said.

Teruko got her prescription and headed downtown to the Happy China Gardens. Sachie was waiting for her. She had changed her hair to a stylish bob and was wearing new earrings.

"How was it? The doctor?" Sachie said. Her earrings jangled, sharp glints of light flashing off them.

"That black hole is still there. He said it might be permanent."

"That's awful! You have to tell the director. What about Antony? Where is he? Does he know what he's done to you?"

Teruko shrugged her shoulders. "Nanni mo dekinai yo. Nothing can be done."

"So what are you going to do?"

Teruko shrugged her shoulders again. She was concentrating on the menu. She wanted number six— egg noodle with pork. It came with bean sprouts and three slices of barbecued pork.

The waiter came and they ordered.

"So you cut your hair, neh?" Teruko said. "It looks very nice."

"I know. Clara did it. You know what? Clara's thinking she might want to open her own shop and she wants me to be her partner. Isn't that a great idea?"

"But you're still in hairdressing school."

"I know, silly, but *after* that."

Teruko smiled. Sachie moved like lightning with everything she did. They had met in an English class at the college they were studying at in Japan. Sachie had always wanted to go abroad. She had relatives in Canada and had visited them when she was in high school. When she found out Teruko had an aunt in Canada, she became Teruko's friend, talking to her about Canada even though Teruko had never been there.

"Canada is so free. Japan is so… so narrow," Sachie once said. "Everyone is so narrow-minded. You can't do what you want. You have to do what everyone expects you to do."

It was Sachie who suggested they go to Canada together. Now, almost a year-and-a-half later, she was going to hairdressing school and was thinking of staying permanently. They had both started out working at the group home, since it was the only place they could find work with their limited English. But Sachie had stayed only a few months. She went to night school and improved her English.

"Teru-chan!" Sachie's voice broke into Teruko's thoughts.

"Huh?"

"What are you going to do?"

Teruko did not answer. She looked down into the now-empty bowl of noodles to the small pool of broth at the bottom. She couldn't tell if the dark spot on the bottom of the bowl was pepper or the black hole in her eyesight.

"Neh, Teru-chan? You don't know, do you? You never know what's coming next. You just let things happen to you. You can't do that here, do you know that? This is Canada. You have to make things happen. *You have to make choices, decisions.*"

Teruko lowered her head. It was true. Things just happened to her. Like being hit in the face.

"You're just the same way you were at home." Sachie complained. "I can't do anything for you now. I can't. I'm too busy."

Teruko smiled uneasily. She remembered how in Japan she had sat paralyzed at her desk at the travel agency where she worked, wondering if she should go to Canada. She hadn't said anything to her boss.

Finally, it was Sachie who had called her boss and told him that Teruko was going to Canada. The tickets had been bought already. When the boss confronted Teruko, she tearfully admitted it was true. She was let go at once.

"Warukatta wa neh. I'm sorry." Sachie apologized later on the plane. "But I had to do it. I wasn't sure if you were serious about coming."

Teruko remembered looking out the plane window and thinking that, yes, she was glad she was going. The sky outside was midway between morning and night. It seemed endless, deeply endless. Teruko felt herself on the edge of a floating abyss between two worlds she did not know. She felt vaguely hopeful, but even still, a little sad.

Mrs. Shimada and Teruko were doing the dishes. They were standing by each other at the sink. Teruko was washing the large, glass pitcher that the mugi-cha was kept in. She would boil some more tonight for Mr. Shimada.

"You know," Mrs. Shimada began, "Shin-chan told me you serve him mugi-cha every night and that you run the bath for him."

Teruko nodded. The water was very soapy and Teruko's fingers slipped against the glass.

"He said to me, 'Remember before the children were born when we lived in Japan how you used to do that for me? Get the bath ready for me and then afterwards we'd have mugi-cha on the balcony and look at the stars? Natsukashii yo. I remember it so fondly.' he said. Every night, right? You give him mugi-cha?"

Teruko picked up the pitcher and was about to move it to the drying rack when she felt a sharp bump against her side. The pitcher slipped out of her hands and fell onto the floor with a crash. The noise was loud and hard.

Mrs. Shimada looked at the broken glass and then looked at Teruko.

"You can't stay here any more, Teruko. You must leave."

Teruko. Not Teru-chan.

Mrs. Shimada left the kitchen. Teruko looked at the broken pitcher. It lay on the ground, scattered in pieces large and small, asymmetrical bits shaped like diamonds and triangles. She went and got a newspaper and pulled apart the pages. And then she began cleaning up. Slowly, piece by piece, she wrapped the broken glass in the newspaper, making sure the sharp edges were covered. There were the headlines and photos, creased and crumpled, folded against the broken glass. And sometimes there was a large wet blotch on the paper that came from her eyes. Unwillingly. Always unwillingly. These tears.

That night, Teruko packed her things. She wondered where she would go. Maybe she would phone Sachie and ask if she could stay there for a while. She couldn't go back to the group home. It had been six weeks now since Antony had hit her and the black spot in her eye was still there.

She wondered what it would be like to see that way for the rest of her life.

Where is Antony now? she remembered Sachie asking. Antony. Teruko closed her eyes and a warm flush came to her cheeks. Antony and she had held hands once. They had gone to the park together, with Emily in her wheelchair. No one had seen them but Emily, who laughed and clapped, her eyes rolling up towards the sun.

HONEYMOON

"Would Canada be all right?" He looks at her. On Shizuko's lap lie travel pamphlets of blue lakes and snow-topped mountains. Bright katakana and kanji lettering flashes across the top: "KANADA— DAI SHIZEN." (CAN-ADA— BIG NATURE.)

Shizuko nods shyly. Years ago she would have preferred Europe for a honeymoon, but now she does not care where they go.

"I shall make the reservations tomorrow."

"Yes, that will be fine." She scoops up the pamphlets and carefully arranges them into a pile on the coffee table.

The two sit in silence. Shizuko folds her hands in her lap. Kosuke Tanaka, her fiancé, shifts positions, parting his legs slightly. He takes out a handkerchief and wipes his forehead.

"And so what have you decided?" Shizuko's mother appears with the tea tray.

"Canada," they reply in unison. They look at one another and laugh nervously.

They arrive at the Calgary airport in the late afternoon and are put on a bus headed towards the mountains. Shizuko has chosen to wear a suit, cream-coloured with gold trim and buttons. She carries a square black handbag. Kosuke also wears a suit— the exact same one he wore the day they met. Theirs was an arranged meeting, an omiai.

Shizuko notices that all the couples around them are younger. They wear jeans and matching sweatshirts. Some are holding hands. Shizuko thinks how old she must look. Kosuke looks his age, forty-seven. Black tendrils of hair scraped up from the side cover a shiny bald spot. His stomach protrudes over his belt. *Not a handsome man,* Shizuko thinks, *but I'm no beauty, either.* The years had passed by, steady as the march of ants. There was no flowering of looks or poise, just the accumulating of age— twenty, twenty-five, thirty, thirty-five. The omiai opportunities became fewer.

Kosuke Tanaka was introduced as something late— a last effort by her now elderly parents. Shizuko had never told them she would not marry. When her mother heard through a relative that an older bachelor working in Asakusa was looking for a wife, Shizuko did not decline the offer to meet him.

They met in a small café in Asakusa on a rainy day. "I'm a shitamachi boy," he said, somewhat proudly. "I've worked all my life in this part of town." He patted the table-top. He told her he lived with his widowed mother who was old. "She is eighty-two. I look after her," he said plainly. Though soft-spoken, the man displayed an earnestness Shizuko found vaguely appealing. There seemed to be no airs. That was what was considered noble in shitamachi people— their earnestness.

In past omiai, Shizuko had easily determined "yes" or "no," but as she sat across from Kosuke Tanaka, she could not tell. All she could think of was herself. She looked at her hands and thought of them as old and wrinkled, absorbed by her lap. When would they touch a man? Would they ever?

The man was looking out the window, his hand propped against the ashtray with a cigarette between his fingers. Shizuko loosened her hands in her lap. They would yet touch a man. Maybe even this man, Kosuke Tanaka.

That was six months ago. Now they are married and on their honeymoon. On the plane, they sat in silence. The brave but mindless chatter that marked their brief courtship has disappeared. Shizuko is secretly glad. What was their courtship anyway, but an endless series of politenesses exchanged? Long and unimaginative conversations endured for the sake of that unspoken goal, marriage?

"We'll be in Banff in approximately an hour-and-a-half," the tour guide says. The honeymoon tour has begun.

Shizuko shifts her attention to the window. The scenery is vast. Broad fields roll into the distance, the sky hanging above, pale and impenetrably blue. No living creature can be seen except for the occasional clump of cows clustered in a protective circle.

"Why do you think they're doing that?" Shizuko says to Kosuke, pointing to the cows.

"Hm?" Kosuke looks out the window. "It's probably to keep away the flies."

Flies? Dai Shizen. That was Canada. Big Nature. Shizuko looks around the bus again at the other couples. Most have fallen asleep, heads against each other's shoulders, arms entwined. They are all wearing casual and comfortable clothing. Shizuko feels over-dressed. Has she even brought a pair of pants? It looks windy outside and the mountain air will surely be cold.

"You know," Shizuko leans over, "I think we should phone your mother when we get to the hotel. Tell her we've arrived safely."

"I've already done that," Kosuke says. "I phoned Mother from the airport."

"You did?"

"I knew she would worry, so I called her right away. You know, we must call your parents, too."

Shizuko nods. She does not particularly care to call her parents. It is just a duty. But perhaps with Kosuke it is different.

While they were courting, she visited his mother only a few times. On the first visit, she brought the customary gift and spent an hour politely listening to the old woman talk about her son.

"He's loyal, he's devoted, he's faithful." Over and over again the mother repeated herself— how good Kosuke was, how much she, as a mother, did not deserve her son's love or attention.

The mother was old and frail. She walked slowly, putting her hand on the wall or on the furniture to steady herself. Kosuke was always at her side, scooping his arm around her to help her sit down, clasping her trembling hand firmly in his grip.

Shizuko thought it would be hard for such an elderly woman to do things around the house, but as she looked around, she noticed how immaculately clean everything was. The butsudan had fresh fruit in it and incense had recently been burnt there. A faded picture of a uniformed man was propped in the right corner. Kosuke's father. He had served in the army. Kosuke had been born shortly after the war when his father returned. His mother was in her mid-thirties then, and had been barren. Kosuke's father died of tuberculosis soon after his birth.

Shizuko knew if she married Kosuke she would be obliged to live with and look after his mother. Married friends told her what an onerous task this was, but Shizuko had not found the idea particularly daunting. She was tired of living for herself. She wanted to live for others. For her husband. Her children. The family.

The bus pulls up to the Banff Springs Hotel. Everyone clambers over to the left side of the vehicle to look at the famous hotel, while Kosuke and Shizuko quietly gather their things. They get off the bus and go to the lobby, following the others.

"The Tanakas. Room 506." The tour guide hands Shizuko the key. "Very nice room— faces the mountains," he adds. Shizuko feels the dull weight of the heavy golden key in her hand. She will guard it carefully, put it near her person, in her pocket or purse.

When they get to the room, Shizuko notices the bed. It is spacious and wide, covered with a white bedspread. There is much light in the room. The curtains are drawn wide open. Kosuke moves to the window.

Shizuko goes to the bathroom to change. She pulls in her suitcase and closes the door. She worries about what to wear. They will be having dinner soon.

She comes out wearing a navy skirt and a fresh blouse. Kosuke is staring out the window. She goes to him.

"Wonderful view, isn't it?" Kosuke says. The setting sun casts a pale yellow glow onto his face. He looks old. Sad. Shizuko feels a trembling of pity for him. She wants to touch him, satisfy him. She will be what he has longed for all his life.

"Kosuke-san," she says his name softly, gently.

"Yes?" He turns to her.

"Oh, nothing." Shizuko looks down.

"That's a different skirt you're wearing."

"Do you like it?" Shizuko unfolds her hands and runs them down the front of her skirt. She looks at him.

"Yes, it's very nice."

"Are you going to wear that suit to dinner?"

"I was thinking of it. Why?"

"You should change. Relax a little more."

"Yes, you're right. I'll change."

Kosuke brushes past Shizuko as he moves towards his suitcase. Shizuko can feel the rustle of his shirt against her, can smell his cologne.

"Which one?" Kosuke says, pulling out two shirts.

"The yellow one."

Kosuke begins taking off his shirt. Shizuko turns to the window. The sun is beginning to set behind the mountains. She can faintly see in the darkest corner of the window a reflection of Kosuke changing, his hands slowly unbuttoning, one by one, the buttons, opening the shirt, exposing his chest. Shizuko looks up. She notices movement on the lawn. Two elk. The large one with the antlers mounting the smaller one. Shizuko stares, her eyes glued to the rumbling mass of brown fur openly mating on the manicured lawn.

"Shizuko-san," Kosuke calls. "Should I wear a tie?"

"Yes, of course," Shizuko replies. The elk have moved away.

"Here, let me help you."

She goes to Kosuke. The light in the room has grown dusky, casting shadows. Kosuke leans back his head, darkness enveloping his face. Only his neck is exposed, thick and warm, the Adam's apple bobbing almost imperceptibly up and down as Shizuko knots the tie below his collar. *He's letting me do it*, Shizuko thinks, *knot his tie for him*. She feels her cheeks grow warm.

They are the first couple down to dinner. The other couples come later, dressed up in suits and bright coloured dresses. Shizuko realizes she has again misjudged the situation. At least Kosuke is wearing a tie. Her skirt looks dull compared to the dresses of the young women.

The tour guide seats them beside two couples from Kansai. They are young, in their twenties. They smile shyly at Kosuke and Shizuko, bowing their heads. Shizuko asks all the polite questions, like an older sister. "Where are you from?" "What do your parents do?" "How long have you been married?" "What are your future plans?"

After dinner, Kosuke and Shizuko take a walk around the hotel. It is dark, the mountains invisible. For the first time, they hold hands.

When they return, Shizuko goes to the bathroom. She looks at herself in the mirror. The warm, red flush in her cheeks is still there. She closes her eyes. Slowly she brings her hands to her shoulders, onto her neck. Her skin feels smooth. She knows that her delicate white skin is a mark of beauty. She opens her suitcase and pulls out a lavender silk nightgown she bought on the Ginza at Mitsukoshi two days before the wedding. A quiet, private purchase. She slips it on. It feels cool on her body, releasing a shudder of goosebumps on her skin. She breathes deeply, turns herself around and looks once more in the mirror. *I look fine*, she thinks.

She enters the bedroom. Kosuke is sitting straight up in bed in his pyjamas, his back against the headboard, hands folded in his lap.

As Shizuko turns off the lights and slips into bed, Kosuke turns and looks at her. When he doesn't move towards her, Shizuko reaches for his hand and gently places it on her breast. His hand feels like a damp, warm cloth, and for a moment it lingers on the curve of her skin before slipping off.

Kosuke swallows visibly. His brow shines with sweat. He cautiously raises his hand again and places it on her breast. Shizuko arches her back to encourage him. Again, his hand falls off.

Shizuko moves closer, pushing her body against him. She slips her arm around his waist and brings his arm up to her shoulder. The arm is heavy, leaden. Kosuke swallows again. His arm slips off her shoulder. He looks away. Shizuko looks at his groin. It is lifeless, limp. A wrinkle of cotton pyjama.

"What is the matter?" she finally says in a high, tremulous voice.

"I... I c-can't... I'm n-not normal," Kosuke wheezes out. He pushes himself down and turns the other way. His whole body trembles.

Shizuko cannot speak. She is dumbfounded.

The dark ceiling hovers like a dead weight over Shizuko. She lies still, a corpse, her hands resting on her breasts as she breathes in and out, pretending to be asleep. Kosuke has gotten up and left the room.

What's the matter with him? How can this be? All night, questions dog Shizuko, the words spinning around her in the darkness. *Why? Why is this happening?*

She tries recalling their dates, to see if there was a sign then. *The French restaurant in Aoyama, cherry-blossom-viewing in Ueno Park, visiting Sensoji temple, seeing that Austrian symphony*— nothing there to indicate that lack. He was always so polite on their dates, running ahead to pay for tickets, buying small things like key-chains, postcards, souvenir charms.

What is it? What is wrong?

Keychains, postcards, souvenir charms. Shizuko closes her eyes. Something forms in the back of her mind—a memory, an image. *Postcards, souvenir charms.* Shizuko stops. Souvenir charms for who?

Why, for the mother, of course. Kosuke's mother. Everywhere Shizuko and Kosuke went, he bought something for his mother, discreetly purchasing it and putting it into his pocket.

The memory comes back. A warm afternoon, sitting in the Tanaka living room, Mrs. Tanaka kneeling on the tatami, bowing deeply, her forehead pressed to the ground, her hand clasping Shizuko's. Over and over again, saying, "Thank you, thank you so much for agreeing to marry Kosuke. He's not much, I know, for a woman like yourself, but he's been good to me, such a worthless mother, I've been keeping him all these years. Thank you, thank you so much."

Shizuko had not known what to say. She remembered looking up. Kosuke stood in the hallway, partially hidden, his eyes dark and wet.

His mother. That's what it is. His mother.

Sunlight streams through the window. Shizuko gets up and opens the curtain. The lawn is bare, the sun harsh on the green surface. No trace of wildlife outside. The elks of the evening before seem an illusion.

"Shizuko-san."

Startled, Shizuko turns around to face Kosuke, standing behind her, his head hanging low. He falls to his knees.

"Shizuko-san, I'm sorry," he says, unable to lift his head.

Shizuko begins trembling. "You brute," she wants to say, but controls herself. She clenches her hands and turns back to the window. The grim curl of her lips is reflected in the glass. Something in her is about to snap.

"Please, please forgive me. I, I wanted to be, to be m-married."

His voice is a whimper. Shizuko feels like kicking him.

"I have never been with a woman. Only my mother. She has no one but me. I am afraid of what I am doing to her by marrying."

"What is wrong with you?" Shizuko turns to look at Kosuke. Her voice is clear, cold. "We are not children. Everything we have done is proper and natural. How can you say that?"

"Natural?" Kosuke says. "Please forgive me, then. I am not a natural man. I discovered this long ago. I am unnatural. That is why I have been unmarried so long."

"It's your mother, isn't it?" Shizuko says, her voice rising. "Poisoning you. Mother complex— that's what you have, isn't it?" The word "complex" fills Shizuko with a superiority of loathing. She has seen that word somewhere in a magazine and it suddenly unleashes her anger. "You're afraid of women, aren't you? Aren't you? You're afraid that they'll control you like your mother, that they will suck you up, that they will drown you with their demands, aren't you? Admit it— you're afraid of women! Aren't you? Aren't you?"

Kosuke stands stone-faced. The pitch of Shizuko's voice has risen higher and higher until it sounds like the shrill whine of a siren. Kosuke grabs her by the arms.

"Stop it!" he says. Alarmed by his own aggression, he lets go.

Shizuko is weeping.

"Listen," Kosuke says. "It is probably as you say. I have a mother complex. Yes, I am afraid of women. They ask me to be things I cannot be. Look at yourself. What did you marry me for? Certainly not for love. We are neither doing this for love, are we? Then what are we doing it for?"

"Because it is a natural thing for men and women to do," Shizuko sniffed, "and it is also natural that I should expect of you at least— at least, this which you cannot do."

"Yes, it is a natural expectation. But I have told you already I am not a natural man."

"Too late. It's just too late."

Kosuke sits down. He pulls out a handkerchief and wipes away the sweat on his forehead.

"I know that. I, I was just hoping things would be different. I thought you could help me. You seemed so kind, understanding. But I see that I am too much a problem. I am not a man. You may leave me if you want."

"That's it? Go? After all this embarrassment, this shame upon our names?"

Kosuke shrugs his shoulders. "I am not unaccustomed to shame," he says bluntly.

Shizuko stops. She feels sheepish, though she doesn't know why.

They go down to breakfast together and eat in silence. The chatter of voices, the tinkling of silverware, the bustling of the hotel staff are a dull buzz in Shizuko's ears. She is tired and has little appetite. She eats a slice of toast and drinks a glass of orange juice. Kosuke does not eat.

"Please meet at the bus in ten minutes!" the guide announces to the group.

Shizuko looks at Kosuke. He is fiddling for his bag.

"What are you looking for?" she asks.

"The camera."

"Then we're going?"

"I would like to," he says. "Please, we should go together."

Shizuko does not answer. She folds the napkin in her lap. What would she do all day alone in the hotel? She decides she will go with Kosuke.

They board the bus with the others. The guide begins talking at once. Shizuko shifts her attention to the window. Slowly, the hotel— a ruddy brown colour— moves away. The bellman waves. Shizuko's hands tighten in her lap. *I will not wave.* She turns to Kosuke. He sits stiff and upright, his face thrust forward. Shizuko turns back to the window. *He won't see a thing, sitting like that.* She notices an elk grazing on the lawn of a house. *Look, an elk!*— the words rise in Shizuko's throat but do not emerge. She swallows them.

They do not speak until the first picture stop.

"This is Castle Mountain," announces the guide. "We'll stop here for photos. Five minutes."

Shizuko and Kosuke step off the bus. Castle Mountain, tiered and pinnacled, stands in the distance, a picturesque block of stone. Shizuko closes her eyes before she speaks. *Civil, I must be civil.* "Did you bring the camera?"

"Oh—" Kosuke begins checking his pockets. "N-no, I forgot. I'll go and get it." He starts back to the bus.

"No, never mind. Forget it."

"I'm sorry." Kosuke hangs his head.

"You're sorry about everything, aren't you?" Shizuko's voice rises without warning. She is amazed at her own cutting quickness, the sharpness of her words.

Kosuke takes out his handkerchief and wipes his brow. They go back on to the bus. The guide picks up the mike. "See how thin the trees out there are? They're called lodgepole pines and were used by the Indians to build teepees. I hear Canadian log houses are very popular in Japan right now, but these trees can't be used for house building. They're too thin."

Houses. House building. Trees too thin, too fragile, too brittle. The row of matchstick trees shudders and topples in front of Shizuko's eyes. *House. No house. That's what marriage is for. Children. A family. It's my right.*

As the bus nears Lake Louise, Shizuko notices Kosuke shoving his camera into his pocket. They get off the bus. Shizuko lags behind, unconnected to the others.

In front of the hotel is a signboard. CHATEAU LAKE LOUISE. Couples are having their pictures taken together there by the guide.

"Mr. and Mrs. Tanaka! How about a picture?" the guide calls out.

Kosuke begins pulling out the camera. Shizuko stops. *No,* she thinks, and gives a harsh, quick glance at Kosuke. But it is too late; the guide has the camera in his hand.

"Now stand together."

Shizuko freezes. She will not move from her position, left of the sign. Kosuke is standing on the right. He inches towards Shizuko. She puts out her hand. *No. Stay there.* She clasps her hands in front of her and looks straight at the guide. *Take the picture, please.*

After the shot, the guide hands the camera back to Kosuke who puts it back in his pocket.

"Shizuko-san," he says slowly. "Perhaps we should not take any more pictures?"

Shizuko does not answer and looks away at the mountains.

Kosuke begins to shuffle off. Quickly Shizuko puts out her hand. *Stop. Take pictures of the mountains. So beautiful you can't ignore them.* The words linger in Shizuko's mouth, but she cannot say them.

Kosuke is looking at her, his eyes searching hers. *I've been sarcastic to him,* Shizuko thinks. *So unlike me, indulging his earnestness.* Earnestness. *Shitamachi people are earnest.* Shizuko remembers that thought from long ago— the day of their omiai.

Shizuko looks at the mountain. Slowly, Kosuke takes out the camera, aims it at the spot she is looking at— a glacier gleaming in the sunlight, a white wall of ice.

When Shizuko gets back on to the bus, she thinks of all the other omiai she had. Names, faces flash through her mind— Miura, Honda, Kadota. She remembers odd things. The way Miura-san held his cup, what colour tie

Honda-san wore, the first words Kadota-san spoke. All the omiais of that time were half-hearted attempts, something Shizuko had done to please her parents. They were forever setting her up with somebody— her father going through his business connections, her mother asking all the relatives. Shizuko wasn't really interested in any of the men. All she could do was compare them to Makimoto-bucho, her boss.

For seven years, she had nurtured a crush on Makimoto-bucho, a married man with two children. He was several years older than she. But Shizuko could not help it. She was so close to him, the most senior of his office secretaries. She served him tea, filed his documents, arranged his appointments. Day in, day out, seeing him always.

One night, he took the staff out to his favourite bar. He was being promoted, moved to a higher department. In a moment of drunken gruffness, he turned to Shizuko and spoke the words she had longed to hear. "You want me, don't you?"

Shizuko paled. She was paralyzed by his words. How had he known? Was she that obvious? Makimoto-bucho's hand moved into her lap. He was drunk. Repulsed, Shizuko stood up and fled.

Seven years mooning over a married man. Seven years of wasted infatuation.

Shizuko closes her eyes. What did Makimoto-bucho look like? She can barely remember now. He was tall, taller than Kosuke. He had some grey hair. He wore blue suits... or were they black? It is Kosuke who wears blue suits. Shizuko opens her eyes to check.

Kosuke is searching through his pocket. Slyly, covertly, he brings some small thing to his lips and pops it into his mouth. He puts his hand back into his pocket. A few seconds later, he puts another one into his mouth. Shizuko looks down at his bag. There is a packet of umeboshi— tart, red plums pickled into wrinkled balls. The kind of snack old people take on trips, the ones who believe umeboshi to be a cure-all, a daily vitamin. Kosuke notices Shizuko looking at him and smiles sheepishly, offering her one. Shizuko declines and turns her head to the window. Embarrassed, Kosuke offers some to the couple across the aisle. Shizuko cringes. *How silly— offering umeboshi to that young couple.*

The sky outside draws Shizuko's attention back to the window. *How blue it is.* Impenetrable. Day after day, the same blueness. Indifferent to change, the perfect frame for mountains.

The guide is talking about glaciers now— how they were formed by the packing of snow, the pressing of snowflakes into heavy layers of ice that began to move down the mountain, grinding the stone behind it. *Powerful.* Shizuko looks at the glacier. She feels small, suddenly impoverished.

The sound of heavy breathing comes from Shizuko's side. Kosuke has fallen asleep and leans precariously against her shoulder. Shizuko shrinks back against the window. The land has grown suddenly flat. There are no trees except a few small, stunted firs.

"We'll be reaching the highest part of the road here soon," the guide says. "This is alpine meadow. You'll notice the lack of trees. Cold winds constantly sweep down from the ice field, making it hard for things to grow here."

Where are the buildings? Why so empty? Shizuko looks again at the flat expanse. *Where are the people? The children?* She thinks of the lakes, the open fields, the mountain air. *For the children. Land for the children.*

The bus toils up the hill, the sound of the engine rumbling louder. The driver shifts gears, making a low, grinding sound. The bus slows down.

Children, Shizuko thinks. *Whose children? Not mine.* The land that has flowed across her eye now seems to creep and crawl to a standstill. Shizuko looks out the window. The reality is barrenness.

It will be an hour before they reach the ice-field. Shizuko is tired but cannot sleep. She thinks she will look for wildlife, fixing her eyes on the spaces between the trees in the forests, on rock ledges and shelves on the mountainsides. Miles, minutes creep by. Still nothing. The land rolls out before her like a scroll of painted scenery.

Shizuko's mind begins drifting. *Maybe I should look at this more practically. Kosuke's deficient. Such husbands are to be divorced. That would only be right. Divorce.*

But who would divorce who? How do you divorce, anyway? Shizuko frowns. *Who would make the announcement? Kosuke? Would he be man enough?* Man enough— ironic.

What if I announce it? How can I do it without sounding bitter? Harsh? They would all think I was over-demanding, unsatisfied. They would think I have no gaman. "Oh, she's a selfish type, can't endure hardship"— *that's what they would say. "Kosuke Tanaka is such a good man. It must be her fault. Ruining him like that."*

Shizuko looks out. They are fast approaching a cliff wall. *If I divorced, where would I go?* The wall towers, sheer and upright, a mass of limestone. *A thirty-five-year-old woman, now divorced?* Dark stains run down the front of the wall where water has seeped into the stone. *Same old routine again, every day. The way it was before.* The wall grows closer, tighter to the window. Shizuko can no longer see the sky.

Then she spots it. A small, cream-coloured speck. Moving. Shizuko squints her eyes. It's an animal! A mountain goat, standing on a ledge no bigger than itself. It stands isolated, suspended, a small white blotch that looks almost like snow.

"Kosuke, look!" Shizuko cannot help but nudge Kosuke. "A goat!"

"Where?" He strains over to see.

"There!" Shizuko points.

"Where? Where?"

But it is too late. They have passed it. Shizuko falls back onto her seat. *He didn't see it. Of course, he didn't see it. He couldn't see it if he tried. Or maybe it's just me wanting him to see. See things only I can see. Maybe it was just a patch of snow.*

They stop at a gorge. People clamber out of the bus to view the small canyon. Kosuke convinces Shizuko to come.

This gorge is small, deep. Water gushes down the sides, churning and foaming against the rock. Shizuko peers over the rail. The sight is mesmerizing.

"So beautiful, so beautiful," someone mutters. An old Japanese man from another tour group stands beside her.

"Makes you want to jump?" he says. "Neh?"

He looks at her. His eyes are small, milky.

Shizuko feels the cold spray on her hands and feet. The white water churns, leaps up from the stone, gushes and roars into her ear. The rock walls recede, stretched back as if elastic, the gorge widening like a mouth.

"Shizuko-san," Kosuke's voice interrupts. "We must go back to the bus."

Shizuko looks up. Her hands are trembling. She has been gripping the rail too tightly.

Back on the bus, Shizuko stares sullenly out the window. Words creep into her throat, seal themselves under her tongue. The sound of water even now thrums in her ear, vibrating against every nerve, every muscle in her body.

"Over there is Bridal Veil Falls." The guide points to a long column of water pouring down the mountainside. "An old Indian legend tells us these are the tears of a weeping warrior's wife. A woman who lost her husband in battle on the eve of their wedding night."

Shizuko looks away from the falls to her lap. Her cheeks feel warm. Tears well up in her eyes and slowly trickle down her face.

Kosuke has been watching. Without looking at her, he extends his handkerchief. Shizuko notices how damp and dirty it is. He has been using it all day.

"We'll be at the ice-field very soon now!" the guide says excitedly. "Please get ready!"

Shizuko's feet crunch the grainy surface of the ice as she walks on top of the glacier, further and further beyond the others. For a fleeting second, she takes a look behind her. The sno-coaches, the special buses they boarded for glacier travel, look like small larvae in the distance. She turns forward and heads towards the mountainside. Peaks rise up around her, their bald rock surfaces exposed to the sky. The glacier, an opaque ocean, throws up waves of hardened ice, fixed like stone monuments. Above her, monstrous cracks and fissures of blue ice gleam like cavernous mouths waiting to swallow up the living. Shizuko squints at the glacier. The thoughts in her head grow thick with dull purpose. *I cannot go back there. I cannot go back to a life I do not want to live. I want to disappear. I want to stop wanting. Become whiteness, pure and indifferent. Become snow.*

Shizuko has come close to the mountainside. She sees ahead a broad tumble of ice. Beyond, Shizuko knows, is the ice-field, the source of the glacier. She will walk and walk towards it, her feet moving her body forward, mapping out the ice, hoping for the moment when hard surface will give way and become air.

The sound of her feet is loud. Louder than she expects. Crunching. Grinding. Crushing.

Shizuko stops. The crunching noise continues. It is not just her feet making the sound. She hears, faintly, voices, and turns to look behind her. Clambering down an icy ledge are a middle-aged couple, dressed in climbing gear and roped together. As they reach the ground, they are chatting amicably to one another. The man is tall, silver-haired, wearing dark breeches, a red jacket and hiking boots. A coil of rope hangs from his shoulders. The woman is about the same age, white hair gathered loosely in a bun. She too is wearing breeches and a red jacket. They notice Shizuko.

"Well, hullo there!" the man says in a startlingly loud voice. "What are you doing here?"

Shizuko does not reply. She remains standing frozen.

"I don't think she understands, dear," the woman says. "She looks Japanese."

"Where do you think she came from?" the man turns to his wife.

"I don't know. I suspect she's from one of those sno-coach tours."

They look at her together. The woman's eyes are kindly, concerned. She extends her hand to Shizuko.

"My dear, you must go back to your group. They'll be waiting for you."

Shizuko nods, though she does not understand. They are speaking English far too quickly for her. She wonders where this couple has come from. Roped together. Friendly. Unafraid. The glacier suddenly recedes from her mind, the blue crack closing up its mouth, the ice growing flat and dull. The sky is a dazzling blue, the sun shining brightly.

Just then, a shout.

"Mrs. Tanaka!" the guide waves his hand, running towards her. Kosuke is a few steps behind.

"Mrs. Tanaka! Here you are!" the guide says. "We've been looking all over for you! You made us all worried. The sno-coach has been waiting for fifteen minutes!"

Kosuke approaches Shizuko. Briefly his eyes meet hers. They are filled with something that makes Shizuko look away. Not anger, but something else. Suddenly he embraces her, the force of his arms jerking Shizuko's back. The guide turns away, embarrassed.

Kosuke breathes hard into Shizuko's ear, the hot rasping sound tingling her skin. Shizuko's lower lip begins to shudder. She wants to push him away but his grip is strong, like an animal's, his body pressed against her, the frantic heartbeat slowing down, the breaths now coming evenly, one after the other. Shizuko closes her eyes. Soon his breath will match hers, and for a moment they will be one.

RONIN

It was mid-afternoon and it had been snowing steadily since morning. Three young men shivering in light windbreakers hurriedly entered the Wei Ming Noodle House. The restaurant was nearly empty, except for a man sitting in a corner reading a newspaper. He looked up briefly at the men, then craned his neck and barked something in Chinese to the kitchen. A small woman in a white shirt and black pants choppily strode out and grabbed some menus along the way. The men had taken a table by the window and watched the woman approach. Her step was jaunty and erratic.

"Harro! Very cold today. You want hot noodle soup, right?" She thrust the menus at them. "What you like? You order?"

The men opened their menus and studied them intently, muttering amongst themselves, pointing to the various words and characters.

"Hey, you speaking Japanese," the waitress said.

"How you know?" one of the men said. He was portly with a boyish face.

"I been to Japan. I go Tokyo. You from Tokyo?"

"Me, yes, Tokyo," the man who had first spoken replied. He pointed to the short, sinewy one wearing the baseball cap, sitting beside him. "He Yokohama." Then he pointed across to the taller one wearing the rugby shirt. "He Tokyo, too."

"I been Tokyo," the waitress repeated. "Before come here, Canada."

"Oh? But you not Japanese," said the taller man.

"No. I'm Chinese. From Vietnam."

"Oh."

"My name Mei Mei. What your name?"

"Masa." He was the portly one. He nodded to the others to make them speak.

"Kazu," said the taller man.

"My nay-mu eezu Ta-ka-hee-ro Ka-neh-da. How do you do?" Taka stuck out his hand. The others snickered.

Mei Mei ignored the outstretched hand.

"What you do? I know!" She clapped her hands. "You study ESL at MacKinnon College, right? I been there. It's very close. What level you?"

"Two," Masa said, pointing to Taka and himself. Then he pointed to Kazu. "He, level four. Very smart. He speak good English."

Kazu frowned, giving Masa a dirty look.

"Well, Japanese boy! You better order." Mei Mei pointed to the menus. "I come back few minutes. Okay?"

She smiled, then briskly walked off. The three men returned to their menus. They made their selections and then turned to look out the window. Small white flakes like shaved wax were falling onto the sidewalk. The men did not speak further; they had known each other since high school and were comfortable with one another. Quietly, they observed the snow with their foreign eyes, still unaccustomed to this world into which they had been haphazardly thrust as students of English.

"How old you think that Mei Mei is?" Kazu asked casually as he lounged on the only piece of furniture in the three men's living room. It was a large black leather recliner with side pockets for TV remote controls. Kazu had stuck a can of beer in the right side.

"Oh, she's old." Taka was squatting over the vent, cigarette in hand. The warm air filled out the cuffs of his jeans. "Close to thirty, I'd say."

"Hmm," Kazu leaned back and stared vaguely at the ceiling.

"What do you care, anyway?" Taka raised his chin. A swath of greasy hair fell into his face. He flicked it away.

Kazu shrugged. He leaned over, took out his beer and poured it into an ashtray.

"Hey, Popo!" he called out to Masa's pup. "Want some drink?"

The gaunt little pup waved its tail excitedly and rushed over to him.

"Kora! Don't give him that!" Masa's voice boomed from the bathroom. He came through the door, his big frame in a damp white bathrobe, wet hair slicked back, hands on his hips. The sweet, slightly medicinal smell of aftershave spilled into the room. "He'll get drunk and he won't eat his dog food!"

Masa scooped the dog away from the ashtray. But it was too late. It had finished lapping up the beer and was grinning stupidly, its tongue lolling out its mouth.

"Oh, my poor, poor Popo!" Masa simpered into the dog's ear. "Now you're going to be so very, very sick!"

Taka rolled his eyeballs.

"I'm hungry," Kazu announced. "Let's go out for dinner."

"No!" Taka protested. "It's too cold."

"We don't have to go far. Let's just go to Wei Ming's like usual."

Taka turned to Masa. "Kazu wants to see Mei Mei."

"Mei Mei?" Masa raised his brows. "Who's that?"

"That new waitress," Taka said.

Masa shook his head. "She's too old for you."

Kazu didn't reply. He began rummaging through a pile of dirty clothes on the floor to find a sweater. Taka butted out his cigarette.

"Put the dog out, will you?" Masa handed the pup to Taka. "All that beer will make him piss."

Taka opened the balcony window a crack and pushed out the dog.

"Jeez—it's cold." He quickly shut the window. "We better take the car."

"Whose car?"

Masa shook his head. "Not mine. Sorry. It's still in the shop."

Kazu sighed. "Okay, my car, then." *He* would have to drive. It seemed he was always doing the driving. Taka did not have a car. His parents had taken away his license before he left for Canada. "They don't want me dying in a meaningless accident over here," Taka had explained piously. Masa just laughed. "Baka-bon! You stupid!" Masa said. "This is North America. How can you not have a car?" Masa had bought himself a brand new sports car the first week he arrived. His father wired him the money. The three men walked into the first dealership they saw. "How much?" Masa asked. "Twenty-three thousand," said the salesman. "Okay," Masa said. "I buy." He drove it off the lot the following afternoon and was in his first accident that weekend. Since then the car had been in the shop four times. It was in the shop yet again this week. Another little accident. Masa had been driving in the wrong lane. "I'm always forgetting this isn't Japan," he said. Kazu rolled his eyes when he heard. He didn't have the kind of disposable cash Masa was getting; he, Kazu, couldn't afford to have accidents. He looked after his car and drove carefully. It was a 1974 Ford Mustang, scrupulously chosen after weeks of visiting dealers and wading through the difficult English of the *Auto Trader*. Buying that car had been the only pleasure Kazu had experienced living in North America. He hadn't meant to come in the first place. It was all his father's idea.

Ever since Kazu had failed his entrance exam to the university, his father had become unbearable. *You worthless, shameless son, good-for-nothing. Never studying, fooling around all the time. Lazy! Disobedient!* The stream of words was endless. Kazu began shutting them out. Why was *he* always under the gun? With Kunio, his older brother, his father was all praise and glory. Kunio went to Waseda; Kunio was the star on their rugby team; Kunio was taking over the family business like a pro. Kunio was the best kind of chonan, eldest son, a father could ever want. And what about the jinnan, the second son, Kazu? Jinnans were supposed to seek out their own fortunes, forge their own destinies. That's what Kazu's father told him. *I was a jinnan and I started this company from nothing. I don't know what's wrong with you. You don't have any initiative. I'm sending you to North America. Maybe that'll teach you something.* Kazu had obliged with a shrug. Getting away from his father made North America sound appealing. Nothing else there attracted him in particular.

"Hello!" Mei Mei waved to the three men as they hustled into the restaurant, a shivering mass of bodies, hands thrust into pockets, collars turned up.

"Very cold today!" she said. "Minus twenty-eight and windy, too!"

Taka shook his head. "I told you we should have stayed home."

"What you order?" Mei Mei said, passing out menus as they sat down.

"I— numbah su-ree," Masa said in his exaggerated English, putting up three fingers. He liked to practise, sometimes.

76

Taka merely put up four fingers. Mei Mei scribbled down the order.

"You," she pointed to Kazu. "You like number one, barbecue pork special. I remember."

Kazu smiled as Mei Mei walked off. Taka and Masa gave each other a knowing look. They jabbed Kazu in the ribs.

"Oh, she *likes* you!" Masa said.

Kazu pompously tossed back his head and combed his fingers through his hair. It was true— he *was* better looking than the other two. Women were more attracted to him. It had always been that way, since high school.

Mei Mei returned with three steaming bowls of noodles. She put the check on the table beside Kazu.

Taka laughed. "Your treat, I guess, eh, lover-boy?"

Kazu frowned.

The three of them went at their soups like animals at a trough, slurping and smacking their lips. From out of the corner of his eye, Kazu noticed Mei Mei watching him. He stopped his slurping. Gingerly, he picked up the ladle and began to quietly sip his soup. Taka and Masa were already picking up the bowls and bringing them to their mouths, finishing things off the Japanese way.

Kazu reached into his pocket to pay the check. For a tip, he left a couple of loonies.

The men went outside. The wind had died down and now there was only the biting cold of the air. They got into the car. It wouldn't start.

"Chikisho!" Kazu swore.

"Well!" Masa huffed. "Let's push the thing, then! It's only a few blocks." He got out, went to the back of the car, and threw his bulky mass against it. It moved forward a few inches. Kazu was encouraged. He went out to help Masa, instructing Taka to steer.

They pushed the car down a block. Kazu had his hands wrapped in his sleeves. He'd already lost the gloves he'd bought a week ago. The wind began to blow up again, raising clouds of snow. Kazu slipped on the icy pavement. *Damn clogs!* he thought. He'd put them on instead of his runners which he'd gotten wet jumping into the snow. His stockinged feet were freezing. He attempted to wriggle his toes, to no avail. An icy blast of snow blew into his face and he sputtered. *This country is unbelievable,* he thought. No one had warned him about the cold.

"Popo! My poor, poor Popo! You must be frozen!"

The dog lay trembling in Masa's arms. He'd forgotten about it when they went out to the restaurant. They'd found it shivering in a corner of the balcony, whimpering loudly, its body covered in snow.

"It's just a dog," Kazu said irritably, still freezing himself. Taka had positioned himself over the vent and, with a half-blissful look on his face, was taking in all the hot air.

"Why don't you take a bath?" Taka suggested. "It'll warm you up."

"Take Popo!" Masa thrust out the dog.

"No way!" Kazu said, slamming the bathroom door shut behind him. He quickly stripped down, ran the hottest water possible and threw himself in. A million pricking needles pierced his skin as the water touched the tender redness of his feet and hands.

That night, Kazu slept fitfully. He kept seeing the three of them battling through a blinding blizzard of snow, their hunched-up bodies creeping along the ground like animals. For some reason, they were inadequately dressed in tattered samurai garb, the tinny metal plates hanging by loose threads under their arms and chests. They might have been wounded for all he could tell. They were going somewhere— there appeared to be a destination— but mostly they seemed to be battling the snow. It fell on them in fits and starts, sprayed them with cold white spittle; words of windy rebuke broke through the chinks of the tattered armour: *lazy, disobedient, good-for-nothing fool.*

Kazu awoke with a start. The tips of his ears and toes were tingling so painfully he could not think.

"Taka," he whispered hoarsely to the other bed.

"Wha-at?" Taka mumbled groggily.

"Take me to the hospital. My toes, ears— they're killing me."

Kazu lay in bed and idly stroked the dog lying beside him. How could he have gotten himself into this predicament? he wondered. The doctor at the hospital had released him that morning, three hours after he and Taka had stumbled into Emergency. "Frostbite," was the doctor's diagnosis. A minor case, not too severe, Kazu gathered, since the doctor did not do much but tweak his toes and finger his earlobes. "You must get proper winter clothing," the doctor said. "A good coat, boots, mitts. Canada is colder than Japan."

The whole rather uneventful visit cost Kazu four hundred dollars. The hospital wanted the money immediately and told him to get reimbursed by his insurance company. The prescription was another forty-five dollars. Kazu couldn't believe how out-of-pocket he was already, and it was only the tenth of the month! His father had put him on a strict month-by-month budget, but the money he sent over was never enough, and there was no way Kazu could work, with his poor English and a student visa. After the rent, the meals outside, and the gas... there was hardly anything left. And now he needed emergency cash yet once again. What a predicament he was in. He hated calling home for more money, but there was no other alternative.

Kazu got off the bed and limped to the phone. He dialled home.

"Moshi moshi—" a man's staticky voice came over the line.

Damn! It was his father. Kazu hung up immediately. What was his father doing home? He wanted to talk to his mother. Only she would send him money. His father's words still echoed in Kazu's ears: *You live on what I send you at the end of each month! You hear? You have to learn how to live within your means. I have had enough of your uncontrollable spending.*

Kazu wondered what he was going to do. He still needed to get the winter clothes the doctor had told him about. Where was he going to get the money for that? His stomach tightened. *I'll have to stay in this apartment forever*, he thought sourly.

"Tadaima!" Masa's voice boomed from the front door. He was home from classes. There was a loud thunk of footsteps as Masa approached Kazu's room. Popo stood up on the bed and began wagging his tail.

"How do I look?" Masa spread out his arms like a great bear, his massive frame covered in a bristling fur coat. On his feet were a pair of clunky white boots that went up to his knees.

"Where did you get that coat?" Kazu said, incredulous.

"I bought it," Masa said. "No more freezing for me. I don't want to get frostbite—" he paused, "—like you."

"Yeah, yeah," Kazu said, annoyed.

"And guess what I got for you, Popo!" Masa pulled out a fuzzy pink woollen vest from his pocket and slipped it on the dog. It looked ridiculous, hanging way down below its belly.

"Wrong size," Masa muttered, "I'll have to take it back."

"Where'd you get the money for all this?" Kazu asked.

"Credit card," Masa said nonchalantly. "I don't have any more cash in the bank till the end of the month."

Kazu frowned. Why hadn't *his* father given *him* a credit card?

"I gotta get out of here," Kazu said. "I've been cooped up all day in this place and it's driving me crazy."

"Be careful," Masa said. "It's cold out there."

"So you outa money this month, eh?" Mei Mei slowly nodded her head as she watched Kazu take another sip of Chinese tea.

Kazu grunted. He could see Mei Mei's reflection in his tea. The thin face had suddenly grown moon-shaped, the black hair soft around the inner rim of the cup's edge. It was like looking through a faraway telescope, wisps of steam curling around her features. Here was the Chinese princess of the Milky Way.

"I know cheap place to buy winter clothes."

"What?" Kazu's head jerked up. Mei Mei's real face loomed close, the skin dry as paper.

"Are you listening me?" she laughed gently. "I take you to store now. Restaurant not busy. It very close."

They walked briskly down a couple of blocks to the Goodwill Store.

Kazu had passed it several times by car, but he had never realized it was a store. Once inside, he couldn't believe how big it was. Racks and racks of clothing, shelves full of used appliances and dishes, tables stacked with books and records. How could so much junk be so organized, so orderly? Some things looked even vaguely fascinating, museum timepieces. Kazu would have never thought to shop here. He and Taka always went to the malls in the suburbs. Masa shopped downtown. It wasn't that Kazu had an aversion to buying used things. He had bought his car second-hand, after all. He just hadn't known that used things could be sold quite like *this*.

Mei Mei took Kazu by the hand. She knew exactly where to go. Near some old suits was a large cardboard box with MITTENS & GLOVES $1.00 A PAIR scrawled on the side. Mei Mei began digging through the box.

"Here, try." Mei Mei handed Kazu a pair of slightly stained ski gloves.

They fit perfectly.

"One dollar! Very cheap!" Mei Mei laughed. She pulled out a loonie from her pocket and gave it to Kazu.

"Here," she said cheerfully, "your tip you give me last night. It was too much."

"No," Kazu quickly took off the gloves.

"No, no," Mei Mei said gently. "You keep— I don't want it money when you have no gloves. It make my heart— what Moogie say word in English? Ah, I remember— *guilty*."

Kazu hesitantly took the dollar. He felt suddenly indebted to Mei Mei, as if she had given him the world. How would he repay her? Now he *really* needed to get through to his mother. He must get money somehow to pay Mei Mei back. He must okaeshi, return the favour.

"Mama!" Kazu said breathlessly into the phone. "I need some cash. I had a little accident."

The line was silent.

"Mama?"

"Kazu-chan——" The voice was weak, shallow-sounding. "I can't send you any money. Your papa found out and he won't let me send you money any more."

"But I had an accident! I went to the hospital. It cost 35,000 yen."

The line was silent again.

"Mama?"

"Kazu!" The loud voice of his father boomed into Kazu's ear "What's happened over there?"

"Oh, Father, it's you." Kazu said flatly.

"Listen, you cannot take advantage of your mother any more. Do you understand?"

"Yes, Father."

Kazu hung up. Then, in a sudden fit of anger, he threw the phone onto the floor.

A few days later, there was a call from the bank. Four hundred dollars had been mysteriously deposited into his account. He rushed over to the bank, withdrew the cash and headed straight for Wei Ming's. Mei Mei was just getting off work.

"I got some money!" Kazu told her excitedly.

"That's good." Mei Mei winked. "Your parents not so bad, eh?"

"I want something do for you— some…" Kazu struggled for a word in English that meant okaeshi.

Mei Mei laughed and put on her coat. "You don't have to do anything." They walked outside.

"Really, I do something," Kazu insisted, stopping by his car. "How about drive you home?"

Mei Mei looked at the car. "This yours?" she said skeptically.

"Yes, my car," Kazu said proudly. He opened the door for her. "Please ride. I take you home."

Mei Mei reluctantly got in. "I live very close," she said. "But I like ride in car. Better than bus."

"I take you anywhere," Kazu said happily. He drove with great care and very slowly. He wanted Mei Mei to enjoy the ride. But a trip home seemed hardly enough. He must take her somewhere else.

"You like shopping?" Kazu said. "I take you."

They arranged a time for the following Saturday. She wanted to buy groceries at the big green Superstore.

"Here, my apartment," Mei Mei said, pointing to an old brick building at the edge of Chinatown. It looked hardly habitable. There must have been a shop on the main floor at one time, but it was boarded up. Tattered remnants of Chinese movie posters were stapled to the walls. Mei Mei pointed to the top floor.

"I live up there," she said, "with my sister."

She stared at the top window with its bamboo blinds before getting out. Kazu wished she could stay in the car for even a few seconds longer, but there was nothing he could say to her, nothing to describe the watery sensation of whatever it was he felt for her. The car felt empty on the drive back. It seemed odd to Kazu, for he had always preferred driving alone.

The following Saturday, Mei Mei skipped out to Kazu's waiting car clutching a canister to her chest.

"Thank you so much you take me shopping," she said breathlessly. "Look— I bring this."

She opened the canister and pulled out a swath of coupons.

"When you buy something and have this, you get it cheaper. See? Whole frozen chicken, $1.50 off! Moogie save lots of money. She buy grocery with these—" she shook the can, "—all the time."

Moogie— there was that word again. Kazu wondered what it meant. He asked her when they were in the store.

"Moogie is name of my friend," Mei Mei explained as they pushed the shopping cart around. "She look after us when my sister and I come to Canada. We live with Moogie. Some other Vietnamese, too."

"Why she have so many people live there? She has apartment?"

"Oh, no!" Mei Mei laughed. "She has big house. She help people coming from other country with no money. It called *refugee*. Me.—" she pointed to herself, "—Refugee."

Refugee. That was not an English word Kazu knew.

"Why she help people?" Kazu said. The thought of someone looking after perfect strangers with no money seemed odd.

"Well—" Mei Mei leaned on the shopping cart. She looked ponderous. "I don't know."

She pushed the cart forward slightly. "She is Quaker. You know?"

"Quay-kah? What's that?"

"Kind of Christian," Mei Mei said.

Kazu cocked his head, still puzzled. Mei Mei suddenly smiled to herself as if she'd hit on an idea. She began pushing the cart faster. "Here, I show you. Moogie show me once and laugh."

Kazu followed Mei Mei down the aisles. Finally, she stopped in front of a row of boxed cereals.

"There." Mei Mei pointed to a smiling old man on a box of oatmeal. "*That's* Quaker."

Quaker's Oatmeal. Kazu read the box. He stepped back to scrutinize the picture, to give it the attention it deserved. A kindly old man in a black outfit. Instinctively, he put his hands together and bowed as if in front of an altar. The Quakers— they looked after her, Mei Mei and her sister. Thank you.

"What you doing?" Mei Mei laughed. "It just cereal."

After they filled the cart with groceries, they lined up at the cashier. Mei Mei eagerly presented her coupons.

"I'm afraid these are all expired," the cashier said.

"Expired??" Mei Mei looked puzzled. "What's that? Expired?"

"See this date here?" The cashier was friendly. "They're no good after this date. You have to pay regular price for all these groceries."

"Oh, no," Mei Mei said anxiously. "I can't. It too much." She hurriedly started shoving items back into the cart. The desperation of her actions alarmed Kazu.

"I pay," he said, thrusting out a hundred dollar bill.

When they got out to the car, Mei Mei said quietly, "I only give you dollar."

Kazu shrugged his shoulders. "It's okay. I have money now."

"I not poor, you know. I have job." Mei Mei said curtly.

Kazu was hurt by the comment. He hadn't meant to demean her by paying; he was only returning a favour, that's all. That was the way of okaeshi.

Mei Mei's face softened. "You Japanese so sensitive boy, eh? You come my house dinner and I cook you this grocery, okay?"

It was an unexpected offer, a fair exchange in Kazu's eyes, although anything now would be fair from Mei Mei. When they got to her apartment, he happily followed her up the stairs loaded down with her groceries, his heart buoyant with the sing-song chatter of Mei Mei's talk. When they got into the kitchen, Mei Mei's sister emerged like a shadow from the other room. She looked about to go out, wearing a tight black skirt and an ivory-coloured blouse that opened in loose furls around the neck. A necklace with a large gold pendant glinted above her collarbone. Her face was thickly made up, white with powder.

"Kazu, this is Yin, my sister," Mei Mei introduced. They shook hands Western style.

The two women chattered in Chinese.

"She go to work soon," Mei Mei said, "so she not have supper with us."

Yin seated herself at the kitchen table, crossed her legs and motioned Kazu to sit across from her with a languorous toss of the arm.

"You are Japanese," she said coolly, almost indifferently.

"Yes."

"Japanese very rich," she said in the same flat tone of voice. She reached into her purse and pulled out a cigarette. Her eyes drifted to a lighter lying by Kazu's arm. Instinctively, Kazu picked it up and lit the cigarette for her. He felt suddenly as if he were in Tokyo— a bar in Shinjuku where he'd once lit the cigarette of a hostess his father had been fond of. It hadn't taken much for him to figure out his father was sleeping with her. He was poor at hiding things from his sons, especially his conquests. That trip to the bar, in its own subtle way, had been another form of showing off. Kazu quite frankly had been disgusted.

"Kazu got money from parents today," Mei Mei said, throwing some vegetables into the heated wok. There was a loud hiss and a cloud of steam as she rattled the pan.

Yin smiled thinly at Kazu.

"Nice parents," she said condescendingly.

"What about your parents?" Kazu replied, slightly irritated. They obviously thought him young, a child— he wanted to divert this womanish curiosity of theirs about *his* family.

The sisters quickly exchanged glances. Mei Mei's hand stopped moving. The hissing grew weaker.

"They dead," she said plainly, looking into the wok.

Yin looked at the ground, the cigarette hanging limply in her fingers. She suddenly looked too young to smoke.

"But we have cousins— many!" Mei Mei said cheerfully. She began rattling the wok again. "Right, Yin?"

Yin nodded slightly, eyes downcast. She sniffled and rubbed her nose coarsely with the back of her hand, making a squeaking noise like a child.

"I have to go to work now," she said abruptly. She stood up and butted out her cigarette.

Kazu watched her disappear out the door. Slowly, his body, which had tightened in the presence of Yin, started to relax. He turned to Mei Mei bustling around the kitchen, taking out bowls and chopsticks. The smell of food suddenly roused his appetite. Now that Yin was gone, he could concentrate all his attention on Mei Mei. Yin had reminded Kazu too much of the discomfortingly urbane world of Tokyo. She looked somehow wrong here in Canada, too sophisticated for a society that couldn't tell the difference. Mei Mei, on the other hand, seemed somehow more *Canadian*— relaxed, natural, easy to be with.

"I wish Yin here with us," Mei Mei said to Kazu later while they were eating. "I don't see her very much. She always so busy— she got two jobs, hairdresser and waitress. She think she can make enough money to sponsor family, but I tell her it's impossible."

II

When the snow began to melt and the weather grew warmer, Kazu began driving more. He skipped school and took long trips out to the country. He drove aimlessly and restlessly. Driving nowhere was a peculiar comfort to him. In winter, he had driven on icy roads for the sheer thrill of it, hoping that he'd slip and slide as he had done once, the car spinning around like a top, his heart beating hard as his hands grappled with the whirling steering wheel. The feeling was giddy, free. When he finally slid into the snow bank, he didn't feel relief, but rather, disappointment. Now, with the thrill of icy roads gone, he would just drive out as far as he could on some gravel road and pull over by a field to stare at its vastness. All that land was peculiarly soothing. It made him feel anonymous.

The only purposeful trips Kazu made were for Mei Mei. He took her shopping at least once a week. He'd push the cart behind her in the aisles at the supermarket or wait patiently for her at the drugstore as she looked at the cosmetics. "For my sister," she'd say, and toss a bright red nail polish into the basket Kazu was holding for her. She bought cheap shampoos and toothpastes on sale. The soap she used— the one he recognized in their soap dish in their bathroom— was a plain white bar that smelled like freshly laundered sheets. Once, when Mei Mei wasn't looking, he sniffed the soap box and got a familiar whiff of her smell.

After their shopping trips, Mei Mei always invited Kazu in for dinner or tea. He grew comfortable in their small apartment. It was better furnished than his with a worn but comfortable brown couch by the window and one large overstuffed chair with pillows. There was a little coffee table on which Mei Mei sometimes served Chinese desserts— coconut buns or egg tarts they'd pick up on the way through Chinatown. A small black and white TV sat in the corner, mostly unused, Mei Mei said, because the reception was bad. She'd bought it for only twenty dollars at the Goodwill Store. On top of the TV was a small statue of a woman draped in flowing robes, a necklace of beads wrapped around the base. Kazu wondered who she was. The woman's eyes were downcast, piteous looking. He'd never seen such a thing before in Japan. "That's Mary," Mei Mei said almost reverently in the same tone of voice she used when she spoke of the Quaker people. "Christian?" Kazu ventured. Mei Mei nodded. "Me, too, Christian," she said. Kazu looked at the statue of Mary again. Christian— he did not know what it meant, exactly, but he felt it must be something beautiful and good.

One warm spring evening, Kazu suggested the three men go to Wei Ming's. They had not been to the restaurant in a while; in fact, it had been some time since the three of them had gone anywhere together. They had been drifting apart, making their own friends, going out by themselves. The drifting seemed inevitable— they were no longer in the fixed confines of the strict and regimented private high school they had attended in Japan, to which their parents had sent them in hopes of their becoming disciplined and respectable. They had all been soft— botchans— the spoiled children of wealthy parents. "They dump us here, like pieces of trash," was what Taka had once said in a bitter outburst. But at least it had made them feel close to one another.

As they walked to Wei Ming's, Kazu thought happily about seeing Mei Mei. His step grew lighter, faster. As he approached, he heard loud voices in the alleyway. One of them was Mei Mei's. He hurried ahead, eager to see her.

"Kazu!" Mei Mei cried out as soon as she saw him. She was caught in the grip of a short man in a leather jacket. Struggling to free herself, she turned to the man and spat something at him in Chinese. He barked back at her and then slapped her, hard.

"Hey!" Kazu lunged forward. "Stop!"

The man let go and then ran down the alley.

"Oh, Kazu!" Mei Mei sobbed. Blood trickled out her lower lip. Awkwardly Kazu put his arm around her.

"We on boat together once. He nice man then. I don't know what happen to him." Mei Mei shook her head ruefully. It was hours after the fight. She and Kazu were sitting in her living room. The sun had set and the room was dark except for the yellow lamp light that bathed the contours of Mei Mei's swollen face.

"He get mad at me see you," Mei Mei said.

Kazu looked away into the darkness, where all the other pieces of furniture were lumps of grey. He could see the statue of Mary glowing faintly above the TV.

"He think you my boyfriend."

Boyfriend? Kazu's face darted back to the light.

"You surprise?" Mei Mei laughed softly. "I tell him you just drive me place, that's all. Then he get mad."

Kazu turned away. In the weak light, he could make out the shape of Mei Mei's foot. It was small enough to fit in his hand.

"I am..." he struggled for words, "kind of boyfriend, no?"

Mei Mei looked at him without speaking. She frowned. The cut in her lip quivered, a shimmering vein of red.

"You a crazy boy—" she said sadly. "You don't know anything."

She got up off the couch to reach for the teapot. As she bent over to pour some into Kazu's cup, Kazu could see the purplish swell of her lip. He felt like touching it, tenderly, softly, but he held back and looked away at the ceiling.

They sat silent for several minutes.

"You go home now," Mei Mei said finally.

When Kazu returned to the apartment, Taka and Masa were sitting in the smoky darkened living room watching a Japanese video. Huge metallic robots lumbered over the carnage of dead humans as the rat-a-tat sounds of machine-gun fire blared from the screen. Taka was sprawled on the floor, his eyes glued to the TV. Beside him was a styrofoam cup filled with leftover noodle broth, butts floating on top. Masa, dressed only in his bathrobe, was planted in the leather chair, Popo in his lap. He smelled faintly sour, of mingled sweat and smoke.

"So what happened?" Taka turned to Kazu. "Is she all right?"

"Yah." Kazu tossed his coat onto the floor.

Masa slowly shook his head as he stroked the dog. "Ayatsu wa abunai—" he said slowly. "That kind of girl is dangerous." He repeated the word "dangerous." Abunai.

"What?" Kazu said sharply.

"Higeki da. It's tragic."

"What's tragic?" Kazu demanded.

"Tragic," Masa repeated, shaking his head again. His hand moved slowly towards Popo's neck. "She is, that whole country, all of them— tragic."

Taka stood up and moved over to his usual spot by the vent. He lit up a cigarette. Then he spoke.

"Kazu doesn't want an ordinary woman. That would be too boring."

Kazu looked away from Taka at the balcony window. He could see his reflection clearly.

"Isn't that so?"

Kazu did not reply.

"You want a woman who you think has suffered as much as you, don't you?"

Kazu clenched his hands. *Not true, not true.*

"But you're not suffering," Taka said. "You're not poor at all. You think you're suffering because you couldn't get into university, because your dad doesn't give you enough money. Ha!— that's not suffering. That's making suffering out of nothing."

Kazu strode up to Taka and grabbed his shirt.

"You shut up now!" he said fiercely, jerking him against the wall.

Taka did not flinch. Smoke streamed out of his nostrils into Kazu's face.

"It's not just *you*, you know." Taka spat. He tossed his head contemptuously at Masa. "Him, too. All of us. Stuck here 'cause our parents don't want us. Stuck here 'cause we can't succeed at anything. Ronin— we're nothing but useless ronin."

Ronin— lordless samurai.

The warm evening sun was just beginning to set. The temperature was mild and the air filled with the sound of running water. Kazu and Mei Mei sat on a bench outside the beauty parlour where Yin worked. The dull buzz of clippers droned through the open doorway.

"It's nice you bring Masa for hair cut," Mei Mei said slowly, "but you know, my sister—" she paused, "— I don't think anyway such thing is possible. We never have enough money to bring them to Canada."

A warm breeze blew a strand of hair into Mei Mei's eyes. She swept it away.

"I don't want come this country anyway," she said. "We just end up here."

"Me, too," Kazu said.

A faint downward curl emerged on Mei Mei's lips; her eyes grew distant. "When we leave Vietnam, we don't care where we go. We just want escape. Yin and I— we go anywhere. So we get on boats. But when we on sea, we don't move many many days. Sun is so hot. We are tired, we want go to some place, but there is nowhere. We are just floating, floating like seaweed."

Kazu looked at a thin stream of black water flowing down the gutter to the grate. He imagined what it must have been like floating on that boat. Endlessly, forever, never arriving. The sensation was dark, but not without pleasure.

Mei Mei continued staring out into space, her voice now hard, thin. "But then the bad ones come. We scream and scream, but nothing stop them, they are so bad. Moogie calls them evil— the evil ones. They take our money, our things—" Mei Mei clenched her teeth, her voice a whisper, "— *our bodies.*"

She turned to Kazu. Her eyes were glittering, wet.

"I want to die, it was so terrible. People jump out of boat into sea. But I was too scared. Too scared to die."

Kazu looked at Mei Mei's face. Then he abruptly turned to the ground. He blinked, jerked his wrist up to wipe his eye. The thin stream of black had become a wash of grey.

"I'm going to stay in Canada another year," Kazu told his father.

"What for?" The voice was gruff. "You got a girlfriend? Is that it? Huh?"

"No," Kazu said, although he thought immediately of Mei Mei, the bruised face he had wanted to touch, the quivering red cut sharp with the words "crazy boy."

"No, I just want to study more English."

There was a pause before his father spoke.

"You really want to study, huh? That's a change."

Kazu did not reply.

"Okay, another year."

"Thank you, Father." Kazu hung up. He looked at his passport. The man at the immigration office had told him he had to go to the U.S. to renew his visa.

The drive to the border was through the flattest land Kazu had ever seen. Before him was an endless plain of grass, an infinity of earth. There was hardly a car to be seen for miles. Kazu pushed on the gas. 120. 130. 140. 150. The car began to shudder. It was an exhilarating feeling. This was the fastest Kazu had ever gone. He was flying, flying into the landscape like a speck of hurtling dust.

HIRO

Hiro stood on a street corner where there were no lights. In his hand was a newspaper that he'd bought for the Classifieds; he was going to look for a job. The cramped English print was of more consequence to him now than ever before. He had never looked for a job like this— so haphazardly, without connections— in Japan, much less in Canada. Shivering, he waited for a break in the traffic before crossing the intersection towards a large apartment building.

Inside, Carol was lounging on the couch reading a magazine. Hiro let drop the newspaper. It fell with a dull thud on the carpet.

"Oh, you're back," Carol looked up. "What took you so long?" She pulled herself off the couch and went to him. Kicking aside the newspaper, she put her arms around his neck. Hiro looked ruefully at the crumpled paper framed by the smooth arch of Carol's underarm. Why had he bothered getting her attention? She didn't care at all about his looking for a job. She was kissing him on the neck— soft, wet kisses, the tongue slithering around his earlobe. He felt like pushing her away, but he couldn't. He was growing hard.

"Carol," was all he could manage to say. She was pushing him towards the bedroom, her hips pressing against his. He tottered backwards, stumbling over a pair of his shoes lying in the hallway. Carol deftly kicked them aside with her foot, and continued pushing him into the bedroom. Once inside, she entwined her leg around Hiro's ankle, gave it a sharp twist, and *thump!*— they landed together on the bed.

"Do you love me, Hiro? Do you?" Carol whispered in a half-mocking voice. "You do, don't you? I know you do. I know you'd come back for me." She laughed. She was always answering her own questions, so assured of herself, not ever waiting for Hiro to put together the English to express himself— he was always having to blurt things out with her, and then, when he did, it was in such bad English, it sounded stupid, childish even— though he was an intelligent man, a Waseda graduate. Angry, he squeezed her breast hard, but she just arched her back more so the fullness of skin under his hand erupted like an overripe fruit.

"Mmmmm," she moaned. There was absolutely nothing delicate about Carol's desire for sex; it was raw, offensive, selfish. She never understood the subtle, unspoken meaning of his gestures the way Kazumi could. *Didn't you see the way I threw that newspaper down? I got it for you. So I can find a job to be with you, stay in this country.* No, Carol was dense, opaque to his needs. So *why* did he come back? Hiro closed his eyes, thrust himself into Carol. She groaned.

"More," she said, "harder."

When Hiro arrived in Canada from Japan on the Rotary scholarship in his senior year of university at Waseda, he was determined to get the best grades possible. He had honed and refined his English conversation skills by spending all his spare time at the foreign students' club on campus. He took out subscriptions to the international editions of *Time* and *Newsweek*. He turned the switch on his bilingual TV so that he could watch American movies in English. "You're getting to sound like a regular old American," one of the foreign students told him— the funny one with the spiked hair who came from Texas. Hiro took that as a compliment, but though his speaking skills were good, he knew he was still weak in writing. He was worried about the essays he would have to write. "You should get a tutor," his supervisor recommended. He gave him the phone number of a woman named Carol Adams. Carol was an English literature graduate in her first year of grad studies in comparative literature. She wanted to specialize in the Japanese classics.

"Actually, Japanese lit is a new thing for me, really," she explained to Hiro the day they met at the library. She was a red-haired woman all dressed in black: low-cut T-shirt, freckled chest, several silver necklaces. Dark, pointed boots.

"I studied the modernists— Pound, H.D., Lowell, and really liked their stuff. They were influenced by Japanese literature, so I followed up and read some of the *Tale of Genji*."

She looked at him with her head slightly to one side, waiting for a reply.

Tale of Genji? Hiro wondered. *What was that?* Then he realized she was talking about— *Genji Monogatari. The Tale of the Shining Prince*— Hikari Genji.

"I'm sorry," Hiro apologized quickly, "I don't know literature very much. I am journalism major."

"Oh," Carol said, disappointed. She looked at him, her pale white face framed with straight red hair. Her lips were perfectly shaped crescents of deep crimson. When she opened her mouth to speak again, Hiro glimpsed a row of ivory teeth.

"So," she said in a tone implying a change of subject, "do you like Canada?"

"Yes?" Hiro replied, not catching her question. He had been watching the teeth emerge, the whiteness from under the waxy red.

Carol rolled her eyes.

"Yes, yes," Hiro said at once hastily, firmly. He wanted to show her that he had understood. "I like Canada very much. Good government. Clean environment. Better than U.S."

"Well, we should go to my office, but just let me get a cigarette." She fumbled through her purse. Hiro noticed her rings. She had one on almost every finger. A silver snake coiled around her middle finger up to her knuckle.

"Want one?" she asked, pack in hand.

Hiro shook his head. He regretted his answer at once. He *had* smoked before; it had been fashionable for a time amongst the journalism students at Waseda. But Kazumi had held her nose and said simply, "It stinks."

Carol strode ahead, the tips of her long black coat fanning out like a crow's tail feathers. Hiro had trouble keeping up with her.

"What's it like there?" Carol's voice came back to him as he struggled to catch up.

Does she mean Tokyo? Hiro wondered. He did not answer.

"Tokyo, you know. What's it like? Is it all *neony?*"

Neony? Again, Hiro did not respond.

"Oh, I'm sorry— that's insensitive of me, isn't it? *Neony*— you know, lights, the big city, billboards, Times Square and all that, Coca Cola, you know..."

Coca Cola? Hiro was really confused. Where did that come from? She'd said "billboard." That means sign. He'd looked up the word once when someone told him about *Billboard* magazine. Then he saw it. The big red and white sign flashing in Shinjuku, the big Coca Cola emblem in lights. Lights. *Nay-on* lights. *Nay-on. Nee*-on. Neon. He understood what she meant now. Tokyo— was it all neony? No, it wasn't. Tokyo wasn't *all* neon. Or was it? When he'd first come from Niigata, Hiro, too, had been struck by the city's lights, the ever-pouring stream of neon blasting out of the pachinko parlours, company logos flashing into the sky like mini-sunsets, huge video screens parading gigantic images of runway models, foreign movie stars. Well, yes, perhaps Carol *was* right.

"Yes," Hiro spoke. "Tokyo has many lights."

"I thought so," Carol said. "That's what it looks like in the movies. Like *Blade Runner*, you know?

They arrived at her office.

"Tell me your address in Tokyo," she said, sitting at her desk. "I'd like to visit there when you go back. Maybe I'll go teach English there."

"Yes, I know people who are doing now." Hiro replied. "Friends."

"Really?" Carol cocked her head and looked at Hiro. "Who?"

"Americans. I met them at Waseda. I belong to the foreign students' club."

"Oh, imagine that!" Carol laughed. "A *club* for foreign students! How quaint!"

Hiro did not know whether to feel insulted or humiliated. It was the first time a woman had ever spoken to him the way Carol did.

The low, steady breathing beside Hiro told him Carol was still asleep. The room had grown dark with the setting sun. Hiro felt vaguely irritated. Another wasted afternoon of lovemaking. How many more days would this continue? It was two weeks since he'd come back for her. Two weeks of nothing but lounging and drifting. Carol was right; he should never have gone back to Japan in the first place after his scholarship had expired, but he'd already bought a return ticket and he had to change his visa. "I have to leave the country for that," he told Carol even though she begged him to stay and live with her. He didn't want to tell Carol that although he liked her, he was not entirely sure of her. She was sometimes as affectionate as a pet, curling up to him, cuddling him on the couch, cooing to him for his attention. "Kiss me, Hiro. Right there." Other times, she was condescending, disdainful. "You don't know *that*?" Or "Oh, never mind, it's too hard for you to understand."

Hiro returned to Tokyo. There was other, unfinished business he hadn't told Carol about. Namely, Kazumi. He had to see her. At least one more time. At least to say goodbye, that is, if he really meant it, if he were really serious about Carol. The night he arrived in Tokyo, Carol was already calling.

"Come back," she said, "come back. I need you. I miss you."

The voice was sad and weepy, genuinely bereft. A sudden ebullient joy swelled in Hiro's heart. She *needed* him.

"I miss you, too." He said. "I— I'm going to come back." The very next day he'd applied for a working holiday visa.

Hiro got up out of bed, slipped on his jeans. His clothes were scattered all over the floor. Carol had taken everything out of his suitcase, wanting to inspect it.

"Wow, what a great scarf!" she said, taking out the one Kazumi had knit for Hiro for his birthday. She wrapped it around her neck. It looked ridiculous on her, making her neck look like an overgrown tuber.

"Take it off," Hiro said rather sharply.

"Touchy now, aren't we?" Carol dropped the scarf on the floor. "What? Did your old girlfriend knit it for you?"

The voice was snide. Hiro looked at the small snow-coloured mound the scarf made on the floor. It looked oddly out of place, pathetic. He picked it up, remembering. Kazumi had given it to him the first year they were in Tokyo. He was so disappointed! A hand-knit scarf, of all the childish things. Callously, he had told her he did not expect this kind of trite gift from her any more. Such girlish handmade gifts were inappropriate, a remnant of senti-mental high-school exchanges between teenagers. They were adults now, real lovers, he a Waseda man, she a shakkai-jin, a working person. Kazumi's eyes grew bright and round as he lectured her. Then she lashed out at him with the knitting needles— "What was wrong with knitting?" she asked. "Would you rather have me knit you a Rolex, Mr. Tokyo?" Her Niigata dialect was thick with anger.

Hiro glanced back at the sleeping Carol. The white nape of her neck pulsed faintly in the dim light, its soft fuzz of red hair trimmed close to the base. She had cut her hair boyishly short while he had been away. He had been disappointed at first, but after touching her neck, curling his fingers around its shapeliness, he found the new look arousing. He had always had trouble resisting her, even from the beginning. At first it had been the lips, always so carefully lined and coloured in that thick red lipstick that he had discovered, to his surprise and delight in her bathroom, to be Chanel, the lone black and gold case standing elegantly aloof from the plastic assemblage of drugstore eye shadows and nail polishes scattered on the counter. Then it was the eyes, a dusky green, almost reptilian in the way they darted back and forth at every moving thing. Her curiosity and appetite for the new and exotic was insatiable. *Let's try that Ethiopian restaurant. I want to take Korean. I'm going to buy that hat.* Each time he saw her, he became fixated on her as if she were a movie starlet. *What is she wearing today? What does she smell like?*

It all began unexpectedly in his dorm room, with Carol looking over a paper he had written. She was talking about an old boyfriend of hers— "His name was Coonie. He was black, a Jamaican"— when she started playing with the top button on her shirt, undoing it and doing it up again. Hiro tried not to notice, but it was hard keeping his eyes off the little shadowed vee of flesh that would suddenly appear and disappear. There was something vaguely familiar about the act that stirred in him something both disturbing and arousing. He wished she would stop, but she wouldn't— she kept doing it, knowing he was watching.

"So, do you have a girlfriend?" she asked, her eyes glinting sharply in the light.

Hiro thought of the stack of Kazumi's letters inside his desk. They arrived weekly without fail.

"No?" Carol said, peering into Hiro's face. The button slipped out of its hole against Carol's finger.

"You know," she said, cocking her head, "you're kind of cute."

Hiro blushed. He turned his eyes to the paper in front of him and tightened his thighs. He was stiff and hard, his loose sweats forming a tent. Carol looked down at his lap. Her lips curled into a smile. Embarrassed, Hiro swiftly lowered his hands to cover himself, but Carol intercepted, boldly putting her hand around the tent pole. She moved her face close to him and smiled.

"Gotcha."

Carol pulled him onto the bed, tugging down his pants. Hiro leaned into her body; complicit in desire, he thrust his hands into her shirt, fumbling for her breasts. Hiro could hardly believe this was happening; it was as if he had been touched by a marble goddess and had been commanded to make love to it. The heart that pounded under the fleshy mound beneath his palm was *for him. This is incredible*, he thought, bending to kiss the pale breast flesh. The nipples, large and erect, protruded from the large blotchy aureolae like rusted nails. A damp musky scent enveloped Hiro as Carol wrapped her arms around his head. It was an unfamiliar smell; Hiro had only been accustomed to Kazumi, her odourless body, its small shapeliness, the breasts like little cakes, the nipples wet pebbles. Carol's body was lean and hard, waist-less, the leg and arms sinewy and long. She worked her limbs like an efficient machine, moving up and down Hiro's body, her fingers probing the skin's every surface, knowing where to touch exactly to excite him. She did not mind his pinching and grabbing; she relished his thrusting, wrapping her legs around his buttocks, squeezing with such tight delight that Hiro felt caught between her thighs. Her groaning and moaning was loud, unchecked. She even talked. "Yes, yes, more! Right there! Uh huh!"

The next day, they met at their usual spot in the library, but neither of them could concentrate. Carol's hand strayed onto his, her calf rubbing against his under the table.

"You want to come to my place?" she said.

The minute they crossed the threshold, it was the night before all over again. They went on like that for weeks, making love on the couch, on the floor, in the shower. The stranger the place was, the more Carol seemed to enjoy it. Hiro remembered scooping her crumb-pocked buttocks off the kitchen counter in the heat of one passion, remembered wiping up semen that had spurted onto the TV in the aftermath of another. When he closed his eyes, all he could think of was Carol's body, the way it smelled, the armpits with their wiry nests of hair, pungent and strong. She liked to be on top of him, bringing herself on him, her arms two pole-like sticks by his head, red hair shooting out into his face like bicycle spokes. He was mesmerized by the reddish-orange colour of her hair— the way it spread all over her head, inside her arms, between her thighs— angry bursting sunsets into which he'd sink himself.

Afterwards, exhausted and hungry, they'd lie on top of each other like wilted vegetables, arms and legs askew on the carpet or bed. Sometimes Carol would get up, fetch snacks she'd bought at the Chinese grocery store: Oreo cookies, potato chips, strange Chinese soft drinks made from guava juice or kiwi fruit. They would munch silently, naked, self-absorbed. Then Carol would turn on the TV and sprawl naked in front of it, figures of blue light quivering on her body like a tattoo.

Hiro quit writing to Kazumi. He took the pile of letters in his desk and dumped them in the trash compactor. He could not bear to look at them any more. They were embarrassing to him— the pink envelopes with their girlish print, little hearts and flowers doodled on the corners and edges. When the new ones arrived each week, he would throw them away without opening them. He knew what she would be writing about— her life in Tokyo working at the factory, gossip about the people in their home town. "Remember Na-chan? Well, she finally got married to Hiro-kun. It was about time; they'd been going out so long. Auntie Machiko had a baby boy, five kilos. Momma says he's very fat!" Hiro remembered how he had looked forward to Kazumi's letters and how he had written back to her in the same tone of voice. "Well, everything is fine here. The university is very big and spacious. I'm adjusting very well. My classes are all very difficult but exciting. I've met some interesting people like my tutor, Carol." It was important to mention whom he'd met. Kazumi was always asking about them. "Is she nice? What kind of food does she eat? Have you met her family?"

If a name came up, Kazumi would always ask whether Hiro had given him or her one of the souvenirs she had prepared for Hiro to give to any Canadian from whom he received kindness and favours. Kazumi had given him a whole bag of Japanese trinkets— key-chains, small wooden dolls, fans. "I know exactly what gaijin like," Kazumi had asserted when she handed the bag to Hiro at the airport. The souvenirs were cheap and trivial, hardly worth giving, in Hiro's opinion. But when Carol asked him if he'd brought anything traditional from Japan, he had nothing to show her but what was in the bag. He tossed it to her, said she could have the whole thing. Carol was delighted. "Look at this fan!" she cooed. Hiro could imagine Kazumi looking at him now, giving him a knowing look. *See? I told you. The gaijins— they all like the same things.* But that was the trouble with Kazumi; she knew with stinging intuition, everything, what to expect. It was uncanny, intimidating almost— that plain practical sensibility of hers that was as fine-tuned as antennae. That was fine-tuned enough to say at the airport boarding gate, "Don't you fall in love with a gaijin." He'd thought it was a joke. "Of course not," Hiro had laughed, looking at her and wishing she had worn something more stylish than the dull clothes she was always buying on sale at the supermarkets. This was not just any send-off. He was going away, after all, to North America. "You promise?" she said, the look on her face strangely indeterminate and lost. "I won't," he said. "And besides, it's only for a year," he tried to reassure her. But she did not look at all comforted. There was not a thing she could do. Not a thing. Tokyo was as far as she could go with him. Leaving Niigata had been hard enough for her.

The light in the kitchen drew Hiro away from the bedroom. He picked up the newspaper in the hallway and sat at the kitchen table. It was still covered

101

with the remains of the Chinese fast-food lunch they had ordered earlier in the afternoon. Carol had not cleaned up at all. With a sigh, Hiro picked up the empty tins and styrofoam buckets and threw them into the garbage. He opened the newspaper and looked in vain for the ads for jobs Carol said would be there. The fine English print— plain and simple journalistic prose— suddenly became unbearably difficult to read. For the first time in years, Hiro felt the words to be utterly foreign. What had Kazumi said when he began attempting to read *Time* and *Newsweek?* "All those little black lines," she'd said, "marching you to America DON-DON-DON." She marched her two fingers across the magazine that lay in his lap. "Like Gulliver," she said.

Hiro futilely flipped back and forth through the pages of the newspaper. *Where were those ads?* He finally threw the paper down on the floor. This was not the way to find a job. There was no one he knew here; no one who could help him aside from Carol. His university professors here had been pleasant but indifferent; they would never help him get a job like the professors back home. *What am I going to do?* he thought miserably. It was the first time he had ever felt such agonizing, paralyzing doubt about himself. Ever since he was a child, he had always been driven, directed in his goals.

The first goal had been to leave Niigata. He had sensed correctly, even in his boyhood, that the prefecture was a backwater, that all the important things in Japan happened in Tokyo. He often thought wistfully of the short time his parents had lived in the glamorous capital before he was born, when his father, a bureaucrat at the Niigata prefectural office, had taken a temporary posting there. His father was newly married then, and had no great aspiration to stay in the big city. "Your father never liked Tokyo," Hiro's now widowed mother had said many times, as if to contrast his thoughts against her own contrary but unspoken ones. In high school, she had been encouraged by her teachers to test for Ochanomizu Women's University in Tokyo, because she was bright. But she did not pass and so ended up attending the local women's teaching college in Niigata City. "I was always a little sorry I didn't study a bit harder," she said, "but you—" she looked at Hiro— "you can do it. Study as hard as you can." She said these words repeatedly because Hiro did well in school from an early age.

Hiro early set his sights to test for one of the big five universities in Tokyo. By high school, knowing his strength was in the social sciences, he knew he would test for Waseda. Everyone knew how bright he was; his teachers were always encouraging him. He was their star pupil. In addition to their attention, there was also a coterie of girls who followed him around, tittering behind his back. In junior high school, he set the school record for the amount of chocolates he had received on Valentine's Day. He was still setting the school record in high school when he began seeing Kazumi. She didn't like him receiving things from other women. In their first year together, she was angry that girls still had the audacity to give him chocolates when they knew she was going out with him. She stood in front of the school with Hiro where everyone could see them and tossed all his chocolates into the garbage. Her voice was loud, clear. "I don't care what people think. You're mine!"

Hiro was shocked, but moved. He secretly admired Kazumi for her toughness and tenacity. Most of the time, she was shy and self-effacing, but occasionally he would get a glimpse of that other self, the one others always referred to as shikkari— well-balanced, sturdy and mature. He remembered the first date they went on together to a nearby ski resort. Kazumi had planned everything; she was friendly with many of the resort owners because the kimono shop her family owned provided all their sleepwear yukata. "Papa will be glad," she said, "if I keep in touch with his customers." As a result of her connections, she got free lift tickets and coupons for the restaurants.

They spent the whole day together on the slopes. Kazumi darted in and amongst the flashy and fashionably clad Tokyo skiers with the ease and familiarity of a local. She showed Hiro secret runs and quiet places away from the crowds. "Over here," she called in a bright cheery voice, motioning him to a pristine patch of snow that had been left untouched by the Tokyo throng. Hiro boldly skied up to her and spontaneously circled her in his arms. He kissed her. Lightly, on the lips. Kazumi's gaze fluttered down to the ground.

"Oop," she said, a little embarrassed.

"I like you," Hiro said gruffly. He wanted to yell it out to the skies, the dazzling blue that sparkled above them, but he held himself back, pulling away his arm, standing awkwardly beside her.

"I like you, too," she said, in a voice barely audible.

When Hiro took the trip to Tokyo to find out his exam results, he went by himself. He didn't want anyone with him in case he had failed. He waited anxiously at the campus building with all the other students who had tested. The names of the accepted would be posted on the boards outside. When they finally went up, it was only a few agonizing minutes before Hiro spotted his name— *Takata Hiro, Kusatsu, Niigata*. He did not yell or scream like the others, but quickly strode to the nearest phone booth and called his mother.

"I did it," he said quietly, assuredly, although his heart was beating hard. "Don't tell Kazumi, I want to tell her myself." Right after he got off the phone, he headed straight to the Ginza to buy Kazumi a present— a bottle of her favourite perfume.

It was late evening when Hiro arrived back in town. The Ikeda shop was closed, but a dim yellow light radiated from underneath the metal shutter that covered the display window. Someone was still there. Hiro rapped at the door instead of at the back where the house was. He peered into the dark interior of the store. The light was coming from the back office. Hiro rapped at the door again. Kazumi's shape appeared, a silhouette in the office doorway.

"Kazumi!" Hiro waved at her.

The silhouette moved swiftly, quietly, to the door, and opened it.

"Well?" she said, breathless. "Did you pass?"

"Yes," Hiro said proudly. "I did."

"That's wonderful!" Kazumi clasped her hands and closed her eyes as if in thankful prayer. She raised her head. Her face was like moonlight, wet patches on her cheeks glowing softly. She had been crying.

"Can I come in?" Hiro said shyly. "I've got something for you."

Kazumi nodded, but moved only slightly. Hiro noticed, in the light behind her, a mess of accounting paper strewn all over the floor by the door.

"I had a fight with Papa," Kazumi said in a low voice, looking down at the ground.

"Who is at the door, Kazu-chan?" Kazumi's mother's voice floated out of the office. A hand emerged from the bottom of the doorway and began scooping up the accounting sheets.

"It's Hiro. He passed his exam!" Kazumi called out behind her.

The hand suddenly stopped moving.

"Come say congratulations!" Kazumi's voice was thin, reedy.

Mrs. Ikeda emerged from the office, her kimono-clad silhouette perfectly symmetrical in the light. Hiro had never seen Mrs. Ikeda in a dress. She wore the kimono as a symbol of who she was. The Ikeda family had owned this kimono shop for generations.

"Ah, Hiro," she said, her voice almost cold. "Congratulations."

She turned to Kazumi and handed her a sheaf of papers.

"You better clean this up before morning."

"Yes, Mother," Kazumi nodded her head. Mrs. Ikeda turned and bowed stiffly to Hiro.

"Good luck," she said. Then quietly, she left the room. Kazumi clenched the sheaf of papers and shook them at Hiro.

"Look at these figures!" she hissed. "I *told* Papa— I showed him I made that money for him last year. I *knew* those yukata would sell. I sold twenty in one day!"

Hiro took the sheets from Kazumi's hand. The year before she had convinced her father to order a new line of summer yukata that were untraditional. The new colours and patterns were all the rage in other parts of Japan; Kazumi knew they would sell quickly. "We can compete with the department stores then, I just know it!" Her father, hesitant at first, finally relented and ordered the new stock. Kazumi took charge of the new yukata, spent spring and early summer promoting the colourful new wear. Hiro had seen little of her during those days, but he considered it just as well; by that time, he was fully engrossed in studying for the then fast-approaching examination period.

"That money is mine." Kazumi's shoulders began to quake. "I want all of it. I want to go to Tokyo with you."

On the bullet train down to Tokyo, they talked of marriage. "After I graduate and find a job," Hiro promised. Kazumi nodded, her eyes bright. Meanwhile, she would try and find work in a textiles factory. They usually had dorms for single women.

Hiro took Kazumi's hand and squeezed it. He felt with complete and utter satisfaction that she was his now, completely his. An airy, ebullient feeling— a mixture of hope and pride— filled him as the rush of the speeding train propelled him towards the capital. Station after station, the buildings grew bigger, more densely packed. Beyond the platforms were blocks of hotels, neon lights flashing in the late afternoon light. *Tokai Hotel. New City Hotel. Shinmachi Hotel.* A faint but slowly overpowering desire began to overtake Hiro. His fingers felt thick and warm, nestled between Kazumi's; he squeezed them slightly, felt the pinch of her soft hands. Another station, the lights flashing again. *Muraya Hotel. Star Time Hotel. Hotel Imperial.* Hiro turned his head to look at Kazumi. She was dozing, her head resting against his shoulders. Her lips parted slightly with each breath.

Hiro looked out the window again. The train was pulling out of the station. The hotel names that had been legible as they had pulled in were blurring as the train picked up speed. Hiro looked again at Kazumi. *Why not make love to her now?* he thought. *At the next station? Find a hotel.* They had waited long enough. After all, he loved her so.

"Kazumi," he nudged her awake. "Kazumi, let's stop somewhere. Let's stop at a hotel."

They got off at the next station. Hiro picked the hotel— a dingy, nondescript building with cheap tiny rooms. The bed, a looming square, took up all the space. Hiro stood against the wall, suddenly unsure of himself.

Kazumi sat on the edge of the bed, looking down at her shoes. Outside was the sound of traffic, the rattle of passing trains, the roar of cars. Small strips of light filtered through the slats in the blinds in the window. The sun was setting quickly. Hiro stood there, looking at the darkened shadow of Kazumi lengthening onto the bed. Finally, she stirred. A trembling hand arose from her lap, moved slowly to the collar of her blouse. Slowly, she began to unbutton. A small triangle of white light grew under her neck; the plain of her chest widened invitingly. She spread her hand above her heart, opening the blouse to expose her bra. The flesh of her breast was pressed against the white trim. She looked up to Hiro, her eyes frightened, but Hiro was looking at her body, its pale, perfect whiteness, the small curved mound of her breast pushing up beneath the bra. His hands were sudden and darting, hot on her cool flesh. Instantly, he pushed Kazumi back onto the bed, his body pressing hard against hers, his busy hands frantic with joy, grabbing, sucking, licking every part of her.

When he broke into her body, she winced, bit down on her lip. She did not say anything but smiled at him bravely. He did not notice the blood on the bed sheet until much later. *I didn't mean to hurt her,* he thought, but in his excitement, how could he have known?

I never promised her anything, Hiro thought angrily to himself in Carol's kitchen. He stood up and restlessly began pacing around the room. The cigarette he had started to smoke— he had picked up the habit from Carol— bobbed in his hand, the ashes falling in bright red sparks onto the floor. Not watching, he stepped on one. Hotness seared through his foot.

"Chikisho!" he swore loudly.

He flicked the grey ash off the bottom of his foot. A tender red spot remained on the skin. He rubbed it with his thumb. Out of the corner of his eye, he spied in the mess on Carol's desk something familiar. It was an old snapshot of Carol and her mother sitting on a bench under a palm tree. He limped over to have a closer look. Carol looked much younger then; her hair was fuller and longer. She wore hardly any make-up. The smile on her lips was faint but genuine. She seemed happy, if only remotely. The picture had been on Carol's fridge when they first met, but when he asked her about her parents she had said in an offhanded way that they were divorced.

"That's my mom and I in California," she explained about the photo. "We don't see each other much. It's because— well, we get on, you know, like a house on fire."

Hiro didn't understand.

"Like terribly. We get on terribly." The waxy red lips shuddered slightly as the words escaped. And the green eyes dropped suddenly, despondently into a small abyss of pain.

Hiro fingered the photo fondly. Its weak shape with the young Carol had touched him then, so much it had never really left him.

"Now why would you want to go back to North America again?" Hiro's mother had asked on his return. She knew nothing of Carol.

"Because there are more opportunities there," he said.

"But what about Kazumi?"

"What about her?" he said with sudden coldness. "She'll be all right without me. She always has been."

He had visited her at the tiny dorm room in which she lived after he had been to the visa office. The room, immaculately clean, felt empty, tempo-rary— the walls devoid of posters or pictures, the shelves lined with only a few knicknacks. They sat on the bare tatami, facing each other. Kazumi hardly spoke at first. She stared down at her hands, defeated, as if she had already known. But he had to press on her the lie— that to go to North America was to advance the cause of his career and himself and that was a good thing, wasn't it, ultimately, that he succeed?

"That's not true," she said, her voice low. "That's not true at all." She looked up. Her eyes were dark, gleaming points. "Don't lie to me, Hiro!" The sudden change of tone in her voice, the anger, was startling. "I know why you want to go back. You found a woman, a gaijin woman, right? Just like I thought you would. You don't think I know?"

Kazumi stood up and grabbed a fistful of Hiro's letters off her desk. She shook them at him. "You write Carol this, Carol that, and then suddenly you stop."

She threw the letters at Hiro's feet splayed open, exposing Hiro's dark, handwritten lines. *Could it have been that obvious?* he thought to himself. *Or was it, as he had always suspected, that she knew him better than he knew himself?*

"You want to go anywhere where you think everything is better. Tokyo's better than Niigata, North America's better than Japan, gaijin's better than Nipponjin. When will it end? When will you stop being so selfish?"

Her words floated into his ears and then out like a vast unbroken field of stones— the debris, the aftermath, the rubble. He took it quietly, stoically, but the worst part had been the collapse of her body onto the floor, the sheer weight of her inconsolable grief, her body a crumpled, trembling mass of sorrow.

Hiro looked down at the kitchen floor, remembering. The stub of his cigarette hung between his fingers, about to go out.

There was a sound from the bedroom.

"Hiro?" Carol called out sleepily.

Hiro did not answer. He had not moved his eyes from the ground.

"Hiro— where are you?"

"Here," he answered weakly.

There was a shuffling, rustling. Hiro turned towards the hallway. Carol emerged from the bedroom, her body glowing dimly in the darkness. The whiteness of her figure grew more and more distinguishable: the pale limbs, almost evanescent, the red hair, glistening.

"What are you looking at?" She glanced at the photo in Hiro's hand. "Oh, *that* old thing!" She flicked at it dismissively and sat down at the kitchen table. "I'm hungry," she said, reaching over to a bowl of fruit. She picked out an orange and casually began peeling it. Hiro watched as she put a piece into her mouth. The juice dribbled out of the corner of her lip. Quickly, Hiro turned away. The sight filled him with a mixture of disgust and arousal.

Section II

FOREIGNERS

I heard it on the radio this morning: two foreigners arrested for selling fake Louis Vuitton handbags at Shinjuku station. A Turk and an Israeli. An odd combination, but then again, maybe not so odd for Tokyo. But all I could think just then was *Thank God, it wasn't an Austrian. It wasn't him.*

Franz would have never sold handbags. It would have been beneath him to sell something fake. He sold his own little creations— sand paintings, or rather sand floating in coloured oil, framed between two panes of glass. He made them himself and sold them at Shinjuku station, outside, underneath one of those huge expressways where the sky is a long beam of cement and the light is yellow green. I saw him there, sitting with his knees drawn to his face, the scarf wrapped around his neck barely covering a day old stubble. He had set up by a shoe shiner— one of those old dusty men whose very faces seemed creased with shoe polish. The decision to set up there was deliberate. Some of the people who had their shoes fixed or polished would have a brief moment to glimpse his sand paintings, and in that moment some would decide to buy.

"They are so busy, these Japanese people— all the time rushing here and there. So when they stop, they really stop and look, since they only have that precious little moment, see?" Franz said.

I never had my shoes polished. In fact, I never bought one of Franz's sand paintings. I only looked and made some comment— a comment in English, which, of course, he noticed.

"Ah, you speak English so well."

"Of course," I retort. "I'm Canadian."

"But you don't look—"

"Japanese Canadian."

"Ah— I see," he said. He looked confused. But soon he began to smile again, and then he made some witty comment about how the cement sky was

113

lovelier today than yesterday, and that maybe we could go for coffee and look at books at the nearby Kinokuniya bookstore together.

When we got to the bookstore, he went straight to the art books and I, not knowing where else to go, tentatively followed him.

When we dream, it is often said, we are in another world. Now that was how it was with Franz and I. We were in a dream, I told myself, because, of all things, Japan is always a dream. It is the place where neon creeps at the temple gate, where the sound of the closing train door is a sharp, ringing buzz, and where the smell of the air is the stagnant breath of the dying sea. Here, unlike any other place, fate works its hands on you, drawing you to people you would have never met except in circumstances such as these.

Franz lived in a small cramped room upstairs from a confectionery— the kind of confectionery that makes sweet little powdered cakes for tea ceremonies. When I first visited Franz's room in October, the cakes were in the shape of persimmons. And when I left him in the late spring, they were in the shape of cherry blossoms. That is how one measures the passing of time here— by season.

The first day I went to Franz's place, he showed me his collection of clay pots. They were of all different sizes and shapes but were of dark earth colours. Franz said they had been made by an old Japanese potter— the kind, he said, you would expect to be enlightened. He said the more enlightened one becomes the more like nature one's art becomes. The pots resembled stones. Inside them, Franz kept his sand— red, blue, pink, yellow— such unnatural colours in such natural vessels.

"All about us is art," Franz lectured me one day. I sat at his table with a pot of sand, running it through my fingers. The smooth flow of colour was fascinating.

"Are you listening?" he said sharply. He abruptly grabbed my hand and held it. Tiny grains of red trickled out of my palm. I looked up. A train passed by and rattled the windows. He let go and sighed. I smiled sheepishly.

On the first night we spent together, there was an earthquake. Not the pleasuresome kind. A real one. The kind that starts drawer handles clacking and light bulbs swaying and walls shuddering. We held each other, then. If the roof had fallen on us we would have died happy. But instead, a pot of sand fell onto the floor and spilled across our futon, and with the moonlight streaming through the window, it seemed like the coastline was at our feet, the ocean lapping beyond the glass's blue edge in a wave slow and languorous as oil. *Yes, we were happy then,* I thought to myself, *so happy.*

At times though, I felt rather like an animal around him—a dumb sort of horse, maybe. Other times I felt like a bear. I saw a bear once in Jasper. At night. A big lumbering bear with all the mystery of the moon in its belly crossing the highway. Bears are nearly blind; they can barely see, and squint at everything, but don't ever cross one with cubs or you're dead. That's what the little pamphlet from Parks Canada said. Franz had never seen a bear. But he seemed to know a great deal about them.

Everything he knew, he'd read in books. Everything I knew, well, wasn't in books. Maybe it was in my belly.

"Teach me about art and civilization," I said one night in a delicious mood of saké and sweet caresses. We were sitting on the floor at his little table. White saké urns and cups lay scattered on the table. A Japanese still-life.

"Art is—" he began.

"Art is," I interrupted, buoyant with drink, "the way stars gather around the moon, and civilization is the way men gather around the fire."

Franz looked at me queerly, then flopped backwards onto the floor, his arms spread out to the side. His face was slightly red, too. He stared at the ceiling. I lay down beside him, curled up close. He did not move. From out of the corner of my eye, I could see a dead cockroach in a crack in the wall where one of his hands lay. I rolled over right away and laid my head in that hand so I wouldn't see any more, and just as I was about to speak, Franz took his other hand and gently clapped it to my mouth, saying, "Hush, you've spoken enough now. I'm tired."

He did not speak after that. Soon I could hear him snoring. I turned to the wall, my face hot and flushed from all the saké. My eyes drooped, heavy as oil, and I saw a black pool of catfish darting across the room. I tried to catch one with my clumsy bear paw, but only managed to flop my hand onto Franz's chest, where it lay for the rest of that night.

In time, I became invisible— invisible in that thronging sea of black that poured like oil out of the subway stations and department stores. At first, he hadn't been able to tell the difference between me and them. Now, he no longer wanted to. My coming and going was like an anonymous drop of snow on his window ledge— a natural marvel in the gritty wasteland of Tokyo. Soon there was another. A Filipino girl working as a hostess in a bar in Roppongi. I met her one day, briefly. She clasped my hand as if grateful for a gift. I merely shrugged my shoulders and walked away.

That day I remembered most clearly. It was windy. Walking through Ueno Park where all the cherry trees were in bloom, I could see the petals falling like bits of flint, letting off sparks of pink and white in every direction.

MISHIMA

Megan looked out the window of the tour bus as it drove down a narrow Kyoto street. In her hand was a brochure about an ancient Japanese pavilion. *I wonder what it looks like now*, she thought. Would it still be that same dazzling gold that had mesmerized her when she was a girl? *Kinkaku-ji.* The Golden Pavilion. She remembered the long-ago visit to it with her Japanese grandmother like it was yesterday. Reflecting on it, she realized she might not be in Japan now— several years later as a foreign student at a Japanese university— if it hadn't been for that visit. Not "visit," so much as *homecoming*, almost, at least for her then just-recently divorced mother.

"Excuse me—" a voice with a clipped accent came from across the aisle. "I saw you at the literature conference."

Megan turned around. A thin, square-faced Chinese man with black, bristly hair cropped close to his head leaned towards her.

"You from Canada, right?" He pointed to her name-tag— *Megan Johnson CANADA.* "What is your study?"

"My area is contemporary Japanese literature," Megan said. She wished she had taken her name-tag off. It was misleading to say she was Canadian, but she did not want to add— *"Even though I've lived in Japan in the past, even though my mother is Japanese."*

"Contemporary literature?" the man said gleefully. "Me, too!"

Without even asking, he moved into the empty seat beside her.

"Poetry? Prose?" the man asked.

"Poetry, I guess. I do translation, actually."

"Oh, I see. My specialty is Mishima. They're fond of him in the West, I hear."

Megan smiled and nodded. *Fond* wasn't quite the word she would have used to describe the way the West viewed Mishima. Still, he was probably one of the more famous contemporary Japanese authors in the West— if only for his sensational suicide in the early seventies. She told the man that.

"Oh, yes," he said most seriously. "It is the most famous thing he did. My research is on Mishima's death. Why do *you* think he killed himself?"

Megan thought for a moment. It seemed an odd question.

"I don't know," Megan began. "I've always thought he did it for art's sake. You know, the ultimate act of art being death— making death art."

"Well, yes," the man replied, nodding seriously. "That is the most common theory accepted by critics, but I myself have another theory."

"Oh, really?" Megan was intrigued.

"Yes, but I cannot tell you now," the man said in a low voice. "No one must know until I finish my research."

"I see," Megan said. She turned back to the window. *He probably wants to go to Kinkaku-ji because of Mishima,* she thought. Mishima had, as she recalled, written a book about the famous pavilion, but Megan had never read it. Her interest in Kinkaku-ji was personal. She wanted to recover that ephiphanic moment when, as a young girl, she had crossed the threshold to claim beauty. "See this? *This* is your heritage," her kimono-clad grandmother said to her that day. She spoke triumphantly. Just hours before, she'd been lecturing Megan's mother at the train station: "Now that the divorce is final and you're staying in Japan, you've got to give the child a sense of herself. She's half Japanese and the sooner she starts knowing it, the better."

Her grandmother had succeeded. At least with the help of Kinkaku-ji, anyway. Up until then, the thought of living in Japan had been intolerable to Megan. Moving with her mother from Canada seemed a nightmare to her then fourteen-year-old self. But her grandmother managed to convince her that there were things in the country that were worth seeing, worth being proud of. Still, Canada would always be home: Megan never faltered in her plans to go back to do her university there. Now, however, as a graduate student she'd returned once more to Japan, this time as a Canadian on a foreign student's scholarship. Her friends on both sides of the world thought her lucky, slipping between cultures whenever it was to her advantage.

Kinkaku-ji was as beautiful as before. The sun was bright, so bright; the gold glittered like glass, casting beams of harsh yellow light. Megan stood by the bamboo rail and squinted. She lowered her gaze to the reflection in the pond. It had been this way before, too; too beautiful to look at. The Chinese man, Yaozhu, had not left her side since they got off the bus. He was still talking about Mishima.

"You know he wrote a book about this pavilion? I am very happy to be here to see this place. It helps me in my research to— to get his feeling, you see. That book examined the power of beauty. A monk burnt the original building down. Did you know that? Would a person in the West burn down a church because it was beautiful?"

"I can't imagine," Megan said truthfully.

"It is most beautiful." Yaozhu sighed. "A man falls in love with it so much he wants to destroy it— that was what Mishima's book was about, this monk and this—" he broadly swept his arm towards the pavilion and said grandly, "this building, his lover."

As if on cue, he quickly pulled out a Fuji box camera from his pocket and proceeded to take several pictures of the building. Then he asked someone nearby to take a picture of Megan and him standing together. Pushing his thin, wiry body close to hers, he rigidly fixed his face, neatly putting his arms in front, his hands clasped together. Megan could smell a faint trace of soap and oil.

"Thank you," he said politely after receiving his camera back. They began walking towards the pavilion.

"You know the book Mishima wrote about this pavilion made him famous— I mean, really famous."

"Oh?" Megan said.

"Yes, he was very concerned about being famous. It is quite understandable. I myself would like to be famous, but I have no talent for writing, so I must be something less... like... hmm..." He looked around. "Ah, like that pebble under a great lantern." He pointed at a tall and imposing stone lantern nearby. Pleased with his little metaphor, he picked up a stone from the base of the lantern and gave it to Megan.

"Now you, you have a chance. You are from the West and everyone listens to what comes from the West. What you translate will be known everywhere."

Megan laughed, nearly dropping the stone. Who would ever know of her translations but a few literary magazines? But of course, publishing in them mattered to her greatly.

"Whose work are you translating?" Yaozhu asked.

"Setsuko Murakami," Megan replied. "Have you heard of her?"

"Hmm..." Yaozhu paused to think. "Oh, yes, I think I know who she is. In fact, she knew Mishima quite well, didn't she?"

"I don't know— she's never— oh, you're right. She *did* mention him once, saying that he liked this one poem of hers very much," Megan said, remembering Setsuko showing her the poem and emphatically stating, "*Mishima* liked this one."

"I must talk to her," Yaozhu said suddenly. He pulled out his name card and gave it to Megan.

"Please give this to her. I would like to interview her."

Megan took the card reluctantly. Looking at it, she noticed that Yaozhu lived in the ward next to hers in Tokyo. He was probably in a foreign students' dorm, as she was. The Kyoto literature conference had attracted quite a few foreign student delegates from across the country.

"We-ll," Megan said slowly. "I don't know. I can ask Setsuko, but I'm not promising anything."

"We can all meet in Tokyo when we return. Now please— your address and telephone number in Tokyo?"

Two weeks later in Tokyo, Megan received a letter from Yaozhu.

Dear Megan-san:
Now is spring and the cherry is pink in the blue sky. Also it is very

warm. I am glad to meet you in Kyoto. We had a most pleasant stroll around Kinkaku-ji. Do you remember stone I gave you? Here is picture in this letter of together us. Do you remember my secret theory I tell you about Mishima? Please let's talk. I would like to meet your poet who knows Mishima.

Yours affectionately,
Yaozhu

Megan read the last line with some guilt. She hadn't called Setsuko since she had returned from the conference. She was afraid to call. Just last week, she had received a rejection notice from a magazine for her translations and this had unnerved her. Setsuko would ask about the magazine sooner or later and Megan feared the consequences. Setsuko was determined to make a reputation for herself in the West. Any rejection of her work by Western magazines was always the translator's fault.

Megan looked at Yaozhu's letter. She frowned. *I have to call Setsuko sooner or later. Maybe if I just talk about Yaozhu, she won't ask me about anything else.* Megan picked up the phone and dialled Setsuko's number. No one was home. A message on the answering machine said Setsuko was away on a reading tour. Megan put the receiver down in relief. Now she would call Yaozhu.

"Oh, Miss Megan-san!" Yaozhu's voice was cheerful.

Megan explained to him that Setsuko was away.

"Oh, that is too bad," he said lightly. "But she must be a busy woman because she is so famous. She would not have time for me, I think. Thank you for trying."

"Oh, but Yaozhu, she's just not at home— I didn't say she wouldn't see you," Megan insisted. She felt suddenly sorry for Yaozhu and his research project.

"Really?" Yaozhu said in disbelief.

"I will try again when she returns," Megan assured him. *What am I doing?* she thought to herself. *This is his research project.*

"Oh, I am very grateful. Of course, *you* must come with me if she agrees."

"Of course," Megan said laughing, "of course, I'll come."

Yaozhu laughed, too.

"Let's meet for lunch," he said. "I know good Chinese restaurant in Shinjuku. I want to tell you some new things I find out about Mishima."

"You see, many different theories why Mishima kill himself," Yaozhu explained as he sucked the meat out of a shrimp and spat the scales onto his plate. He wiped his mouth on his sleeve cuff, leaving a translucent grease spot on the shirt. Megan did not know whether she was more intrigued by his words, or disgusted by the way he ate.

"Main theories is 'he-is-mental-sick' theory, the 'he-cannot-do-any-more-good-art-so-he-give-up' theory, the 'he-do-it-for-Japan' nationalism theory, and the 'death-is-beautiful' theory."

Megan nodded. The theories all seemed to make sense, even in his highly condensed versions of them. Except there seemed to be one missing.

"Yaozhu, what about for *love?*"

Yaozhu raised his hand, chopsticks dangling in mid-air. "Yes! Now, how you guess?"

"I don't know— it just seemed one of those things, you know, people do things for."

Yaozhu looked at her admiringly. "You are very, very good— that is what I am trying to make my theory."

Megan crossed her arms over her chest. *I wonder what he's found out,* she thought. *These literary biographer types are always trying to figure out a writer's motives. It's fruitless speculation.* Megan had never been interested in literary biography or history. She chose to do translation because at the time, it seemed easy enough. She'd grown up translating languages between her parents, her friends. But literary translation, as it turned out, was much harder than she expected, especially working with a living writer. Setsuko was as difficult to fathom as one dead— one minute she would be telling Megan, "You don't understand what I'm saying," and the next minute she'd be shaking her head vigorously, saying, "I meant *this* before, but now I see your meaning." Other times, Setsuko plain yelled at her. Megan sheepishly acknowledged it was deserved. Art's meaning was so slippery that Megan stumbled over the paper with leaden words, unable to convey much but her own incompetence.

Yaozhu bent forward, his eyes bright. "Now you must know already, because everybody know, Mishima was homosexual. He also had special army called Tate-no-kai. When he do hara-kiri, he had someone... someone from his army, man named Morita, he cut off Mishima's head." Yaozhu gave himself a blunt chop on the back of the neck with his hand. "Then Morita— someone cut his head off. I try to think how I feel if I die like that. Maybe I think I don't want die alone. I want special person with me. I love that person, don't you think? And he love me because he do anything for me? Yes, even kill me. No?"

"Hmm," Megan replied, staring at the pile of scales on Yaozhu's plate.

"Mishima's death was love suicide," Yaozhu pronounced, slapping his hand on the table. His plate shook, a few scales falling to the floor. "A shinju, Japanese call it."

"Do you have proof?" Megan asked.

"I'm working on 'proof' now. I contact family of Morita soon," Yaozhu said, his voice lowered.

"Really?" Megan said, her voice hollow. Was she impressed? She couldn't tell. She herself was working with a great literary figure, but working with Setsuko didn't have the same quality of feeling as working with Mishima— there wasn't that mysterious and macabre odour of death. No, there was just Setsuko bustling around her house with her fax machines and publishers, her on-the-train scribbled documents carelessly lying on desks and tables.

"It very difficult getting interview," Yaozhu said. "They don't want to talk to Chinese."

He looked suddenly despondent. Then he looked at Megan and smiled, "But at least you, Megan-san, are interested. That is the way of the West, no— to find the truth?"

Megan shrugged her shoulders. She looked at Yaozhu. He was leaning towards her, his lopsided chopsticks dangling in his right hand. His face was bright, eager, almost innocent, the cheeks flushed pink like a Chinese mooncake she had seen wrapped in a store in Chinatown. Megan thought he could be any of a number of Chinese students she'd met in Japan, except for his subject area— literature. Literature was the odd bird in the world of scholarly pursuits. Studying literature was like studying life, except life in the mirror. Most literary scholars Megan had met were aware of this fact and were appropriately cynical, but Yaozhu seemed blithely ignorant of the reasoning behind his discipline. It was as if he had selected at random the topic "Literature" and thrown himself into it with the same energy he could have put into any other subject— chemistry, entomology, history. But it was Yaozhu's energy— that sincere, enthusiastic drive— that Megan found compelling. Where, Megan wondered, did it come from?

Yaozhu smiled, picked up a shrimp with his chopsticks, and dropped it onto Megan's plate. "Here, you take— you haven't eat very much," he said. "I finish now."

"Oh, of course, I talk to him!" Setsuko said to Megan on the phone. "I know Mishima very very well when he was alive. He was my good friend. I tell you that once, right? You must come to dinner with your Chinese man soon. I will tell him what I know."

On the arranged day, Yaozhu arrived at Megan's dorm room early.

"I am nervous," he said, standing at the door. "We must not be late."

He wore an awkwardly fitting brown suit whose sleeves were too short, the cuffs worn and frayed. His white shirt was wrinkled, and his tie, a loud red and yellow, was slightly stained. On his feet were dark leather oxfords with traces of dust on the tongue behind the laces. His hair was slicked back with an oily lotion that smelled medicinal.

Megan could not help but laugh.

"Really, Yaozhu, it's only a dinner. It's not a big thing. Setsuko is a casual sort of person."

"Oh," Yaozhu replied, unconvinced. He took a quick glance in Megan's dresser mirror and proceeded to comb back his hair.

"And that tie is… too funny. You must change it."

"Change it? I have no other tie!"

"Well, don't wear it, then."

"That would not be right."

"Look, I could get you a tie from one of the Americans down the hall. I'm sure they'd lend you one."

Yaozhu nervously fingered his tie. He took a look at himself once more in the mirror.

"Perhaps you are right," he said tentatively.

Megan skipped down the hall to the room of an American who was living with her boyfriend. She felt suddenly elated because she was being so helpful.

"Kate, will you lend me one of Bruce's ties?"

"Sure, what for?"

"Oh, it's for this Chinese guy. We're going out for dinner—"

Kate raised her eyebrows.

"Don't get me wrong—" Megan hastily added. "We're going to see my poet. And you know the Chinese— they're always wearing clothes that are out of date."

The comment was so flip Megan blushed in embarrassment. It felt like a betrayal. But Kate merely laughed in agreement. She gave Megan a dark blue tie with small diamond patterns.

Megan quickly fitted the tie onto Yaozhu. She had learned how to do ties as part of her junior high school uniform. Yaozhu closed his eyes and thrust out his neck, as if the act of Megan's fitting him was proper, familiar.

"There, that's much better." Megan stood back. "Now, do you have everything? Notes, paper, pen, tape recorder?"

"Tape recorder?" Yaozhu said, looking panicked.

"What? You don't have a tape recorder?"

"I forgot it," Yaozhu said at once. He stiffened, squeezing his vinyl bag under his arm. Megan suddenly noticed how shabby it was. Yaozhu probably could not afford a tape recorder.

"I'll lend you mine, then."

"No. I will take notes only," Yaozhu said firmly. "My method is to take notes."

"Oh, all right, suit yourself," Megan shrugged.

Yaozhu took one last look in Megan's mirror. A few obstinate strands of hair were sticking up at the back of his head. He raised his hand to pat them down. It was then Megan noticed his fingers— how long and slender they were— like the bamboo brushes she used in calligraphy class. The fingers seemed incongruous, almost too delicate, too sensual to belong to the rest of the man.

When they got on the train, Yaozhu produced a long list of questions he had prepared the night before for the interview. *How did Ms. Murakami feel about Mishima? What did she think of his writing? What did Ms. Murakami and Mishima speak about?*

"You have to be more specific," Megan said. "You have to ask when and where Setsuko *first* met Mishima. Then you ask her how often she met him after that and in what circumstances. Then you can go on to the feeling stuff. And bring up your theory about Morita. Don't wait for her to give you her theory about his death."

Yaozhu nodded his head seriously. "Your technique is very good. Very—" he paused, "aggressive."

He vigorously rubbed out his questions with an eraser and began to write down Megan's questions.

The train ride was short. They arrived at Setsuko's house and rang the doorbell.

"Come in, come in!" Setsuko answered the door. She was wearing a large neon pink apron and was holding a frying pan. Her long hair was swept into an untidy bun, pinned at the back with a rainbow-coloured barrette covered with little birds. She led them down a narrow corridor into a room with a small veranda. Megan knew the room well; that was where she and Setsuko worked on the translations. Piled on the floor were papers and files of assorted sizes. A large desk took up space by the veranda. On top was a fax machine and a portable photocopier. The table they were to eat off had been cleared away. It was the first time Megan had seen it that clean; she was used to seeing a stack of hand-scrawled manuscripts all over it. Beside the table were two chairs Setsuko had set aside for her and Yaozhu.

Setsuko was friendly and gracious to Yaozhu, telling him about her trip to Beijing and her very good Chinese writer friend from Shanghai whom she had met at a writers' conference in Seoul. At dinner she told anecdotes about her travels around the world, about artists and writers she had met from different countries. Megan was used to this kind of talk from Setsuko and was not particularly engaged by the conversation. She felt impatient and wished Yaozhu would get on with his interview. When they had finished eating, she offered to do the dishes so Yaozhu could get on with his job.

Megan carried the stack of dishes into the kitchen. The room was small and dirty, filled with the dank odour of rotting vegetables and old grease. It was the first time Megan had ever been in Setsuko's kitchen. She noticed that all around the fridge were shelves filled with colourful, odd-sized books. The kitchen seemed a strange place to keep such things. Megan looked closer.

Tanikawa Shuntaro— With Silence My Companion. Megan pulled out the thin volume of poetry by Tanikawa and cracked it open. The binding made a fresh popping sound. The book had never been opened. Megan quickly put it back. She spotted another book in German with the bold letters *GRASS* on the spine. Opening the front cover, she noticed a flourished inscription: *To my wonderful and beautiful Madame Butterfly, Setsuko, Gunter Grass 1978.* A small fruit fly was squashed on the corner of the front page— the rest of the pages were bunched together in a sticky clump.

Megan felt a sickly rush of curiosity— she began pulling out book after book, checking the front pages— *"To Setsuko, the great poetess of Japan From Octavio Paz Mexico City Writers Congress July 1979." "To the Fire Lady Setsuko Love Salman Rushdie, London 1980," "To Setsuko Seamus Heaney," "Setsuko, with sincerest affection, Nadine Gordimer Paris 1982," "To Setsuko Margaret Atwood Toronto 1989."* Megan lingered over the inked lines of Atwood's signature, tracing them with her finger. She then flipped through the book, going over some of the poems she had studied in university. Had Setsuko looked through this book even once? Megan was about to put it back when she noticed a dusty red and yellow roach hotel pressed against the wall where the book had been. Further inside, she could see a brown scaly body squashed against the cardboard, imprinted like a picture. Quickly, she shoved the Atwood back into its place.

Megan drew back from the bookshelf. She noticed a thin layer of kitchen grease on all the books, making each of them appear, in orderly perfection, shiny and slick to the touch. *Is Mishima here, too?* Megan wondered. She searched carefully. On the bottom shelf, nearest the fridge door, was a black space where books had obviously been recently removed. One lone book lay flat on the shelf— *The Temple of the Golden Pavilion*. Megan picked it up. The cover was faded and worn, the pages rather grubby. Inside was an inscription:

Art's meditation, could it be you?
Oh, how I wish, oh, how I wish it were so.

It seemed an odd inscription, but Megan thought she had perhaps read it wrong. Of course, as she could now see, writers wrote all sorts of silly sentimental things in book covers. But there was something disconcerting about the words in *this* book. Could Yaozhu's hunch be right? Was it love? But *who* was Mishima in love with?

Megan took out the book and went back to the other room.

"Oh, Megan-san! Come be with us!" Setsuko said. She was sitting in the one easy chair in the room, the Mishima books stacked on the floor beside her feet.

"I brought this one of Mishima's that I found in your bookshelf—" Megan said, handing her the book.

"Oh, *that* one— I didn't think that one was important to bring out," Setsuko said, her voice lowered. She did not mention the inscription.

There was an awkward silence in the room before Setsuko finally said, "*I* wanted to *live. That* was our essential conflict."

"Yes, Mishima *did* want to die," Yaozhu said solemnly.

The phone rang. Setsuko sprang up from her chair to answer it.

"Oh, Mr. Rodriguez!" She spoke brightly into the phone. "Yes, I remember you. It was very nice of you to show me around Mexico City— I have never forgotten that trip. Another festival? But of course, I'd like to come very much. I enjoy last time so much— you know I enjoy meeting Mr. Paz. Yes, yes. I know, I will try to bring some more English translations. Yes, yes. I will wait for the fax. Thank you."

Setsuko hung up the phone. She looked slightly flushed as she said, "I am going to Mexico for writers' festival again. They invite me."

Yaozhu began to clap. Megan looked at him strangely. He seemed entranced, as if watching a diva.

"My! Your friend flatters me," Setsuko said. "Now I must get my writings together. I will need translations. Megan— have you heard from that American magazine yet?"

Megan hesitated, dreading what was to follow.

"I'm afraid they didn't want my translations," she admitted quietly. To Megan's surprise, Setsuko merely screwed up her face momentarily before she smiled and said, "Oh, well. I *still* need translations for the festival. I'll get you to translate the shorter, lesser poems."

Lesser. Setsuko had a way of being gracious with a knife.

"You know—" Setsuko began. "I know someone who will help you— an American. His name is Basil Howard. Do you know him? He's done many translations. Mishima's works, too. They knew each other— Mishima and Howard-san. Anyway, I think you need someone American to help you. He knows people; he'll help you get published."

The fax machine suddenly beeped. Yaozhu stood up and went to look at the machine as it produced its paper message.

"A writer can be famous all over the world now," Yaozhu said, mesmerized by the paper with its Spanish and English message. "Not just in your own country."

"Yes," Setsuko said, her eyes bright.

The train was nearly empty when Megan and Yaozhu boarded. It was very late.

"Did you get what you wanted?" Megan asked Yaozhu when they were seated.

"Oh, yes, many good things she told me."

"And what of Morita?"

"She says it is possible although she says no evidence, of course."

Megan leaned towards Yaozhu. "Are you sure?"

"Why do you ask?" Yaozhu looked at Megan oddly. "Have I done my research the wrong way? I ask all your questions."

"No, no," Megan said, shaking her head. "It's not your technique or my questions. It's—"

"What is wrong?"

"We-ll," Megan said. "Did you ever think maybe *she* might have been his lover once?"

"Setsuko?" Yaozhu drew back, surprised at the thought.

"You know, she might've been."

"No, that is not possible." Yaozhu said firmly. "Mishima was a homosexual."

Megan sighed and leaned back. Her gaze shifted to the window. They had stopped at a brightly lit platform. A young couple stood next to one another, the woman leaning her head on the man's chest. The scene was intimate. Megan stared, half-curious, half-wistful. She had never had a boyfriend. All that travelling back and forth between countries had hardly permitted her the time to become intimate with anyone. Her eyes fluttered down to the empty space of plush seating between her and Yaozhu. Yaozhu sat stiff and upright, oblivious, his eyes distant, a curl of a smile on his face. He looked peaceful, detached, a student buddha.

Megan looked at the scrap of paper with Basil Howard's college address and phone number. She picked up the phone reluctantly. *Why do I have to show anyone my translations?* she thought. Weren't the magazine replies judgement enough? Now she would have to face a real person whose judgement meant everything— Basil Howard, of all people, the man whose translations of Japanese literature she had studied in all her university courses.

Megan met Howard at his college office the following day. He was a tall, thin man with a long, carved face and silver hair that hung in wispy strands around his neck. There was an elegant stoop to his shoulders as he bent down to shake Megan's hand. His voice was smooth and deep, with a faint trace of a Boston accent. But when he opened his mouth to laugh, Megan noticed one front tooth that was rotting, a chip of black in the corner. Without thinking, Megan ran her tongue over her teeth.

Howard smiled at Megan.

"Have a seat," he said warmly. "Tell me about yourself. How did you get into translating?"

Nervously, Megan began babbling about herself. She started with the usual, "I'm half Japanese," and then went on. "My father's a Canadian; he met my mother when he was working here on contract for a securities company. My mother's from Yokohama. After they got married, they moved to Canada, where I was born." Megan stopped for a moment. She didn't like talking about the divorce, but there was no way to avoid it. "Well, it didn't work out, the marriage, I mean. My mom came back to Japan with me when I was fourteen. She put me in an American school so I could learn everything in English. My father got me into university in Vancouver. I graduated there and then got a scholarship to study here, to do translation." Megan watched Howard's eyes, hoping for acknowledgement, but he looked benignly back at her, his cheek resting on the palm of his hand.

After she had finished, he said, "I see. And now, let me look at your translations."

Megan's hand shook as she passed the folder across the desk. Howard's hand lightly brushed against Megan's as he tried to take the folder from her. But Megan's fingers were curled tightly around the edges. Howard tugged. Finally, Megan let go.

"Setsuko told me on the phone you're quite a translator," Howard said reassuringly. "She said your being nearly bilingual helps enormously when you work together."

"Well, yes," Megan said shyly.

"I'll have to spend a couple of days on this. Do you mind if I call you when I'm done?"

"Oh, that would be just fine." Megan picked up her briefcase to leave. She suddenly thought of Yaozhu. "Dr. Howard— a Chinese student I know is researching Mishima's death and Setsuko said you knew quite a lot about the man."

"Yes, I did know Mishima rather well—" Howard said, his eyes narrowing, "and this Chinese student friend of yours— what is his angle? Literary? Biographical? Psychological?"

His. Megan wondered how Howard knew Yaozhu was a man.

"Well, he seems to think Mishima committed a love suicide with his second, Morita. He thinks love was the cause of the death."

"Yes, that is one of the theories, but not one often deeply explored."

"It is?" Megan said.

"Yes, I'm sure your friend has run into it in the biographical literature on Mishima. I wrote a book on Mishima myself, and touched on the notion."

"Oh, really?" Megan said. "I'll tell him about it. He seemed to have come up with the idea himself. He never mentioned any books, but he did say he had interviewed some members of the family."

"Oh? I wonder who?" Howard raised his eyebrows. "They are rather tight-lipped. And I suspect they wouldn't really know. The whole thing was a tragic embarrassment for them. Mishima lived out his obsessions in a public literary life that ran counter to a rather private and mundane family life. He kept the two quite separated."

"Then it must've been a shock to them when he killed himself."

"No— it wasn't entirely unexpected." Howard shook his head. "I suppose for them it was really just a matter of *when* it would happen."

Megan wondered how such a death could not have been a shock. A deep shock, no matter what Mishima's strange impulses for art and life were.

Perhaps she was not Japanese enough to understand; she could only picture herself aghast, like the Western journalists who must have witnessed the grisly scene only to feel that sudden great gap between cultures.

"The translations are quite fine," Howard said a week later to Megan over the phone. "I'd like you to come over and see me to go over some corrections I've made."

When Megan arrived at Howard's office, he showed her the translation of a poem he speculated Setsuko might have written to Mishima.

Red memory licks
at bright wounds of metal
swordside shudders
of ecstasy inside me
now gone, now gone

"People said they were lovers, you know," Howard said. "In fact, that was how I got to know Setsuko. She and I met through Mishima, a long time ago, when he was alive. I've helped her now and then with foreign matters, and she's familiar with my translations of contemporary Japanese fiction writers."

"But I thought Mishima was a homosexual," Megan said, her words a hollow repetition of Yaozhu's.

"Yes, but he was also married. You must understand that in many ways, Mishima was a conventional man. He was the type to respond to anyone who loved him, whether it was a woman or a man, but when *he* had to reciprocate, he would withdraw."

"Really?" Megan said excitedly. "So perhaps the Morita theory is right?" She felt a quick rush of curiosity for Yaozhu.

"Of course, there hasn't been any real conclusive evidence," Howard said slowly. He leaned back on his chair and brought his hands together, forming a tent on his stomach, "but I believe without a doubt that Morita was the cause. Mishima was a man deeply devoid of love— all he knew was the tyranny of it from his over-possessive grandmother.

"Whatever he had with Morita— probably the purest and most private love he had experienced— would have sooner or later been corrupted by something from the outside— his family, his reputation, whatever. Japanese lovers are always committing suicide for this reason. There is no way for their perfect love to continue except in death— especially in Mishima's case, with its being homosexual love. Mishima coveted love. He had to protect it from everything. Even himself, oddly enough. The only way he could protect it was in death. Love was his innermost longing, I believe— not death— but this longing for love was unconscious."

"But surely he was more independent than that. I mean, from his family!" Megan blurted out. She was suddenly zealous, consciously aware of the progress she was making for Yaozhu. "Mishima had such great artistic success. That must obviously have given him the freedom to love whoever he wanted."

Howard laughed. "One never escapes the tyranny of one's success. And besides, this success is relative. Let me tell you— there are whole worlds of people out there for whom art means nothing. Haven't you heard of the notion 'silly artist'? Well, that was what Mishima was to his father— a silly artist with silly notions. You humour a creature like that until he does something perverse, and then you scratch your head and ask yourself what's wrong. For many people, Mishima was just queer."

Yaozhu's words "insanity theory" popped into Megan's head. She struggled to understand how one could look at genius as queer.

"I like this poem," Howard said, returning to the translations. "You might want to change this word here. Have you been using a dictionary? It seems to me this word could mean something else in this context."

"Oh, yes, I do use a dictionary," Megan said offhandedly, "but I rely on my intuition sometimes." It was true; there were times when she did not look words up.

Howard looked at her. "Do you write poetry yourself?"

"No—" Megan began, "but—"

"Then don't rely on your intuition. It's too dangerous," Howard said with a tone of finality. He quickly gathered up the papers and made a neat pile.

"And have you been sending out to magazines?"

"Yes, but I'm not having much success."

"Which ones?"

"*The Kenyon Review, American Translator's Review, Poetry Chicago.*"

"We-ll, I think the translations are fine. Why don't you go over the changes I made and give them back to me? I know some of the editors of those magazines. I'll give you a reference. These editors can really be pompous asses sometimes. They often toss out work by people they don't know."

"You'll give me a reference?" Megan said, flabbergasted. "Really?"

"Sure, I will." Howard smiled. The black tooth now seemed less ominous, just rotted with decay. Megan took her translations and put them in her briefcase.

"Remember to call me when you're done," Howard said, watching her.

"Oh, I will. And also— maybe I should have you meet my Chinese friend."

"Oh, no— that won't be necessary. He can read my book. Do tell him, though, that he's on the right track."

Yaozhu was delighted with the new information Megan had received from Howard. She told him about how Howard was going to help her.

"It is good! You make friend like I make friend, and we all help each other get what we want."

"Yes," Megan said cheerfully. "I guess that is what it boils down to."

"I am glad because I'm not having good success these days. I meet Morita's family and they say Morita was not homosexual. They say over and over again. They say he had girlfriend. They even give me her name."

"Really, you talked to Morita's family?"

"Yes… is that maybe surprise? I learn many good technique from you how to do interview, so now I use them with this family."

"Oh," Megan said. She wanted to say "bravo," but she felt suddenly deflated.

Yaozhu put his hand into his pocket and pulled out a plastic packet of school pins. He gave it to Megan.

"This is where I go to meet girlfriend. Her name is Makiko Tsurukawa. Her husband is principal of some kind of military school. They have big Japanese flag in the school and they make the students sing "Kimigayo" every morning. They sang to me when I come to visit. She's a nationalist, believes in Emperor."

"Well that explains her relationship to Morita, doesn't it? A marriage of ideologies, no doubt. What did she say about Mishima?"

"She said Morita admired him. That's all. Morita admired Mishima too much. But she said, though, Morita loved Japan and was not afraid to die for his country."

Howard listened to Megan's account of Yaozhu's story. He thought the story made up.

"Nice touch, though," he said almost sarcastically, "the military school."

Megan was offended. Yaozhu would not have lied about something like that.

Howard brought out Megan's translations.

"I've looked over your poems and taken the liberty of faxing over a few to the editors of The Kenyon. They said they'd take them. I sent some down to Kyoto magazine as well. They're always looking for new translations of things."

"Oh, that's wonderful!" Megan clasped her hands. "I can't wait to tell Setsuko. Thank you so much!"

"Not at all," Howard said. "I've not written for many years now myself, but people still respect my opinion. I do that now and then— help out a beginning translator." He sighed. "Being burnt out myself, it's consoling."

"Burnt out? You're not burnt out!" Megan protested. "People still study your anthology of contemporary Japanese short stories in university. It's the standard text."

"Heh!" Howard laughed. "I had a good distributor and the field of Asian literature was starting to boom when I translated those works. In those days, if you had a good mind to know languages and weren't into European culture— and most people still were then— you could translate Asian things and people would eat them up. You just simply were the first, *not* necessarily the best, translator. But somehow being the first makes you the best. My success was a mixture of fashion and promotional politics."

"And talent."

"Talent, what is that?" Howard laughed bitterly. "If I had talent, I would have written novels, not translations."

"Well, it's not as if you can't continue translating, is it?" Megan said, wondering why Howard had chosen to speak about himself in this way to her. "With Japan's profile increasing in the world, there'll be even more of a demand for work like yours."

"Yes, it ultimately does boil down to these socio-economic realities, doesn't it? But I'm too old to be cheered by that— translations are for you to do, not me. Someone younger."

He handed back Megan's translations. "Let's meet at my house next time. The college will be closed for semester break."

Howard's house was set deep into a hilly suburb outside Tokyo. Megan had to take a bus from the station before she reached the address. The house was new, but when Megan stepped inside, the place felt stale— darkly cluttered with books and cumbersome furniture. It seemed as if Howard had just moved in without any concern for how things should be placed. Megan had been in houses like that with her mother when they visited Canadian friends in Tokyo. Her mother called them gaijin places. "They try and make it home," she had said, "but it's not their home."

Howard led Megan into a room filled with bookshelves. The air was damp. An old couch with its back pushed against a wall faced a large wooden desk. There was little natural light in the room except for a window above the couch. On the window ledge was a clay pot filled with painted branches covered in dust.

By the desk were two chairs. Howard did not move towards them, but sat on the couch. He took out a cigarette. Megan stood still, wondering what to do. Should she sit on the chair or on the couch? She opted for the chair. Howard did not move.

"Do you mind if I smoke?" he called out to her.

"We-ll," Megan began.

"Of course, you do," Howard said. "I'll open the window."

Howard remained sitting as he reached over to the window to open it. A cool stiff breeze blew in, rustling the branches in the clay pot, scattering dust onto the couch. Howard sucked at his cigarette and then blew smoke out the window. He looked sharply once at Megan sitting quietly in the chair. Then he stood up and abruptly shut the window. He butted out his cigarette.

"I'm not usually so considerate," he said almost gruffly as he walked over to where Megan was sitting. "Shall we begin?"

He took out her translations from his desk and gave them to her. Megan read silently, noting each mistake. She felt no compulsion to speak. Each mistake now seemed less of an insult than before. She would soon be published and that would absolve her of this tedious revising.

"And how is your Chinese friend doing with his research?" Howard said at last.

"Oh, him— he's fine. His research seems to be going well. I think your information helped him a lot."

"So you live near him?"

"He lives a few stations away from me," Megan said. "But I've never actually been to his place. We met at a conference and have just been keeping in touch because of our mutual interest in literature."

"A Chinese interested in Mishima," Howard said, stroking his chin. "I wonder why— and the Morita theory, of all things."

"Yes, it is interesting, isn't it?" Megan said. She now knew more of Mishima's life than of Setsuko's.

"What power of insight, of intuition, your friend must have," Howard said, "to have guessed about the Morita possibility."

Megan did not say anything. She thought of Yaozhu and his silly clapping.

"You know your friend is quite right about Mishima," Howard said slowly and deliberately, looking directly at Megan's eyes. "He committed suicide for love."

"But there's no proof!" Megan said adamantly. "You said so yourself! It can't be as simple as that."

"Oh, I have proof." Howard stood up. "Proof that no one else has." He reached to the top shelf of the bookcase beside him and pulled down a dusty lacquer box.

"You know about Mishima's private army, the Tate-no-kai? I was working as a freelance newspaper correspondent when Mishima formed that army. I had translated some of his stories by that time, so we knew each other. He asked me to come out to one of his training camps in Gotemba, because he wanted me to write an article for the Western press, to interview him and some of the other army members. It was quite an opportunity, so of course I took him up on it. I was able to interview quite a few of the men, including Morita. I had an interpreter with me. It wasn't Mishima, but one of the other students who spoke fairly good English. We talked about several things— I can't remember now what— but we got around to talking about Mishima himself. Morita was very proud to be Mishima's 'disciple,' I guess you'd call it. He talked on and on about Mishima's abilities, mostly about his skill and strength, but not at all about his writing. *That* I thought was odd. He talked about devotion to the Emperor in relation to Mishima. There was something there I couldn't quite understand. Then Morita suddenly told the interpreting student to leave the room. When he left, Morita slipped me a large stuffed envelope. I have never understood why he gave it to me, a foreign journalist, except that he thought that that would have been what Mishima wanted."

Megan's heart was beating hard.

"I've kept those papers in this box for years. I've always thought about writing about them, but every time I take them out I can't bear the thought of exposing this vulnerability of Mishima's."

Howard opened the box and took out the wrinkled, yellowing papers. He passed them to Megan. She could barely make out the faded brown lines. One set of brown lines alternated with another in slightly thicker brown. One line must have been Morita's, the other Mishima's. She could not coherently read the sentences but could only make out characters such as *glory, gold, sword,* and *desire.* Then she found the character *love,* strangely thick in its lines, as if whoever had used the brush had dipped it deeply in the ink. A sudden cold shudder rippled through Megan's body when she noticed the next character, *chi*— blood. *The whole letter was written in blood!*

A warm hand fell on Megan's shoulder, the fingers crawling into the groove of her collarbone. She stiffened. Slowly, the fingers moved up the shoulder to her bare neck. Megan screamed. The hand suddenly withdrew. Megan whirled around to face Howard.

Howard laughed nervously. "Why weren't you ready for me, love? You came here, didn't you? You are so beautiful."

He moved towards her. Megan stepped backwards, forcing herself against the desk.

"I— I don't want you," she said weakly, leaning farther back, her hands pressing hard against the desk. Her body was exposed to him. She had nothing to protect herself with. Howard moved closer, his thighs now touching hers, his hands moving around her waist, forcing her into his embrace. Megan blindly felt behind her and grabbed the letters on the desk. She scrunched them in her hands and shoved them hard into Howard's face.

"You b-bitch!" Howard sputtered as the papers fell to the ground. "Don't you know what those are?" He reached down blindly for them.

Megan squirmed out of his grasp and stumbled through the house to the door. She ran outside. How could she have been so stupid? Tears jarred her eyes as she staggered down the street. She didn't know where she was running. Anywhere. Anywhere away from her stupid self wanting vain things— reputation, approval, fame, publication— dead things. Dead. A nauseous sea of black invaded her body and she fell against a garbage can, wanting to vomit.

Two young boys playing with a red ball stopped to stare at her. They looked at her and then one another. The oldest one pointed at her and jeered, "Gaijin da! Gaijin da!"

When Megan raised her face, the boys became alarmed and ran away.

By the time Megan reached the station, it was dark. Neon lights glowed around the milling throngs of people as they hurried out into the darkness in taxis and buses. Megan went directly to a phone. She picked up the receiver and dialled.

"Hello? Hello? Who's there?" a voice answered.

"Yaozhu, it's m-m-me, Megan. Are you busy?"

"Oh, Megan-san! How are you?"

"I-I'm fine, I-I guess, and you?"

"Very good! I saw your poet, Setsuko-san, in the paper today. She is going to Australia to accept a prize for some poetry that was translated into English. Did *you* do it?"

"W-what?"

"A prize. She won a prize. Setsuko-san won a prize."

Megan thought she heard the sound of clapping, but it was her heart beating.

"I don't know anything about it," she said. She felt like crying again.

"Megan-san?"

There was silence.

"Megan-san?"

"Oh, Yaozhu!" Megan said, her voice shaking. "I want to see you now, is that okay? Can we meet somewhere? Please! I have to tell you something very important— something about Mishima."

"What? What is it?"

"I can't tell you, I must see you."

It's true, it's all true what you said all along. You were right, Yaozhu, you were right. The words sang loud in Megan's head. She wanted to clap her hands to her ears, the resounding truth unbearably loud, so evident and yet so hidden. *Love, love, love,* said the clacking wheels of the train pushing her toward Yaozhu— there was no proof ever of these things; everything was felt, and then proof found, like brown words on white paper clenched in her hands; that was proof, wasn't it? *Wasn't it?*

Yaozhu was waiting for her at the Chinese restaurant. He stood up when he saw her.

"Yaozhu!" Megan could barely hold back the tears. She stumbled towards him, her hands dropping onto his shoulders.

Yaozhu stiffened.

"You were right, Yaozhu, you were right!" Megan said, her voice quavering. "Mishima *did* commit suicide for love, he did, he did." She grabbed Yaozhu's hands. "What's the matter, don't you believe me? Yaozhu— I did this for you. I know the truth now. I've found it."

Distressed, Yaozhu abruptly pulled back his hands.

"Megan-san," he said stiffly.

"What? What's the matter?" Megan reached for his hands again, but he pulled them away.

"Megan-san— I, I am a m-married man."

"What?" Megan drew back her arms. Her cheeks burned red. "Why didn't you tell me?" she cried.

Yaozhu looked bewildered. "But I don't understand, Megan-san, why are you surprised? Such information is not important— not for you and I. Our concern is literature, no?"

Megan was not listening. She saw in her mind the picture of a face, placid and resigned. A Chinese woman's face. A wife's face. A face that knew the quiet duty of waiting, and not wanting. Megan's cheeks burned red with shame. The collapse was quiet and sudden— the way Mishima must have felt when he realized he was truly dying. Everything then must have tasted of blood. A metallic sweetness. And then, the strong, cold reproach of death.

BLACK WATER ANGEL

She met him on a hot July afternoon. He was from Paris, an artist. He wanted some translations of titles done for a small exhibit he was going to hold in a gallery on the Ginza. A mutual acquaintance had told him she could translate French into Japanese.

His studio was in Askakusa near Sensoji Temple. One had to walk down a narrow lane to get to it. It was tucked far back into a building at the end of a hallway. When she finally found the place, the door was wide open. Inside, everything looked cluttered and in disarray. Canvases lay stacked against the wall and piled on the floor. A large sculpture draped with cloth stood on a pedestal near a window.

She walked in tentatively. He was sitting at the far end of the room on the floor by the veranda, his leg stuck out of his kimono into the garden beyond. In his hand was a fan which he waved languorously, back and forth.

"Ah, you must be here to do the translations," he said, getting up. The blue cotton of his kimono rustled into shape as he walked towards her. He took her hand and introduced himself.

A dank wet smell came from his neck, where his kimono lay open. A v-shaped patch of chest hair glistened with sweat. It was unbearably hot.

He gave her the sheets to translate and made room for her at a low table where she could sit on the floor and work on them.

"So, tell me again, where are you from?" he asked.

"Canada," she said.

"Rather cold there, isn't it?"

"Yes," she replied. "Quite cold."

"I see." He picked up his fan and gently waved it. The corners of her sheets began to flutter. She put out her hand to press them down. His hand, slower than hers, landed on her fingers.

"Sorry," he said, quickly removing his hand. He put down the fan.

"It's okay," she answered. She could still feel the heavy warmth of his inner palm tingling on her fingers. She lowered her head, looked at the sheets.

He had turned away and was staring out at the garden. The heavy drone of cicadas filled the air.

She began translating the title— "Black Water Angel"— she tried to imagine the painting. Then she looked at the next title.

"I can't read this one," she said, pointing to it.

He turned to her. Slowly, he drew up beside her, his blue kimono rustling on the tatami. He strained to look at the letters. His neck, long and thin, tightened as he spoke, "Alphonsine. It says 'Alphonsine.'"

She wrote it down.

"My dead wife," he added, "but don't put that down."

"Oh," she said. "I'm sorry."

"Nothing to be sorry about. She died years ago. Drowned."

"What?" she said absently. She had barely heard. It was hard to pay attention with the heat.

"She was a writer. Quite gifted. And beautiful, too."

"Oh," she said, trying to concentrate. He seemed unbearably close. She could see the sweat gathering like small pearls on the stubble on his cheeks. A faint odour of blackness tickled her nose. It seemed a butterfly was trapped in the veranda window. She could hear its wings beating like the soft drumming of rain. But it was really his fingers marching across the edge of her skirt. His arm, slow and graceful like a train edging along the shoreline, disappeared into a tunnel. A dark gulp of air and the soft flutter of arms against the tatami, a wash of blue cotton over her eyes and nose— the rank smell of salt and dead fish.

When she came to, she was lying on the tatami, her head propped on a pillow. A small electric fan buzzed by her ear.

She could see him across the room. He was standing, working at the sculpture by the window. His back was to her, bare and exposed. He had slipped out of the top part of his kimono, and it hung at the sides, strapped to his waist by the obi. The light from the window reflected sharply off his torso, the hard muscles of his arm and back twitching with each movement he made with his chisel.

She lay for a long time watching him, without moving. There was something familiar about the shape of his skin, as if she had swum in it with him in a dream she could only barely remember. When she remembered the name— Alphonsine— she suddenly realized where she was. Who he was.

Without trying to appear too conspicuous, she sat up.

He turned around.

"Ah, you're awake. You fainted."

"I'm sorry," she said sheepishly. She returned to her kneeling position at the table and picked up her pen.

"You don't need to do any more if you're not feeling well," he said, putting down his chisel.

"No, no. There are only a few left anyway," she said, hurrying herself along.

She finished the last few titles and got ready to leave.

"Would you like to stay for dinner?" he offered.

"No, I must get going," she said. She hastily picked up her things and made her way out.

It was dusk and the streets were noisy and crowded. She hurried off to the subway station.

When she arrived at her apartment, she felt tired and hot. Her clothes were damp with sweat. She bent down to take off her stockings when, strangely, she noticed she wasn't wearing any. Had she even put them on that day? She could not remember.

BESSO

He had a besso, a summer house, in Zushi, and was inviting them to come for a weekend. All of them— Marianne, the Canadian; the two French women, Hélène and Sophie; and the Congolese, Guillaume.

"He feel sorry for us," Sophie said in her strongly accented English, "that we live in this terrible place." She motioned vaguely to the cracked walls of the tiny dorm rooms in which they all lived as foreign students. A stray cat yowled loudly from the window.

"It's nice for him to offer though, don't you think?" Marianne said.

Hélène shrugged and lit up a cigarette.

"Let's go," she said. "I'm sick of Tokyo. I want a break."

They knew him only vaguely, as Desaulnier. He was Guillaume's friend, a French literature professor at the prestigious Todai, Tokyo University. Marianne had met him only once, when he was visiting Guillaume. She had gone to Guillaume's room to drop off her recent edits of his thesis.

"Ah, chère Marianne!" Guillaume greeted her, "Come een! You meet my fraynd, Desaulnier. Desaulnier, dis eez the woman I tell you about, the one who helps me."

A small man, bearded with short brown hair, stood up from a chair and extended his hand.

"Mademoiselle," he nodded his head.

Marianne took his hand. He squeezed it, the fingers pressing warmly against the side of her palm.

"Vous êtes Canadienne, oui?"

"Oui, um, yes, je suis Canadienne." Marianne replied. Her French was terrible.

"Ah." He smiled. His eyes glinted under the thin pointed arch of his brows. He sat down again and crossed his legs. The lamp on Guillaume's desk projected a thick yellow light onto part of Desaulnier's face. When he spoke again, he appeared to be talking out of only half his mouth.

Marianne could not catch what he had said; she turned to Guillaume.

"You must speak da English, mon ami." Guillaume said gently to his friend. "*Please*."

"Ah." There was a slight quiver in the brow, whether of contempt or disdain, was hard to determine.

"It's okay," Marianne apologized quickly. She was feeling uncomfortable. "I didn't mean to interrupt. I just wanted to drop your thesis off."

She reached over to put the clipped sheaf of papers on Guillaume's desk. Desaulnier followed her movement with his eyes, his gaze moving down her arm and up again. He did not speak a word until she was about to slip out the door.

"My pleasure, Mademoiselle; it was nice meeting you."

So he does speak English, Marianne thought as she padded down the corridor to her dorm. Why didn't he use it earlier? Not until she reached her room did she realize what she had felt in the presence of the man. It was languor *and* humiliation— an odd combination. She remembered the warm press of his hand followed by the questioning in French, a language in which she moved like a clumsy reptile— gawky and blundering, joints bulging out with each awkward step. She had felt entirely exposed, vulnerable, but then there was his gazing down her arm— slow and deliberate. *That* was titillating. Marianne wondered if she would ever meet him again.

"What should I wear to Zushi?" Hélène stood in front of her closet. She was half-naked in a black bra and panties, one hand planted firmly on her hip, the other airily holding a cigarette. On her feet were a pair of purple socks. She was a big-boned woman, Slavic looking, with high broad cheekbones and ruddy orange hair always kept in a ponytail.

Marianne and Sophie sat watching her from the bed.

"What about that?" Marianne pointed to a cotton shirt.

"This?" Hélène replied, pulling it out. Marianne nodded. Hélène then glanced at Sophie, whose small, slight frame leaned slightly forward. *No*, Sophie shook her head. Immediately Hélène threw the blouse onto the floor and began rattling through the closet again.

Marianne turned her eyes back up from the shirt on the floor to Sophie. What was wrong with her choice?

"No," Sophie shook her head again. "It is too—how do you say—casual?"

"Really?" Marianne frowned slightly. "This trip isn't a big deal, is it? I mean, we're just going to his summer house."

"It is not a 'deal'—" Sophie grimaced slightly at the word. "It's an *occasion.*"

Hélène pulled out another shirt. This time, Sophie nodded approvingly. Happy, Hélène slipped it on and posed in front of the mirror. "Parfait," Sophie murmured. She got up off the bed and started looking for a matching scarf on Hélène's dresser. She picked up a green one, then a yellow one. "No, not that one, I don't like it." Hélène shook her head. "And that one's too old. There's a nice red one in my drawer." Sophie opened the drawer and pulled out a crimson scarf with gold fringe. "Yes, this is beautiful," she concurred, draping it over Hélène's shoulder. They paused to look in the mirror—Hélène staring critically at herself, head slightly slanted, and Sophie peering out from behind her shoulder.

Like sisters, Marianne thought.

It was Sophie who had first introduced Marianne to Guillaume. "You'll like him," she said, as they walked to his room. "He's a most interesting man, very passionate and full of secrets. I think he's a political exile from a wealthy family, but he would never say so. There has been much persecution in that country." She told Marianne a story of how Guillaume had gone into a liquor store where the proprietor was selling South African wine and how he had angrily protested by dropping the bottles one by one onto the floor. "What's dis crap? CRASH! This is South African wine. CRASH! Do you know what they do to blacks in that country? CRASH!"

The picture she had of the man was hardly the one who greeted them at the door.

"Ah, Sophie, chère amie!" The loud, portly man with the round face and chubby cheeks bent over to kiss his friend. When Sophie introduced Marianne, he took her hand and vigorously pumped it, saying, "Dis ees da American way, non?"

His English sounded clipped like a Jamaican's. They were not a minute into the conversation when he begged her to help him with his thesis.

"You Canadians speak good English," he began, "and moi, I am so poor at English— especially writing. Eet ees not mah language. Please help me with mah teesis."

Mah teesis. Marianne smiles even as she remembers now. She agrees, stupidly enough. He has been told by his professor that he must write the work in English or Japanese. French is not an option. He chooses English. "I want to publish it in an American journal. America, she is king! You make it there and you make it everywhere," he says in poor imitation of Frank Sinatra. Unfortunately, English is his third language after French and his tribal tongue. "I have some difficulty writing it," he tells her. "Some" is an understatement. "Great" is more like it. Soon they are padding back and forth to each other's rooms, the thick, clipped sheaf of papers in their hands. The others on her floor raise their eyebrows. They hear muffled noises, voices sometimes loud and raised. If only they knew the conversations, they could rest easy, go back to bed. "You're not making your point here clearly enough." She shows him the paragraph. "Point, point!" he rants. "Why should there be a point, eh, you tell me! You English must always have DA POINT and then the French, they don't want such a thing, they want atmosphere. You ask me now— shoot with a gun— point this, point that— like a bullet when I have in French to write like a blanket over mah head." He reacts badly to criticism. She sits his fits out quietly, picking at her nails, and then, when he calms down, she begins editing again. Afterwards, he leaves, his face beaming piously with gratitude as he clasps her hand. "Ah, thank you, mon amie, you have saved mah teesis, mah life, you have saved me." And on, and on. Such hyperbole.

She wonders when he will ever finish. Eight years on a Ph.D. is a long time. His scholarship money dried up long ago. He has made ends meet by doing everything from kitchen duty in the dorm to brokering deals for Japanese companies investing in Africa. One thing is for certain— he does not want to return to his country. "It is unstable there," he says, not bothering to explain things further. Perhaps Sophie is right about his being a political exile. His plans for the future are equally vague and nebulously grandiose— to teach at a university like Harvard, work for the IMF, be a government cabinet minister. "Anyway, I am in no rush," he shrugs. If anything, he wants to go back to Paris, where he studied as an undergraduate. He rhapsodizes about the city each time he mentions it, a glazed look coming over his eyes. "Ah that city, she is the light of mah life, so beautiful, I can kiss her, make love to her, every night, she is singing like a bird to me. She is everything— food, art, love. I don't know why I leave her. She is the best place in the world."

Paris, for Guillaume, is always rekindled by Desaulnier's visits. They had met there at the university years before. "They talk about the city tout le temps," Sophie says to Marianne as they stand chatting in the hall one night. She rolls her eyes in contempt. She, herself, is not from Paris, but from Nancy.

"Parisians," she sniffs, "live in a world of pleasure like a dream, and they never wake up."

"They're hedonists," Helga, the German across from Sophie's room pipes up on her way back from the showers. She's always interrupting hallway conversations with her abrasive opinions, but this time Sophie concurs.

"Oui, that's the word. Hedonists."

Sophie tells Marianne that she does not understand how Desaulnier even tolerates coming to the dorm at all; it is so old and cramped, especially Guillaume's room, where there is hardly any space but for the oily standard-issue futon and the large cluttered desk piled with his papers and books. Cockroaches skitter everywhere. Marianne imagines the two of them sitting in the cell-like room, conjuring up nostalgic fantasies of glorious Paris while dim, dull Tokyo throbs listlessly outside. "Are they lovers?" Marianne wonders aloud, rather abstrusely. "No," Sophie says adamantly. "Would you bring a lover here?" Of course not; the question seems absurd. "And besides,"

Sophie adds, "Desaulnier is the type of man who has had many women. You can tell by the way he looks at you."

"Ah," Marianne replies. So she, obviously, is not the only one who has noticed.

And as for Guillaume? Sophie laughs at the idea. The robust, lustful African whose occasional loquacious outbursts included physical appraisals of the world's women— "Japanese women are softer than the French, you know, especially in the buttocks"— was hardly homosexual. No, theirs was an odd and mysterious friendship, all the more endearing for its inexplicableness. Whenever Desaulnier was around, Guillaume could be found happily whistling in the dorm kitchen, brewing up café for his friend in the little steel coffee-maker he had brought with him from Paris.

They went to Zushi in separate groups because of their various schedules. Guillaume, Desaulnier and Marianne set out early in the morning. Hélène and Sophie were to follow later, meeting them at Zushi station in the late afternoon.

"Zushi is where the imperial family has its besso," Desaulnier explained to Marianne on the train. He has decided to speak English to her, after all. And it is impeccable, like his French, or so Sophie has told Marianne.

"All the rich people of Tokyo go there." Guillaume shrugged his shoulders. "It is for the elite. Comme lui." His head leans slightly towards Desaulnier.

"Where is Zushi exactly?" Marianne asks.

"It is close to Kamakura," Desaulnier said. "Have you been to Kamakura yet?"

"No," Marianne shook her head. She had wanted to see the great stone Buddha, the Daibutsu, for some time, but she had been too busy with her studies. Or rather, busy editing Guillaume's thesis.

"Why don't we stop there?" Desaulnier suggested. "We have time."

They got off at Kamakura station and headed in the direction of the

Daibutsu, looming beyond them like a giant grey cloud. The weather was mild and since it was mid-morning on a weekday, the crowds were light, strolling in small groups, chatting with each other. Desaulnier and Guillaume began an impromptu but highly animated discussion about Buddhism. Marianne walked a few paces behind, listening.

Not like the Christian, different self, shame not guilt, desire not temptation...

"And what does Marianne-san think?" Desaulnier suddenly stopped and turned to her. He smiled gently, condescendingly.

"This girl— elle est catholique," Guillaume said, lowering his voice when he spoke the French.

"Ah," Desaulnier nodded gravely.

"Vraiment catholique," Guillaume said, his voice even lower.

Marianne blushed without reason, and looked down at the ground. *Catholique?* Were they saying she was Catholic? Guillaume knew she went to mass. He admired for it. He had once been a Jehovah's Witness himself, he had told her, as if assuring her that he, too, possessed a spiritual side. At the moment, he was into a new Japanese religion that believed in the latent spiritual power of the hand. Palm Power, it was called. "See, I put my hand on the computer when it crash and go 'Ohmmmm' and voila, it work again. It's a miracle!"

She wondered what Desaulnier thought about her Catholicism. She did not have a deep intellectual understanding of the faith. Her father's family, Japanese Canadian, were Catholic, converted by the nuns in the internment centre of Greenwood. Her mother, a postwar immigrant from Japan, had been received into the Church when she married Marianne's father. She was the only child of a rather strict Buddhist family, and so her conversion had caused a rift. That was what Marianne had gathered from scraps of conversation from her Canadian aunts. "She became one of us for love of him," was the way one aunt put it, as if the act, in some profound way, echoed Christ's. Her mother rarely spoke of her parents, and when Marianne had the chance to visit them for the first time when she came to Tokyo, she was surprised to see how warm and friendly they were to her. She did not know what she had been expecting— it was not as if her mother had portrayed them as being wrong, but rather it was the absence of her speaking about them at all that had disturbed Marianne during her childhood. She could see now by her grandparents' quiet solicitude towards her that her mother's actions had caused her grandparents more grief than anger— grief she knew her mother also bore, in the way of quiet guilt.

"You choose one or the other and pay the consequences," shrugged Hélène when she heard the story from Marianne. "Either way, you hurt somebody."

"Or you could not act at all," Sophie mused. "One's desire remains only a desire and not an action with consequences then…"

Marianne remembered this conversation with clarity. They were always discussing the difference between love and desire. And she found they were always gleaning examples from their lives— patterns of relationships, intertwining threads, which, when inspected, had the quality of gossamer— shiny, self evident truths. Men did not discuss things this way. They spoke conceptually, politically— hard truths jettisoned like bullets into the air. The way they were just now talking about religion. They had no notion of what it was to practise faith; it was all merely an idea to them. If she were to answer anyone as to why she went to church, she would say simply what a priest had told her once— deep habit. The deep habit of prayer, the deep habit of love, the deep habit of discerning good.

"There is a cathedral in Zushi, very close to my place," Desaulnier said to Marianne. "The priest there is French. You can confess to him in French, Japanese, or English— all languages, even Latin, I am told."

"Have you met him?" Guillaume asked.

"Only once, at a church fair," Desaulnier shrugged. "I don't like to go to mass in Zushi. I go there to relax, not think about my sins."

He laughed lightly. They were now standing in front of the great stone Buddha.

"Ay, we must look small to him!" Guillaume squinted up at the statue.

Desaulnier pulled out a cigarette and was quietly puffing on it as he looked. His gaze was completely indifferent, abstract, almost, as if he were staring at the sky to determine the day's weather. Guillaume, on the other hand, had his hand perched over his brow and was staring at the statue with his mouth slightly agape.

At such close range, the whole of the Buddha's body consumed their vision. The giant square shoulders jutted out into the corners of the sky, the broad chest filling out the horizon, stone nipples and navel perfectly shaped; the large fingers of the hands were pressed together in balanced tension against the shallow groove of the Buddha's groin. All was stone flesh, grey as a dismal winter's sky. The great slits of the Buddha's eyes stared down at them— dispassionate or compassionate, it was hard to tell. It was in striking contrast to the many crucifixes Marianne had seen hanging in cathedrals— the mortally wounded Christ dangling from the beam— a god so completely and utterly involved in human affairs. From out of the side of her eye, Marianne noticed an old Japanese woman, her hands folded in prayer, bowing deeply several times. Her lips were moving in chant-like repetition. Beside her, Guillaume and Desaulnier began arguing about some tenet in Buddhism. Their disembodied voices rose up in the air. "Craving is not the same as temptation." "But how can you tell da difference?" "It's cultural." "Even morality?" "Yes, even that." The old woman's chanting grew louder, more audible. "Namu Amida Butsu Namu Amida Butsu Namu Amida Butsu."

They met Hélène and Sophie at the train station in Zushi. After dropping their things off at the besso, Desaulnier offered to show them around. "There's a beach here and a marina," he said.

The beach was not spectacular, but rather dull looking, and there were few people about. The five foreigners stood out as they gazed at the sea, a light wind ruffling their clothes. Bright colourful windsurfers raked out lines on the water, criss-crossing the bay.

"We can rent rowboats and go out," Desaulnier said, pointing to a small shack by the marina where upturned rowboats lay stacked on the beach.

"I'd love to go!" Marianne said. Desaulnier smiled at her. He turned to the others. "Anyone else?"

"No way! I'm not going!" Guillaume said, "I can't sweem!"

Sophie shook her head, "Moi, aussi, I don't like boats." She looked at Hélène. "Toi?"

Hélène bit her lower lip and stared down at the sand. She was wearing shoes that were too good for the beach and sand was collecting in their sides. She looked at Marianne and Desaulnier, and then back at Sophie. Sophie shrugged her shoulders slightly.

"Okay," Hélène said. "I'll go."

They rented a boat and set it out into the water. Desaulnier took the oars. He was a small man, but his strokes were robust, vigorous. "He did his military service in the navy," Sophie had told Marianne. The idea of this clearly intellectual person once being so physical fascinated Marianne. She watched the thin fingers curled around the oars as they jerked them back, the abdomen tightening and loosening with each pull. *Ka-thuck* went the oar. *Shwoosh*, the paddle into the water. *Ka-thuck. Shwoosh.* A slight breeze ruffled Desaulnier's hair; fine wisps of it fell across his forehead. His shirt gently billowed out as he leaned back to pull. *Ka-thuck. Shwoosh.* The figures of Guillaume and Sophie grew smaller in the distance.

It had grown silent in the boat. Hélène was not talking at all, but was staring stonily at the water, her left hand curled so tightly around the rim of the boat that the knuckles were white. In her right hand she shakily held a cigarette that bobbed nervously, like a buoy, with every stroke of the oar. Desaulnier was breathing heavily now, but he did not let up. It seemed he was heading somewhere. Occasionally, he would stop, get his bearings, and would then begin rowing again.

Finally, far across the bay, a narrow secluded spit of sand came into view. It was sandwiched between two jagged stone outcroppings. Marianne focussed her eyes on the approaching land. She began to discern the shape of bodies, men's bodies, lying naked in the sun.

Desaulnier stopped the boat and laid to rest the paddles. He looked out at the men.

"Homosexuals," he said, "actors from Tokyo. It's a well-known spot for them."

Hélène turned her head sharply towards Desaulnier. "Do you know them?"

Desaulnier shook his head. "No, I just hear from somebody."

Hélène appeared relieved with the answer. She loosened her grip on the edge of the boat.

"May I have a cigarette?" Desaulnier asked.

Shakily, with one hand, Hélène fished out a cigarette out from her pocket. The action rocked the boat slightly. Quickly, she gripped the side.

Desaulnier, meanwhile, calmly lit his cigarette.

They stared a while at the men. The curl of smoke from Desaulnier's cigarette wafted across the water in a viny thread towards the men. The men did not seem to mind being watched. They lay languorously and indifferently in the sun. One of them even waved. The dark blue of the ocean— the pale, pink flesh of their bodies on the yellow sand— all seemed to Marianne like a framed painting of the Mediterranean.

"Quelle liberté!" Desaulnier said wistfully. He leaned over slightly, and then tossed his cigarette into the water. There was a momentary hiss. He picked up the paddles and began rowing back to shore.

Sophie and Guillaume were waiting on the beach. Guillaume helped Desaulnier pull the boat up to the boathouse. Hélène, looking sickly, went off to the bathroom.

"How was it?" Sophie asked Marianne.

"Fine!" Marianne said cheerfully, "You should have come."

"No, I don't like boats. I get sick."

"Really?"

Sophie leaned closer to Marianne, "So does Hélène, mais…"

"But what?"

"But she wanted to go, you know, to be with him."

"Desaulnier?"

"Oui."

Marianne looked at Sophie. Sophie suddenly turned away, her cheek flushing pink. There was a twist of regret in her face, a look of inadvertent betrayal.

They decided to go to the shops to buy food for the evening. The women went to the supermarket to get the vegetables and meat, and the men to the sakaya to get saké. Marianne followed after Hélène and Sophie, who were nattering loudly together in French. When Marianne reached for a plastic basket in the store, Hélène brusquely grabbed it before her. "I'll get the food," she said abruptly. "Whatever," Marianne shrugged. She was getting used to Hélène's blunt ways. Hélène strode off towards the vegetable section, Sophie quickly behind her. The two women stopped in front of an array of greenery. Leafy bundles of spinach and chrysanthemum lay beside stacks of shapely cucumbers and eggplants. The two women began to bicker over what vegetables to get. *Non, non,* Sophie would say, tapping Hélène's hand as if she were a naughty girl when she reached for something less than perfect in shape or size. Hélène would snap something back in French but would inevitably drop the vegetable. The two women carried on this way in front of Marianne, in blatant disregard of her. She floated behind them, feeling almost like a ghost. *I should've gone with the men*, she thought, forlornly. On the way to the meat section, she caught a few words of their conversation— "It's not possible," "She does not know," "He will make her." Their hands ranged over the various packages of meat as they exchanged words. Marianne stood by quietly, waiting for them.

It was near dark when they arrived back at the besso. Desaulnier showed them around. This place, he told them, was once the summer house of a high-ranking officer in the imperial government of the Meiji era. Although it was dark and run down, it still retained an austere and spacious elegance. Desaulnier had not done much to furnish it— most of the rooms were the traditional empty tatami, except for the kitchen and a small living room in which there was a leather couch set and coffee table. The low Japanese-style veranda that went down the length of the house opened up onto a large yard with a cherry tree in the middle. The tree was in full bloom. On the ground was a spongy, mossy undergrowth that looked like grass. There were no other shrubs or trees.

"It looks pretty spacious for a Japanese yard," Marianne said, standing on the veranda with the others.

"The previous owners were American," Desaulnier explained. "That is why the landscaping is so plain."

The two French women shook their heads, clicked their disapproval.

"But this much room is fun!" Guillaume leapt off the veranda into the yard. He jumped around in his stockinged feet. Then he went to the cherry tree and pulled off a few sprigs. He gave one to each of the women. The biggest, he gave to Marianne, with a flourish.

"To mah teesis woman, you are the saint of mah life!" he exclaimed. Then he hopped back into the house. "Let's make the food. I'm hungry!"

The women prepared an onabe, a dish cooked in a large earthenware pot set on a portable gas range. The range was put on the little kotatsu table in the tatamied room nearest the kitchen. The two men were the first to sit down. Desaulnier lay back on his elbows and watched Sophie deftly set the vegetables and meat into the simmering broth of the pot. The rice cooker he had set by Marianne, and once the food was ready, he languidly handed the rice bowls to her— one by one— so she could fill them up to pass to the others.

"You'd make a good wife," Hélène said to Marianne.

"Oui, c'est vrai," Sophie concurred.

The two women's laughter was like a brass tinkling.

"Well, you can serve yourself, then!" Marianne said in mock anger, putting down the rice paddle. But she had finished; everyone had their own bowl of rice.

"I'll serve the saké," Desaulnier sat up. He carefully lifted up the heated bottle and eyed Marianne. Then he leaned towards her.

"Your cup," he said, nudging her slightly.

Everyone was watching him. The vegetables in the onabe simmered loudly.

Marianne shyly pushed her thin white cup forward. She had not had any intention of drinking, but she could not say "no" now.

Desaulnier poured the steaming liquid into her cup. The sweet aroma of saké filled the air.

"Anyone else?" Desaulnier's eyes flickered around the table.

Abruptly, Hélène reached for the bottle in Desaulnier's hand.

"I'll serve you," she said, her fingers curling around Desaulnier's. He swiftly let go, shrugging his shoulders.

"If you like..." he said indifferently.

They ate and drank heavily. The talk was heady and witty, laced with allusions and references to books, history, and art. When Kamakura was mentioned, Desaulnier brought up the topic of religion again. Buddhism, he proclaimed, was the religion of the truly liberated, the human set free from all desire. Perfect detachment, he believed, was the only real goal in life. This set off a debate about the meaning of desire. "But how can you live without desire?" Guillaume said loudly, in disbelief. "Mah desire is mah strength." He made a fist, and then rudely gestured towards his genitals. Everyone laughed loudly. Guillaume was always bragging about his sexual prowess, although the women of the dorm found him quite harmless compared to some of the other men students. As he drank, he became full of bravado, putting his arms around the two French women, calling them his sweet chéries.

"Tonight we will all sleep together, non?— a ménage à trois," he said festively. "But first we must dance! Ay, but Desaulnier, where is your musique? We must put it on now!" Guillaume leapt to his feet and went to the stereo in the living room. Loud African juju music suddenly filled the room.

"Come 'ere, everyone," he shouted. "Let's dance!"

The others made their way into the living room where Guillaume was turning up the volume. Desaulnier slid open the door to the yard. A warm salt breeze mingled with the faint scent of cherry blossoms and wafted into the room.

Guillaume began gyrating around, shoving his hips against anyone who came near him.

"Like this!" he yelled above the pounding beat, and circled his arms around Sophie. He thrust his hips back and forth against her like a machine gun.

"*Tat, tat, tat*," he said, pointing to his hips to encourage her. His movements were light, quick. Sophie tried to mimic him, but she was too slow; her hips moved thickly, like gel.

"Ay— you must practise!" Guillaume said. He latched onto Marianne, swinging his arm around her, bringing her to his side. Marianne closed her eyes, the beat of the music coming in like a staccato rush; she tried concentrating on the pulse, the downbeat, the *ka-thump, thump, thump*.

"You're doing it good, mah Canadian!" Guillaume clapped his hands. "Look at this girl!" he shouted to Desaulnier and Hélène, who were out smoking in the yard. Desaulnier sauntered over and looked at Marianne. She stopped, embarrassed. Desaulnier stepped up onto the veranda and took Marianne's hand to dance with her.

"C'est bien," he whispered in her ear. His breath smelled smoky and sweet. "You are doing good."

They moved out onto the veranda and into the yard. Desaulnier had taken a waltz position and was slowly circling Marianne towards the cherry tree. The warm flush from the saké coloured Marianne's cheeks. A shudder of wind released a shower of petals from the cherry tree. Marianne tilted her head back and looked up at the canopy of branches. She felt a giddy clumsiness, swirling and twirling in the midst of this cherry petal tempest, her body encircled by Desaulnier's arms. She felt as she had when she was a child—

when everything seemed to be connected— the earth to the root, the root to the trunk, the trunk to the branches, the branches to the sky. She was connected, too, as they all were— the Japanese to the French, the French to the African, the African to the Canadian, the Canadian to the Japanese— all connected the minute they exchanged words, gestures, glances; the minute they held hands, danced. Marianne smiled, her lips curling at the corners like a Buddha at this blissful blending of all into one spacious expansive feeling of pure ecstatic indifference. Beyond, she could hear the gentle thudding of the sea against the shore, and in the easy pounding midst of the music she slipped closer into the curve of Desaulnier's pressing body.

Guillaume was wildly dancing by himself in the middle of the yard, his hands outstretched to the sky, the whites of his palms shining like stars. Hélène and Sophie sat poised on the stone step by the veranda door. Sophie had entwined her arm through Hélène's and was leaning against her. Hélène occasionally moved her free arm to put her cigarette to her lips. She was staring straight at Marianne. Coldly. Marianne closed her eyes. *I don't care what you think*, she thought. *I'm enjoying myself.*

Guillaume stumbled up to Marianne and Desaulnier. He put his arms around them.

"Mes amis, what would I do without you?" he said in a maudlin voice. "I am in this country too long— but you are friends— ah, I am drunk, portez-moi, Desaulnier."

Desaulnier quickly left Marianne's side and shifted positions. They took Guillaume's arms over their shoulders and carried the drunken African back into the house. When they reached the veranda, the two French women stood up and parted to make room for the awkward threesome. Desaulnier gently lowered Guillaume onto the couch.

"Merci, mon ami," Guillaume whispered, taking Marianne's hand and kissing it. Within minutes he was snoring.

Desaulnier changed the music to a tape of ethereal sounds from nature— the tinkling of ice, the rush of water, whale sounds. Everyone moved inside.

Hélène and Sophie slumped down on one of the other couches. Desaulnier sat in an arm chair. Marianne sat on the floor by the couch on which Guillaume was lying.

The French began talking amongst themselves in soft whispers. Marianne leaned back and closed her eyes, listening to the perfect curling of the "r"s , the sashaying "s"s. She was no longer understanding, just hearing. It occurred to her only vaguely that they were perhaps talking about her. She heard the word *Canadienne.* But they could have been talking about the music. Marianne could see the tape cover from where she was sitting. There was a picture of an alpine meadow on it with blue snowy peaks in the background. The title was *Musique de la Nature.* There were words she could recognize: *grand, lac, montagne, neige, forêt...* and others she could not. Sometimes they looked at her, almost fondly, as if she were a specimen— au naturel— of a country whose only identity was its landscape.

Desaulnier began speaking in English. A monologue.

"Ah, Marianne, we are sorry to be speaking in French. We have been talking about your country, its people, the savages."

Savage? Marianne thought. *The native people?* He had pronounced it the French way. *Sauvage.* She did not bother to correct him.

"Le sauvage is free," he said. "He travels where he wishes, sleeps and eats where he wishes, loves whom he wishes. The savage is natural man with only his instinct to guide him. He is pure then, not this over-civilized trash we are now"— here he peevishly waved his hand at the others— "but close to the harmony of Nature, its beauty, its rhythm, its innocence. The savage is naturally enlightened, already a buddha."

He stared at Marianne the whole while he spoke, the level tone of his voice like a hand patting a dog, steady and gentle. His vision of the savage was so compelling she was almost moved by it. *Sauvage*— the sound of the French word slipped into the cracks of her own clunky language and then emerged like a new idea— scintillating, arresting. Still, she was only half-convinced. In the recesses of her mind, she could see the smoky bingo hall in which she'd worked as a volunteer for her brother's hockey team; she remembered the men with their braided hair, sullenly stamping out numbers on their cards, hoping for a win. *Bingo,* one would call out at last, his voice lusty with triumph.

Marianne closed her eyes again. She would not interrupt his intellectual reverie. She would let him go on as long as he wished. He could say anything and she would agree; it all sounded so sophisticated, ideas like streams of silk flowing over her skin. She could sleep in those ideas, trade them for dreams, even.

Desaulnier stopped. Slowly, he got up out of his chair and walked over to the veranda to breathe in the night air. He closed his eyes briefly. The smell of cherry blossoms wafted in the room. Desaulnier walked to Marianne and laid his hand on the armrest of the couch where she had leaned her head. He spoke in French. A proposition loud enough for the others to hear clearly.

Marianne slowly turned her head. *What did he say?*

The others were silent. No one was translating. All eyes were on Marianne.

Desaulnier coughed, but did not repeat himself. Turning abruptly, he left the room and walked down the corridor towards his bedroom. Everyone could hear the creak of his footsteps on the floorboards.

Hélène and Sophie exchanged glances. Then they looked at Marianne.

"What?" Marianne said.

Sophie smiled.

"He said it is time to sleep," she said evasively. "I'm going to get my things."

Desaulnier had not assigned anyone specific rooms. There were two Western-style bedrooms in the whole house— one was Desaulnier's, and the other, off the kitchen, was a spare that had a double bed. The rest of the house was Japanese-style, tatamied, the rooms separated only by sliding fusuma. Desaulnier had shown them the closets where the futons were rolled up.

"Where shall we sleep?" Marianne asked Sophie.

Sophie looked at Guillaume snoring on the couch. She shook her head and laughed. The bold, braggart lover had fallen asleep in a drunken stupour. So much for his ménage à trois.

"He will be here till morning," Sophie said.

Hélène was carrying her bag into the room by the kitchen. Sophie's eyes followed after her. Quickly, she took Marianne's hand and squeezed it.

"I will sleep with Hélène," she said. "You sleep out there—" she pointed to the dark vacuous space of the tatamied room beyond, "— where you will be free."

Marianne rolled out the futon and changed into her nightclothes. It seemed ironic that she was now completely alone, after all that festivity. She crawled into the cool space of the futon sheets. They smelled slightly acrid, like incense mingled with sweat. Marianne remembered Sophie telling her how Heian courtesans perfumed their robes with incense. Whole poems were written about the lingering fragrance of a parting lover. Perhaps, after a night of pleasure, *this* was the smell.

Marianne turned over on her side and slowly ran her hand over the curve of her breasts up to her neck, where a small gold cross on a necklace lay in the hollow of her collarbone. She fingered the cross idly, remembering how her old lover had given it to her the eve of her departure to Japan. They had finally broken up. Months before, he had found someone else and was secretly having an affair. Marianne remembered the dizzying, nauseous feeling, reeling in the kitchen when she found the scribbled love note in his jacket. It felt as if she were no longer in her body but in someone else's— a character in a novel where she was both reader and participant. This was a novel full of the cheap melodrama she most hated, the kind that inevitably prompted the question— *how can people do this?* Yes, how could they? How could *he?* If they had only been together a few months, she might have shrugged it off, but they had been together five years, a good five years full of the warmth and security she felt was every bit as much of marriage as she could possibly hope for. And now it was broken completely, or rather *she* was broken completely, a mess of tears and anger, resentment, hate, fear, and loathing. She knew that clarity of cognizance that comes even in the most hurtful moments. *He did it to me. He was wrong. He committed the sin.* The litany was powerful, a march, almost, that took her right up the cathedral stairs into that sanctuary for the wounded and hurting. *I will be delivered from this, I will.* She returned home, cleansed, self-righteous. Sometimes even confrontational. *Why are you doing this to me? It's wrong, don't you know? How can you love two women? How is that possible?* But it *was* possible, that was the crazy irony of it all. He truly loved her *and* the other woman. The torment, however unbearable it was for her, she could see was worse for him. A man at the mercy of his own tyrannical desire, paralyzed, unable to move in either direction. Late at night, after he had been with the other woman, he would come to her in their room and start to touch her slowly, gently and without a word; his hands, tenuous and apologetic, would work their penance on her until she was consumed with an over-whelming pity. Afterwards, she would look at her body in the mirror; it seemed dirty, all of it, every crack and crevice filled with the musky aroma of his apology. His lovemaking, however tender and gentle, had made her a victim, not the martyr of pity she had somehow hoped to be— that gracious, forgiving, all-consuming, all-loving, mother of sorrows that would inspire true devotion, singleminded faithfulness. No, it was not to be.

Then the letter came. It was the long overdue response to a scholarship application Marianne had made months before and almost forgotten. A scholarship to study in Japan. Yes, she had been accepted to study for a year in Japan. Yes, she could be *free.*

But sometimes, like now, she thought of him. She missed him. He had been a good lover.

From far across the room a sliver of light shone between the cracks of the closed fusuma. Marianne squinted. It must have been Desaulnier's room. He had a separate entrance, but the room was attached to the main tatamied room Marianne was in now, separated only by the fusuma.

Marianne stared a long time at the light. *What is he doing up?* she thought, unable to sleep, thinking of him, his eloquent English, his small hands gesticulating in the air whenever he spoke of language, culture. *He's reading now— a novel or poetry,* she imagined. She turned over on her side. She still could not sleep. *Maybe if I go to the bathroom,* she thought. She got up. She had no idea where the bathroom was. *I'll ask Sophie,* she thought, and stumbled into the dark kitchen towards the French women's room. The door was closed. Marianne paused to knock when she heard soft groanings, a shuffling of sheets, whispers. *What's going on?* Marianne's mind filled with images of Hélène and her rust-coloured hair undone on her shoulders, turning and tossing on the bed, and of Sophie, her hands slim and long-fingered, alighting on Hélène's arms. Quickly, almost with embarrassment, Marianne turned away and padded over to where Guillaume was sleeping. He was still on the couch, snoring gently, his belly slightly exposed. Tight black hair curled in small knots around his navel. One of his thick muscled arms was crossed over his chest; the other hung limply at his side. He grunted, turned over and curled up slightly. Marianne looked at his body and remembered how often Guillaume had sat with her at his desk while she edited his thesis, rubbing his hand up and down her back, telling her, "But wee are fraynds, no? Why can't wee sleep together?" Annoyed, Marianne would usually say, "Then you'll never get this done..." "Ah, you English, you are so..." His voice ended with the customary *bouff* sound of French contempt.

She'd thought about it a long time afterwards— his touching her. He told her things about love that were different. He told her that in his country, if a man was a bad lover, everybody in the village knew. "So you gotta perform, man!" he said, slapping his thigh. She told him once about her old lover. "But he fell in love with another woman," she said. "Ah, mah chérie, that's too bad," Guillaume had replied. He shrugged his shoulders. "But in love, such is the way. Love is unfair, no? If not, life would not be so interesting." She'd never thought of love-hurts as interesting. At the time, they were just painful. Simply painful. Nothing more. But like a wound that needs bathing, tending, opening up over and over again like a blossom in its season, he saw love in some other way— multi-faceted, luminous, pleasureful, even as it was fickle, torturous and dangerous. Perhaps that was why he touched her, even though he had a Japanese girlfriend whom she had met once, standing mutely in his room, looking vaguely suspicious of Marianne and yet hopelessly defenseless in her presence. Perhaps Guillaume was right. Love was only as fair as you wanted to make it.

Marianne peered down the corridor Desaulnier had walked down when he had departed for his room. It had become a tunnel of light, the moon streaming through the shoji, illuminating the narrow passageway with a web-like silvery light. Far down the hall, Marianne could make out the shape of a pair of plastic toilet slippers. *So that's where the bathroom is.* Slowly Marianne padded down the corridor. She could hear the rustle of the cherry tree outside, its branches casting shadows on the moonlit papered squares of the shoji. Her steps were soft, one after another, the boards creaking gently with her weight.

A faint light shone from the last room at the left end of the corridor— Desaulnier's room. The Western-style door was ajar. Marianne approached. She peered into the room. Desaulnier was sitting up in bed, lotus position, a book on his lap. He was wearing a loose kimono, open at the neck. His bare chest glowed under the light of the reading lamp above his bed. He looked up. Half of his face was obscured in shadow, but one eye stared hungrily at Marianne. Slowly, without averting his gaze, Desaulnier closed his book and slowly placed his right hand, palm down, beside his thigh. Come beside me, it was saying.

The next step... Marianne trembled at the thought... *The next step is mine.* She put out her foot. In a moment she could see, breathless, the tumble of her own aching body into his, skin pressed against the other's, breast into chest, hip into thigh, perfect momentary ecstasy, theirs, completely theirs and no one else's— but down came the foot suddenly and without warning, twisting her whole body outwards, the toes leaden, shaped like bird's feet in only one direction— away.

The bathroom was at the end of the hall.

When Marianne returned, Desaulnier's light was out, the door closed.

In the early morning, Marianne awoke to the sound of bells. *Must be the church,* she thought. She lay awake for a few minutes, staring at the ceiling, listening. She remembered those long-ago mornings in those last troubling weeks with her old lover, walking by herself to mass, an angry, huddled, hurt mess of a person, mumbling the catechism, kneeling, repenting, or, *trying* to repent, at least, in word only. She did not feel at all sorry for what she had done, but for what her lover had done, and she blamed him even as she repented of sins she did not believe in. *Whatever I have done, I have done out of love, so there is nothing wrong with me,* she justified to herself.

The Catholic church in Zushi was small, but crowded. Marianne squeezed into a back pew and listened quietly to the French inflected drone of the priest. She could only make out a few words of the Japanese sermon, but they were bracing enough— *holy, honourable, brotherly love, self-control.* Marianne thought it ironic how she lived her life in Japan in only half-languages, only half-understanding. The rest was guessed at, hinted at, presumed or assumed, like yesterday night with the others. In truth, Marianne concluded, most things anywhere were only half-known, and one just groped along in a blind discerning.

When Marianne returned to the besso, she was surprised to see Sophie up in the kitchen making breakfast.

"Ah, Marianne! Quelle surprise!" she said brightly. "Where were you?"

"I went to mass." Marianne sat down at the kitchen table.

Sophie's eyes suddenly softened. She put down the apple she was peeling. "You were not with— *anyone*— last night?"

"No."

Sophie looked at Marianne, almost as if in amazement. Then she picked up the apple again and began slicing it. She put the pieces on a plate and set it in front of Marianne.

"Hélène— is she still asleep?" Marianne nodded towards the closed bedroom door.

"Oui."

Sophie poked idly at the plate of apples, staring abstractly at them. Finally, she spoke. "Hélène was crying. All night in my arms. She is tired."

"Oh?"

"Because of you."

"Me?"

"Yes, you." Sophie said curtly. "I told her that it was foolish to think he would like her. She wants him because he is something— a Todai professor, a Sorbonne graduate, this and that. Who cares? He is not right for her. *I* know that. *I* know her better than anyone else. *I* should be her lover."

Sophie's voice was quavering. Marianne looked down at the table. She felt a vague sense of guilt or shame, but over what, she was not quite sure.

Sophie lowered her voice, then spoke softly. "Marianne, sometimes you are so good you cannot see what you are. This is a beauty— how do you say?— de l'esprit. I thought you needed someone, especially after all that sadness you told me about with your old lover. But now I see I should not have put you in that room by yourself. Forgive me."

What? Marianne's mind reeled.

Hélène walked into the kitchen, sleepy-eyed. At the sight of Marianne, she cocked her head slightly and then turned to Sophie.

"She went to mass," Sophie shrugged her shoulders.

"Oh, did you?" Hélène said, contempt creeping into her voice. "You had something to confess?"

"No," Marianne said firmly, with conviction. She reached over for one of Sophie's apples. Her hand, she noticed, was shaking. *Thank God,* she thought, in sudden gratitude for not having acted in a way that would have been disastrous to that web of fragile connection she had formed here, between friends.

JAPONISME

Her favourite café was called *Chine Bleu*. She no longer remembered where in the Paris rabble it was, but that it was blue, she was sure— a twilight blue, the color of the evening sky before the stars— a royal and imperious blue, the silk gown of a boy prince.

It was run by a Chinese man, long-haired, who had seen the world muscled and fisted in bullets and bloodshed. His face was muzzle rough, a bulldog's bristle, and his body thin and sinewy as hemp. "I am refugee," he said, "from Vietnam." He spoke perfect French. She supposed he was learned; she could never tell with refugees. He came to her table, bending over to take her order, his shirt billowing open at the neck where she could see the small smooth muscles of the neck twitch and twitter with each growl from his throat. She called him *Wang*.

In the early mornings, Wang would open up the café, and would sit in the front window to read the newspaper with a cup of tea, his enfant in his lap. He used to smoke, he told her, but it was bad for the enfant, so he quit. When it got busy, he would hand the enfant to the grandmother who sat in the back behind the cash register on an old red stool. It was she who took in the money, the wrinkled fingers smoothing out the bills, caressing the change. If there was a wife, she was nowhere to be seen.

She and her lover lived in an apartment across the street from the café. Their bed was near the window, and in the mornings they would stare out at the café from under the covers, a snow-white drift over their sleepy heads. Through the hole they had made in the snow, she could see all the people walking along Paris's grey boulevards. Her lover had a long, broad arm that he swept around her head— the shape of which made a frame through which she could see the world, a painting crying out, *Look, look at me!*

Her job was translating Japanese court poetry. She worked at the Musée Guimet, in the back where shelf-loads of manuscripts and scrolls were stored.

From out of the densely dancing black strokes of the calligrapher's brush she extracted poems of autumn leaf, spring cherry, the moon's silver reflections— laying them out into the sun-dusky light of the tiny back room for the curious Western eye to peruse.

Her lover was French— French like a spring vine that curls up to a woman's window and blooms on the sill of a day-dreaming heart. Standing one day at her desk in a long black coat, with a belt knotted at the back of the waist, he was a shining prince of the court. Love-lorn dilettante, here he was— and, oh! in her heart's foolishness— she dropped her pen. He picked it up, and set it on her scribblings with his name card.

Michel de Lavison
Antiquaire d'objets orientale

In those first and luscious days they sat in the window seat of the café sipping warm jasmine tea, their legs entwined underneath the table. The scent of white flowers floated up into the air; the delicious whiff of that faraway spring would bring their eyes dancing from cup to hand, from hand to face. The walls sighed, a shudder of their blue breath slipping over the chairs and tables, melting into the cupped white tea bowls, mingling with the gold trim. Their eyes closed to hear the soft and silent colours when *KA-THANG!*— ear-splitting crash of stone against glass, youths with swastikas running down the street, Wang after them, broom angrily in hand. Sometimes she and her lover would stay and watch the drama of the police— notepads and sunglasses, black boots on splintered glass. Other times they would slip out, leaving money in the teapot. *Hurry, hurry, let's go home*— nestle together in that warm snow.

Hours and hours she spent in the dusty chambers of the musée, poring over the gentle moonlit nights filled with soft scents of summer flowers, the whisper and shudder of a courtesan's gown as he hurried for the evening rendezvous to meet his lover, coy and demure behind her screen— how his words trailed like silk across her face, sheltered her from him— his warm, broad palm cupping, like a bowl to be appraised, her chin, her mouth and the small breaths that escaped between his fingers.

When they fought, she went to the café by herself where she would be beckoned into the kitchen by the grandmother. The kitchen was that private place, not for customers, oh no, but for the black-haired ones like her, like the old woman, like Wang. There the old woman would serve her pork soup and snow-white buns filled with meat. They hardly exchanged words. The old woman would hold the enfant and watch her sip the steaming soup. She'd smile her golden-toothed smile, clucking and cooing. Then, stretching her gnarled, hawk-like hand with its one long fingernail, she would touch her— her young smooth hand that held the pen, that was now holding the porcelain ladle with the dragon swimming in its shallow depths.

From that steamy kitchen the old woman released her, let her out onto the cobblestone alley strewn with garbage and old huddling men. In the low dim light, she would scurry like a frightened cat into the apartment, throw herself into the snow and press her face against the warm bitter smell of Michel's pillow. Later, he would come in, smoke-filled locks of hair rustling against her face, smelling the ginger of her closed eyes, and waking her to finish his silly argument.

His hands were so big the world fit in them, and yet like sand she filtered through, returned to the sea. She and Michel parted the day Wang closed down the café. The enfant was getting big now, too much for the old woman to handle by herself, and Wang was getting tired of the rock throwing. "You see, they hate us," Wang said, waving his arm at the grey buildings, at the snow in their windows. *Us.* Tears sprang from her eyes as if she had suddenly stepped out of a palanquin to become a stone, hurling her way through his blue window to shatter into sand, the people they no longer were.

A CHILD OF THE AGE

Not long ago, at the university, an acquaintance who had only been married a couple of years told me she and her husband had separated. "Oh, I'm sorry," I said sympathetically, but she just laughed. "Don't feel bad," she said lightly. "It's all right. We're living with other people now." She told me she was thinking of quitting university and travelling to Europe with her new lover. Later that day, I saw her husband standing near the library. He usually waited at that spot for his wife, but that day, a new woman came and the two of them walked off hand-in-hand towards the elevator.

When I casually mentioned this incident to my mother, she shook her head in sad dismay. Just that morning she had received an aerogramme from her brother, my Uncle Shin, that contained news of his son's recent divorce. My cousin Akinori and his wife had not even been married a year— nine months to be exact— and although all the details of the separation were not given, one thing *was* clear. My cousin had had an affair with a co-worker and his wife had found out. My mother was deeply disappointed. She had made the long trip to Japan for the wedding just the year before, only to be dismayed by the paltriness of the event— a small, hastily arranged affair in a hotel banquet room. There were only twenty guests altogether. My uncle had said, as if in excuse, "At least it was cheap," but he felt badly for Mother and took her on a week-long trip to an expensive resort in Kyushu. My mother felt guilty. "With that money, he could have easily put on something better for Akinori," she said. "Why, for goodness' sake, was he spending that money on me?"

Now the marriage had failed. With the aerogramme still in hand, my mother turned to me, a disappointed look on her face. "What is wrong with your generation?" she asked.

My cousin was twenty one when I saw him last. I was in Japan that year, teaching English in Tokyo, and I made a special trip to Osaka for New Year's to visit with my mother's family. My cousin and I had not seen each other since we were children, and my memories of that long-ago childhood visit were fragmentary at best. I thought meeting Akinori as an adult would be like meeting a new person— awkward and difficult— but after only a few minutes of chitchat, we fell into an easy bantering conversation. My cousin spoke as freely about himself as he had when we were children. It was as if time had not passed. Akinori still lived at the same house with his parents and my visit was in the same season of winter as it had been when I first met him.

We were sitting in the warm kotatsu by ourselves. My aunt had set out a basket of mandarins on the kotatsu table top for us. Akinori had just come home from his part-time job at a men's fashion boutique, *Comme l'homme*, in Kobe. He looked very chic— no doubt because of the job— with his gelled hair, his white silk shirt and red designer tie. As we chatted, my cousin took a mandarin, peeled it, and began eating it in that peculiar way Japanese eat their oranges— sucking the meat of the fruit out of its small wedge of skin before discarding the skin into a pile in the shell of the peel. Between the sucking and discarding, he talked casually of this and that— what kind of car he would like, what sort of woman he preferred to date, what film stars and sports celebrities he liked to watch on TV. I couldn't remember what we had talked about when we were children, but it seemed the tenor of the conversation had not changed. Only our bodies had changed. From out of the wisps of our childhood selves, we had become adults.

The trip I made to visit my relatives that winter was a special time. I wanted to meet everybody and collect stories about the family. The small peculiarities of personalities and particulars of events that make up family lore had long been denied me simply because of geography. Mother was the odd one out, the one sister in Canada. News came to us by aerogramme in bits and pieces. Only the significant truths were told— births, passing of exams, graduations, marriages, job changes, or moves. Details were rarely included. I was always curious to know where these letters came from and who they were about, but it seemed I would never know unless I went to Japan. The members of my mother's family were like vaguely envisioned characters in an unwritten book, faintly radiating but never completely there.

My mother's youngest sister, Minako, was the one who wrote the most regularly. She was the only one of the family who had visited us in Canada and she had a special fondness for Mother, whom she always called Neh-chan— older sister. When word came to my mother's family that I was going down to Osaka, my Aunt Minako was the first to offer me a place to stay. She wanted to return my mother's kindness to her when Minako was in Canada by being hospitable to me. I was only a child when Aunt Minako visited, but I remembered calling her Auntie Mimi and holding her hand on our walks to my kindergarten. My Auntie Mimi was very youthful and vivacious when I was a child, and she appeared that way even now— married with two children— almost eighteen years later. The only sign of her age was the few wisps of grey hair in her short bob and a few wrinkles around her eyes. She talked freely and easily about the family, and so was a good source of stories, but there was a kind of reverence in her voice when she spoke about her older siblings as if, by simple virtue of their being older, they deserved respect.

One afternoon, while strolling through the grounds of a local shrine, my aunt began talking about my Uncle Shin. We had stopped near a small altar where a young man was praying, his eyes closed and his hands pressed together. He was wearing a black high school uniform with the standard stiff collar and gold buttons down the front.

"Jyuken no oinori," my aunt whispered to me. "He's praying to pass his entrance exam."

I noticed a cluster of wooden prayer boards dangling near the altar. They were inked with requests by students to get into various different universities.

"I wonder..." my aunt said aloud to herself.

She began rifling through the boards.

"Atta! I found it!" she said breathlessly. "Even after all these years!"

She showed me a warped grey board and read the nearly faded writing on it:

175

For Hiromatsu Shinichiro to pass his entrance
examination into Osaka University.

25th day, second month, 1958

"I was there the day Nii-chan wrote this," my aunt said proudly. Nii-chan meant older brother. "We came here often. When I finished school, he'd pick me up after he had been studying all day at home. He'd say, 'Let's go to the shrine. Nii-chan wants to pray and then he'll buy you a cola afterward.' Of course, I couldn't refuse, I wanted the cola so bad! We went so often though, you know, I got tired of cola. Nii-chan failed his jyuken four times. But he kept trying. He said he *had* to pass. 'Nii-chan must go to university,' he told me, 'Nii-chan has to get in so he can get a good job and look after you, and Father and Mother.' That last year that he tried— it was his fifth time, and I was in my first year of junior high school— we went on a marathon pilgrimage of shrines. We went everywhere— shrine after shrine, putting up prayer board after prayer board. I had a little change purse and by the time we finished, there were hardly any coins left. I had thrown them all into the wells in front of the altars. I clapped my hands so hard they stung. 'Please, please gods, this time let Nii-chan pass!' And finally, that year, he did."

"Well, Aki-chan is just like him then, isn't he?" I said, for I'd heard that Akinori had failed the entrance exams he had written that spring. This was his third time.

My aunt laughed rather cynically and then shook her head. "No, it's different with him. That boy really doesn't study. He just has big dreams. He thinks it's good to get into university because it will make him appear more attractive, that's all. Every time I visit or call, Aki's always out buying clothes or playing pachinko. He's not like Nii-chan at all. Aki does not think seriously about his future."

I remembered a conversation I'd had with Akinori a few nights earlier. "I'll go to Canada and open an Issey Miyake store," he said to me. "What do you think?" He showed me a photo from a magazine of a boutique in Monte

176

Carlo. "I'd like it to be like this one— with a black interior and cement walls. Do you think it's possible?" he asked. I cocked my head, not wanting to reply. The question seemed absurd.

"These exams are expensive to write," my aunt continued, "and Nii-chan and Kimiko-san are tired of spending so much money each year for every exam he writes. It's been three years now. His score has not improved and he cannot pass the exams for even the easiest universities. Kimiko-san put him in a prep college this fall with all the money she's earned from teaching piano. They are hoping it will help."

I wondered if it was working. Akinori had told me he'd been going to prep school but he said it was boring. "I get tired at nights," he said, "because I'm working at the boutique. Sometimes I don't make it to the morning classes. They don't teach anything worthwhile anyway, but some of the girls are nice. We usually go out for coffee."

My aunt stopped walking. She glanced back at where the student at the altar had been. There was a wistful look in her eye.

"Things are so different now," she said. "I shouldn't say things about Akinori. I'm sure he has his own point of view. He is a child of the age. And we— well, we were all part of another age, another time in this country."

I remembered some of Mother's stories of the war. She talked of running to bomb shelters and of neighbours looking for things in the charred ruins afterwards. Food was scarce; dogs and cats were conspicuously absent from city alleyways. "You can see why none of us own pets now," my Aunt Sanae said. Aunt Sanae was the second oldest sister after Mother. She was quieter, more shy than either my mother or Aunt Minako. She looked similar to the other two sisters, except for the eyes. Hers were curved and perpetually sad-looking. The look had gotten more pronounced, Aunt Minako said, after Aunt Sanae had converted to Catholicism. Catholicism, in my Aunt Minako's opinion, was a more fatalistic form of Christianity than the brisk evangelical Protestantism she and my mother had embraced.

Aunt Sanae was close in age to Mother, but because of Mother's strong personality, she too, addressed my mother reverentially as Neh-chan. "Neh-chan looked after us—" that was what they all said— Aunt Sanae, Uncle Shin and Auntie Minako. Uncle Shin respected Mother especially. When he was young and the schoolyard bully was beating him up, my mother cuffed the bully's ears so hard that he never bothered my Uncle Shin again. And when he broke his leg in high school, my mother's first pay cheque went to his doctor's bill.

"Shin-chan was such a sensitive boy," Aunt Sanae told me one night while we were having tea. "Your mother and I spoiled him, I think. He preferred to follow us around rather than spend time with other boys his age. I don't think he had any other friends until about high school. Then he changed. Girls started paying attention to him. I guess it was those big eyes. We used to tease him about that: told him he had eyes like a cow. The girls found that attractive, I guess. He quit following us around then. He had his own little group of girls following him. Once your mother said, 'Don't you miss him?' and I said, 'At least we trained him how to be good with girls!'"

My cousin, Mayumi, who was sitting with us, laughed.

"That's funny," she said. "Shin-ojisan is just like Aki-chan. Kimiko-obasan says that when Aki-chan was in high school, he got a mountain of Valentine's chocolates every year. She said she got tired of picking up all the wrappers."

Aunt Sanae laughed. "Well, I hope he was at least as good to his girlfriends as Shin-chan was."

"I doubt it," Mayumi huffed. "I sent him a chocolate one year as a joke because I felt sorry for him. I didn't think he would have any girlfriends, but you know what? He got plenty of chocolates. In fact, he never bothered to thank me. He told me he never even *looked* at the cards. Do you believe it?"

"Well, this Valentine's Day business is all new to us. We never had that custom in the old days. I think it would have appeared frivolous..."

"So tell me more about Uncle Shin," I pressed on.

"Well, what more is there to say?" Aunt Sanae said. "Even though he had lots of girlfriends in high school, he didn't get serious with anyone until he passed his entrance exam. He told us it was very important for him to remain pure during his time of study. This meant he was not to be bothered by women. You might think that kind of thinking very silly, but Shin-chan was quite serious about it. He was never very good at school and it took everything he had in him to pass that exam. It was only after he'd started working that he met Kimiko-san. She worked in the cosmetics section at one of the big department stores, Takashimaya. You know, Takashimaya has a reputaion for hiring beautiful women. Anyways, I don't know how he managed to court her— he was very private about that sort of thing, but for a while he was bringing home compacts and lipsticks for us, telling us exactly how to use them. It seemed very odd behaviour for a man. After a while your mother figured it out. She looked at all the Takashimaya wrapping paper in Shin-chan's room and suddenly put it all together. "He's seeing someone there," she said to me and of course, it all made sense. I remember the day your mother and I secretly followed him to the store. When we saw her, we couldn't believe our eyes; she was so beautiful, like—"

"Yes, yes, we know," Mayumi interrupted, "beautiful like Michiko-hidenka."

My Aunt Sanae smiled. It seemed the story had been told many times before.

Beautiful like Michiko-hidenka, the crown princess, now empress of Japan. For my Aunt Sanae, Michiko-hidenka seemed the measure of a Japanese woman's beauty, poise and elegance. Aunt Sanae revered the imperial couple. When she and Mother were yet young and single, they had made the expensive trip up to Tokyo to watch the newlywed then crown prince and princess drive by in their carriage. In a cup in her china cabinet, there was a little hi-no-maru flag that she had enthusiastically waved when the royal couple had passed by. Aunt Minako, on the other hand, was not so enthusiastic about the imperial family. "A waste of taxpayer's money!" she said. "And what about those war crimes?" Nonetheless, she did agree that there was some resemblance between Kimiko-san and the crown princess. "But Nii-chan wasn't exactly bad looking himself, you know!" Aunt Minako said one afternoon. We were in a coffee shop. Aunt Sanae, who was with us, smiled and said, "Yes, there were some women disappointed when he announced his engagement."

"Some?" Aunt Minako said. "What about that table of women from his office at the reception?" She made an exaggerated motion of dabbing tearful eyes. "Really, it was very embarrassing, especially when that one woman sniffled *so* loud."

The two sisters laughed.

"That *was* funny, wasn't it?" Aunt Sanae said. "But still, it was such a beautiful wedding. So many guests and such wonderful speeches!"

"Yes, and the best part of it all was that they were so much in love. I promised myself that if I were to marry, it would be like Nii-chan."

"You mean, a love marriage?" I asked.

"Yes, none of that arranged omiai business for me," Aunt Minako said. "I thought that was just too old-fashioned."

Aunt Sanae took a sip of her tea. Her marriage had been of the old kind, through the standard means of the omiai. Uncle Kei was a banker. He and Aunt Sanae had a comfortable but loveless sort of marriage. Their children were grown up. They had not slept in the same room for years.

"Well, yes, but it was different for us. Marriage was a—" Aunt Sanae paused, searching for the words.

"A matter of function," Aunt Minako finished the sentence a little too abruptly.

"Soh desu neh," my aunt replied in agreement, although the look on her face said otherwise.

"A matter of function," she echoed, looking down at her hands. The thirty-or-more-year-old wedding band was still there, hardly gleaming but looking comfortably worn. If *that* was what a whole generation of loveless marriages had produced, the omiai didn't seem to be so bad.

Later, on the way home on the train, Aunt Minako reflected on the conversation. Omiais, she conceded, could be successful.

"Mine, for example, went well," she said. "It even led to love."

"*What?*" I said, surprised. "I thought you and Uncle Yoshi fell in love at the university."

"No," my aunt shook her head. "That was somebody else."

For a brief second, my aunt looked wistful, forlorn almost, the eyes suddenly looking much like Aunt Sanae's. *Who was it?* I wondered. Then I remembered vaguely, when I was a child, Mother being on the phone, talking a long time in Japanese. I was only about four or five; the phone call seemed interminably long, and I desperately wanted my mother back. "Mommy, play with me. Get off the phone. I want to play right now. Pleeease, Mommy, pleease." But she wasn't listening. In fact, she absently kicked at me while talking. I could hear every word. "If she came to Canada, it would do her good. She can forget about him. We'll put her up for as long as it takes. She can go to university here." All of a sudden, I stopped whining and drew near. "Who, Mommy, who?" I asked, curious. "Who's coming?" It was Auntie Minako, of course.

"Mina-chan was a very lucky girl. She got to attend university, and go to Canada. She did many things your mother and I could never have done when we were her age." That's what Aunt Sanae told me. Aunt Minako was of a different generation, she said, born after the war. Everyone agreed that Aunt Minako was bright and Grandfather especially wanted to give her the chance to be educated. He had some money left over from his trading company that he kept in trust, and when Aunt Minako passed the entrance exam to the prestigious Setoyama Gakuin University in Kyoto, he released the funds for her. All along, Aunt Minako had thought that the money had come solely from her father, and she had no idea her brother and sister had pitched in a considerable sum until one night Uncle Shin erupted in anger at her for participating in the student riots. "What are you trying to do?" he yelled. "Get expelled? Are you crazy— throwing away our money like that?" Kimiko-san refused to talk to Minako for days, until she promised to stop participating in the demonstrations. "It was a terrible blow for her," Aunt Sanae said, "but she just didn't realize how much we all had sacrificed for her already. And what was worse was that terrible infatuation she had with that student leader who was arrested. All that investment in her education— we were afraid she'd throw it all away for him. Thank goodness, your mother offered to take care of her in Canada."

That was 1969. I was about five. I remember Aunt Mimi giving me a birthday card with a big, pink number five on it. And, as I recall, Akinori would have been about the same age. It was the second time he celebrated Shichi-go-san, the festival for children aged three, five and seven. We got photos of him in the mail, all dressed up in bright silk, clapping his hands at the temple near my uncle's house. Because Akinori was the first grandson, we were constantly receiving photos of him from Grandfather, who was then still alive and living with Uncle Shin and Aunt Kimiko. The photos were always carefully wrapped in tissue paper, sent along with letters to Mother. In 1970, when the world's fair was held in Osaka, we received photos of Uncle Shin and Aunt Kimiko posing with a chubby-cheeked Akinori on the festival grounds. Aunt Kimiko was thin and beautiful, wearing chic sunglasses and a bright sundress with multi-coloured stripes. Uncle Shin stood nearby, looking sharp in his navy golf shirt and white pants. Behind them was that famous ivory-coloured tower with the golden face at the top, the trademark symbol of the fair, a gleaming pillar of progress.

A few years later I would visit that family for the first time.

"You and Akinori got on royally, as I recall," said Aunt Minako. I remembered Akinori wanting to show me everything— his candy, his toys, his games. I tentatively followed him around the house, wondering where he would take me. He seemed to be good-natured, but I was leery. Perhaps it was all his chattering in Japanese. I had never been so bombarded with the language at one time.

Still, despite Akinori's friendliness, he was nonetheless a boy and I could not immediately relate to him and his toys. I remember pleading to Mother to buy me something *I* could play with. I tugged at her arm in front of all my aunts and uncles. "Toys," I said in my simple Japanese. "I want my own toys!"

That afternoon and the days following, I was flooded with all sorts of toys imaginable. Aunt Kimiko bought me a fluffy stuffed kitten, Aunt Minako a plastic kitchen set, Aunt Sanae a doll. It seemed everyone was giving me things. My own little cache of playthings grew so big, it began to take up a part of the guest room we were staying in at my Uncle Shin's house.

Akinori stomped into the room one afternoon when I was playing with my kitten. He was holding one of his robots in his hand, a big heavy metallic thing, one arm half-wrenched out of its socket, its chipped blue fist with its plastic yellow dart pointing into the air.

"Play with me!" he demanded.

I looked up, rather annoyed. I was busy combing my kitten's hair and didn't enjoy being interrupted.

"No," I said calmly, returning to my kitten.

Ping! A plastic dart suddenly whizzed by and lodged in my kitten's ear.

"Hey!" I said angrily. "What are you doing?"

Akinori laughed coarsely. He had the robot by the arm now and was madly swinging it around.

"This'll break, you know," he said, looming closer, "and I'll say it's because of *you*."

I was suddenly terrified. The metal robot was so heavy that if it hit me, I knew it would hurt. In my memory, I can still see the bulky blue frame gleaming ominously above me as I ducked, holding the kitten over my head. "Help!" I screamed loudly in English. "HELP ME!" There was a patter of footsteps down the corridor. Just as my mother entered the door, the body of the robot clunked harmlessly onto the tatami, leaving Akinori with only the torn arm in his hand. "It's broken!" he said, bawling so hysterically I knew it was false. "She broke it!" I didn't say anything, but sat shrinking in the corner.

A few days later, Akinori got a new robot. This time, from my mother.

"Remember all the toys we had?" Akinori said, laughing, as we sat in the kotatsu. He had finished his orange and was lying back on his elbows. "Remember Gantama?" He suddenly sat up and shot his arms up into the air, forming pistols with his hands. "Bang! Bang!" he shot at the ceiling. I flinched slightly. I wondered if he *really* remembered.

"Let's go for a walk," Akinori said, getting up. "I'll take you to my favourite pachinko parlour."

It was early evening. We walked down to the station area where the lights were bright and people were bustling down the streets doing their shopping. On the way, we stopped at a tako-yaki stand where my cousin fished out some yen for a tray of the little doughy balls. He handed me a toothpick and we both picked at the balls, stuffing them into our mouths. My cousin ate hungrily. As soon as we finished, he tossed the pink tray into the garbage.

"You know," he said slowly, as we began walking again, "do you ever wonder what it would be like to *be* nothing?"

"What do you mean?" I asked.

"Well, we all have to *be* something, don't we? That's what they all tell us. *Be* responsible. *Be* an adult. *Be* a salary man. *Be* a husband, a father. But I wonder. What would it be like to *be* nothing?"

I shrugged.

Not far in the distance, I could hear the roar and hum of the pachinko parlour. Akinori quickened his step. Soon the gaudy neon building with its garish light was in sight. Inside was row upon row of pachinko machines, men and women sitting in front of them staring determinedly at the glass walls, their right hands fixed on the knob on the corner.

Akinori sat down at a nearby machine and motioned for me to sit at the one beside him. I had no idea how to play and sat mutely by. I looked at my cousin. He had begun already and was oblivious to me. He was sitting sideways on his stool, one of his legs casually crossed over the other. His tie hung loosely from the collar of his shirt. He had lit a cigarette and was holding it in one hand; the other was on the knob of the machine. The movement of his hand on the knob was slight, so slight it seemed almost a tremble, but it was enough to propel just one of the shiny round balls out of the chute and into the air where it curved up and around the top of the machine and then hurtled downwards, pulled by its own heavy metallic weight. The sound of it going down was half-musical, half-noise—the golden tines vibrated with a shivering clang each time the silver ball hit them, until the ball finally disappeared into the dark hole at the bottom of the game.

The point was to get the ball into one of the holes on the way down, whereupon a set of butterfly-like wings would snap open, triggering a flash of light and a loud pealing ring. A thunderous rush of balls would follow and the player could once more try his luck with the newly released cache at the bottom by the knob.

The thrill was small, cheap. But for Akinori it was completely engrossing.

I turned away, stood up.

"I'm leaving now," I said.

He grunted. "You know your way back, don't you?"

No, I thought, but didn't care. I had to get out of there. The light was just too blinding, the noise unbearable.

FURYO

"So you're a Canadian Nikkei, are you?" he said, peering at me above his round, gold-rimmed glasses. There was a sort of permanent smirk on his face that made everything he said seem sardonic.

He had noticed me when I was standing by myself at the water trough at the shrine entrance. I was leafing through my tour book, trying to find information on this particular site, when he came up to me— a small man in a checked shirt and jeans, a large black bag hung from a shoulder strap. His short hair was coarse, bristly.

"Need any help?" he said in clear, crisp English.

"S-sure," I stuttered. How did he know I wasn't Japanese? "It was the way you looked," he told me later. "Nikkei women are different. More relaxed in their bodies. And besides," he added, "it's not often you see a Japanese woman sightseeing alone."

His name was Peter Arakawa. A Sansei from Seattle. He had been in Kyoto for about a year, teaching English at an evenings-only conversation school near the main station.

"It's called the Kyoto Language House," he said as we walked together towards the shrine.

"I see," I nodded seriously.

He paused to look at me. The lenses of his glasses were polaroid. They were dark and it was hard to see his eyes.

"Pretty goofy name, don't you think?" he said at last.

"Oh, yes, of course," I replied, slightly embarrassed. I looked down at my hands.

"That's what struck me at first about Japan. All those funny usages of words. *Happy Bacteria. Dongari Blues. Sugar Days.*"

He looked at me again, a slight smile on his lips.

"So tell me, what are you doing here? Searching for your roots?"

The question was so abrupt, so blunt, I didn't know how to answer at first. What *was* I doing in Japan? All my friends back home had started university already.

"I— I guess," I replied, remembering what I had told my family and friends after my first visit to Japan a few years before. *I'm definitely going back and for longer.* My aunt and uncle in Kyoto were encouraging. They offered me their place to stay, suggesting I spend a year there before going to university. Kyoto, they told me, had been the ancient capital of Japan and there was a lot to see and do. It was a good place to find my true identity— my true Japanese self.

"Uh-huh," Peter nodded knowingly. "Good for you."

Good for you? The words sounded patronizing. I slowed down, slightly indignant.

"I-I don't think it's just good for me. I mean, isn't it important for anyone to find out where they came from?"

The polaroids turned to me again. I squinted. It was hard to tell what was going on behind them.

"I was just joking— the *good for you* part. I didn't mean for you to take it seriously. It's just that I've heard it so often from hakujin, that well, anyways, it's just become a bit of joke for some of us Nikkei that come over here. Not that I'm against personal quests."

"Well, then, what are *you* doing here?"

"Me?" Peter laughed. "I came here to drink."

Met a pretty interesting guy today, I wrote in my journal that night. *Pretty quirky though but first Nikkei man that actually could hold my attention. Talked a lot about things in common. Grandparents immigrating. The West Coast life. Internment. The war years. He knows a lot, I think, but kind of doesn't let on. Maybe he thinks I'm not mature enough...*

I paused, thinking about that afternoon. Just before the shrine entrance, there'd been a statue of an ox that people rubbed for good fortune. I thought It was a silly superstition and stood off, but Peter rubbed it right away. "Need all the help I can get," he said. That made me think. Later, when he wasn't looking, I rubbed it myself.

I suppose the thing is, he could be influencing me, but I'm not sure if this is good— *like when he told me I shouldn't use the word "Oriental." They don't use it in Seattle, he told me. They use "Asian." "Asian American." It was the way he told me that bothered me*— *his voice went low and sort of dark*— *as if it were an insult to refer to oneself as an Oriental. I told him where I came from we used the word "Oriental" all the time.*

My hand slipped into the drawer of my desk. A few years before, after my first trip to Japan with my father, I'd written a piece for the local Japanese-Canadian newsletter. The article was called "A Second Home." It had won an essay prize in my high school. I had brought the piece with me to show people. But now, as I looked at it, I was dismayed at how suddenly out-of-date it appeared. I had used the word "Oriental" liberally throughout the article. Peter would be appalled. I shoved the piece way back into the drawer and decided then and there that I would show it to no one. Not, at least, until the offensive word was taken out.

Peter and I saw each other regularly. He offered to be my sightseeing partner. I wanted to get through my Kyoto & Nara guidebook and see all the historical sites. Peter taught English in the evenings and had his days free. We planned our excursions on those days. We'd meet at some mutually arranged spot, usually a station convenient to the site we were planning to go to that day. I got so used to seeing him waiting for me at some station that it was hard not to imagine a Japanese eki without him. He was always early, standing off in some corner, holding a book, completely engrossed in it. I could recognize him from far off— small, slightly rugged looking, hair rumpled, round gold-framed glasses, jeans, black shoulder bag. He looked Nikkei, too, different from all the other Japanese men who streamed by in their business suits or colourful casual wear. His was a look that was completely natural, not at all self-conscious. *This is just the way I am,* his look said. So North American. "Hi, Peter," I'd have to say loudly to get his attention. He'd raise his head and then, when he saw me, he'd smile, his nose wrinkling up, the glasses sliding down just enough for me to see the small twinkling black centres of his eyes. He'd put the book back in his bag and would come towards me. Inevitably, I would ask, "So what's *that* book about?" And he'd launch into a critical explanation of the work that almost always left me in the dust.

Peter was an avid reader. The clunky black bag he was always carrying with him was filled with books. His major in college had been in English; in fact, he had an M.A. from the University of Washington.

"Not a particularly useful degree," he said, shrugging. "But good for a reader like me. Give me a book and I'm happy. I'm not into working hard. Not like a med student, anyway. That's my brother," he added with a laugh. "Someone's got to be the good Asian."

"I like to read, too," I said. "Actually, I want to be a writer."

"Really?" he said. "Have you heard of John Okada?"

"Who?"

"John Okada. He's a Nisei writer from Seattle. Wrote *No No Boy*."

I hadn't heard of the book.

"I'll lend it to you," Peter said. "You have to read it. It's a classic."

A few days later, at a coffee shop, Peter handed me a dog-eared copy of *No No Boy*. On the cover was a wild-looking black silhouette of a man with red rising suns for eyes. The picture looked very intriguing. It was the first book I had ever seen by a Japanese American.

Peter leaned back on his chair after he handed me the book.

"So tell me, what do *you* like to write about?"

"Stuff," I replied vaguely. I hated it when people asked that question. It surprised me that Peter would even ask. An English major asking such a simple question.

I put the book into my purse, wondering if it was important enough to read. I wanted to read all the classics while I was in Japan— Shakespeare, Jane Austen, James Joyce. That's what I wrote to my friends back in Canada. *Right now I'm reading* Portrait of an Artist. *It's very absorbing. In some ways, I feel very much like Stephen Daedalus.*

One of my high-school teachers had told me that to be a good writer, one had to read all the great works.

"I read *Portrait*," Peter said. "First year university. Didn't understand a thing. I still don't understand Joyce. He was a genius, all right. But in his case, it takes one to know one."

The waitress came with our coffees.

"Ah-meri-can?" she said.

I raised my hand slightly. I had ordered the "American," the weaker-style coffee. Peter always ordered Wee-na coffee. It was thicker, richer.

"Wee-na?" I said at first. "Sounds like wiener."

Peter laughed. "It stands for Wien, you know— Vienna, capital of Austria."

After our coffees, we tentatively planned our next trip. The weather was getting colder now and it seemed better for us to choose more indoor sights. I flipped through my guidebook. Where should we go next? National art museum? Medieval castle? Historic village? The choices were endless.

Whenever I called Peter, an old Japanese woman answered the phone.

"Arakawa-san desu neh? Just a minute, please."

Her footsteps would shuffle down a corridor; then there was a knock. *Ton, ton, ton.* A rattling door would slide open. "Arakawa-san, denwa desu." More footsteps, this time heavier. Then Peter's voice would come on the line.

"Hello?"

Peter told me he lived in a gesshuku. My aunt told me that meant he was renting a room. To gesshuku, or take a room, was what university students did when they came to the cities to study. My aunt was surprised Peter would live that way as an American. She told me that the rooms are usually quite small and that there was little privacy.

"The rent's cheap," Peter told me. "And the location is convenient. As long as I've got a pillow for my head and a place for my books, I can live anywhere."

His room was near the University of Kyoto. His next-door roommate was a philosophy student named Kentaro. Peter tutored him in English.

"I don't charge him much," he said, adding with a chortle, "I just let him pay for my drinks afterwards."

Peter liked to talk about his drinking. He usually mentioned it at least once in our conversations. "It was so cold last night I had to get a drink to warm up." "I went out to the bar with Kentaro the other night." "My students took me out for a drink." "I was out drinking until two in the morning." The way he spoke about it made you think he was constantly drunk. He sounded like a different person at night than the one I knew in the afternoon. I could never meet Peter in the evenings. He taught at night in different places all over the Kyoto area, and because my aunt worried about me, I always returned right home after our daytime rendezvous to have supper with the family. Afterwards, I'd help my aunt tutor some local kids in English.

When I told my aunt about Peter's drinking habits, she frowned and said, "He sounds like a bit of a furyo." I looked up the word *furyo* in the dictionary. It meant *rebel*, delinquent.

Once I called Peter that by mistake. It just slipped out.

"What did you call me?" He said.

"Furyo."

"Must mean something bad if it starts with *fu*." He said, his eyes darting up past the little black lenses of his glasses. "Fu" was a negative prefix in Japanese.

When we met the next time, he told me he'd looked up the word. I felt embarrassed.

"Yeah, that's about right," he said rather jocularly, "furyo. That's me."

After that he often referred to himself as "The Furyo," as if he were a disembodied character acting out a personality not his own. "The Furyo and Kentaro were discussing Nietzsche one day until they got so drunk they couldn't understand each other." "The Furyo doesn't like gin, but prefers Scotch." "The Furyo met some cute girls at the bar yesterday."

Peter and I always spoke in English. I never did find out how much Japanese he really knew. He told me he envied me being able to speak so much.

"I didn't learn a word of the language until I was in university," he said, shrugging. "By that time, it's too late."

I had been forced to go to Japanese language school by my parents. It had been started up by new immigrants. Peter was surprised.

"You had a language school?" he said incredulously. "I thought those things disappeared after the war. We didn't have a school when I was growing up. My parents wouldn't have anything to do with us learning Japanese. We had to be American."

When Peter said that, I remembered the tantrum I had when I was fourteen and didn't want to go to Japanese school. It was on Friday nights for three hours and it was boring. "I'm a Canadian," I yelled at my parents. "I won't ever need this language. I hate Japanese!" For my mother's sake, I yelled all this in Japanese. She was a post-war immigrant who had married my Dad, a Kika-Nisei. Dad had been born in Canada, but his family had been "repatriated" to Japan after the war. When Dad was old enough, he later "repatriated" himself back to his country of origin— Canada. *Kika* meant "return."

When I spoke to Mom, I used garbled Japanese— enough to get me by; when I spoke to Dad it was English, clear and smooth. Things sounded so different in those languages. When I spoke to Mother, my voice went higher and the syllables grew rounded and were mispronounced like a child's. When I spoke to Dad, my voice was low, authoritative, in command of my thoughts and ideas.

It was Dad's idea to take me to Japan when I was in grade ten at high school. He himself hadn't been back in years. He wanted me to visit the land of my roots. "It's important to know where your ancestors come from," he said. After that trip, I changed my attitude towards being Japanese. That was when I wrote the article "A Second Home."

Peter told me a lot of interesting stories about his family— stories of his grandfather's immigration, of his family's internment in Tule Lake, of his uncle's death in Europe as a soldier in a famous Nisei regiment. I told him what I knew of my family, bits and pieces I had heard from my one Nisei great aunt, the only one in my family who spoke freely about the past, who told me in half-whispers how terrible the whole internment experience was. There was a similarity between our stories. When we talked about this common past, it felt like we had been friends forever. It was the way an old class reunion must feel like, I thought— people getting together, asking each other questions like, *So where were your folks relocated? Where did they resettle?*

"Do you ever think about writing these stories?" Peter asked me once.

I shrugged. "I don't think I have enough information."

"Sure, you do," Peter said. "Listen to yourself; you already know quite a bit. You should interview your relatives. You'd be surprised at what they'd tell you."

"Baachan!" I yelled out to my grandmother as she pushed her dusty cart full of gardening tools towards the garden. She didn't hear me, but kept going, the wheels creaking and groaning. I hurried to catch up.

"Baachan!"

She stopped and turned her head around vaguely. Slowly she drew a hand to her ear. She was so small, her tiny frame clothed in the faded kasuri— the cotton garb of Japanese farm-folk— that she looked almost childlike, except for her wrinkled brown skin and her silver grey hair clumped in a matted bun at the back of her head. Her face was round and weathered, like an old stone that had travelled down a steep mountain.

Baachan had spent half her life in Canada, half in Japan. She had been born in Vancouver Cannery. My great aunt (the one who spoke in half-whispers) was Baachan's younger sister. She told me that Baachan had been separated from the family when she was eleven and sent to Japan by my great-grandfather for her education. Instead of being put with a childless family as was initially agreed, she was mistakenly put with a family of ten, who, of course, had no feelings of tenderness for her. She basically became their live-in help. When she came back to Canada, she was sixteen. Her English was ragged by then and my aunt said she and her brother had difficulty communicating with her. "We pretty well left her alone," my aunt shrugged. "What could we do? We could barely communicate." Baachan had an arranged marriage to a cousin a few years later. They bought a strawberry farm near New Westminster and started a family. Then, of course, the war came. They lost everything; the family was interned in Slocan. Grandfather was sick of Canada by then. When the Canadian government offered repatriation, he immediately signed up his family. They went to Japan and started farming a parcel of land their relatives had procured for them. Baachan had not been back to Canada since.

Everything I knew about Baachan came from my aunt. Baachan herself was not a big talker. When I first came to Japan, she shook my hand and welcomed me. Yoh-ko-so, she said, and that was all. I was sixteen then and wasn't particularly interested in talking to her much; my cousins seemed far more fascinating. But this time, I realized I wanted to talk to *her* more.

"Baachan, what do you remember about Canada?" I blurted. The question seemed startlingly direct. I thought of Peter immediately— his influence on me.

Baachan stared right up at me, her eyes glinting like dark, wet pebbles. She did not speak for a long time, but slowly breathed in and out. She was looking past me, beyond me; I was afraid she had not understood my question.

"From Canada someone come," she spoke slowly in barely a whisper. I bent down closer.

"What?"

"Last year, visitor from Canada."

"Who?" I didn't know of any relatives who had visited Baachan recently.

"Visitor my friend long ago Canada Surrey," she said, slurring the words together. *What visitor?* I wondered. *Was she talking about me?*

"Long time ago, my friend. Nakajima-san. Want to take me to Canada, but too old, too old." Baachan shook her head and with that, firmly began pushing her cart down to the garden.

That night, when the family was watching TV, I casually asked my uncle about what Baachan had said.

"Visitor from Canada? Hmm." He rubbed his chin thoughtfully.

"She said the name 'Nakajima.'"

"Ah— *Nakajima-san!*" My uncle's face suddenly lit up. He shook his head slightly. "It was very strange. Last fall, he came. An older Nikkei. Maybe seventy, seventy-five. Anyway, we didn't know who he was. Just drove up in a car, come up to the house like that. He asked to see Shoko-san. So we took him out to Baachan. She was out in the garden as usual. They started talking. We didn't know what was going on; we just watched from the house. Then Baachan and he finally came in. She makes him some ocha— she insisted on doing it herself— and then she tells us that this fellow Nakajima-san is an old friend from Canada. Actually, he's an old boyfriend. He tells us so. He spoke very plainly, directly. He and Baachan wanted to get married, but her father had arranged something already for her. She couldn't say no to her father, so they broke it off. He got married to someone else a few years later, moved to Victoria. He and his wife had some children. Then the war came. They were interned in Tashme. After that they went out east, Toronto, he said. They stayed there a long time. His kids grew up. Then his wife died three years ago. He started wondering what happened to Baachan. He'd heard she'd come to Japan. He phoned a few people— maybe one of them was your dad— anyway, he finally got an address. He wrote to her, told her he was coming. He wanted to propose, he said. That was why he was here. He wanted to take her back to Canada with him."

"So, what happened?"

"She said no. She said she was too old and she would miss her grandchildren." My uncle shook his head. "Yes, it was all very strange. Strange, indeed."

"No kidding!" Peter said when I told him the story. We were strolling through one of Kyoto's parks at the height of the cherry-blossom season. "That's very romantic! Why don't you write about it?"

"We-ll, I don't know," I said, shrugging. "The way my uncle told it, it sounded anti-climactic. If I hadn't asked him about it, he probably wouldn't have ever told me. I don't think they're used to thinking about their lives as stories…"

"Too busy living them to think about the beauty of them, I guess, eh?" Peter smiled. He paused to stare at a tree laden with cherry blossoms. "That's their generation for you. Work till they drop. But someone's got to tell their stories, make them real, you know."

"Still," I said. "I'm not entirely sure this would make a good story."

I pictured Baachan's story to be the kind I'd seen occasionally in the drugstore— the long immigrant saga of a family trying to survive against cruelty and prejudice in the new world. The opening pages would contain a family tree and the cover would have a glossy image of a geisha-looking female in the embrace of a swashbuckling muscled Californian at the turn of the century. Gaudy chop-suey-like letters would be embossed in the spine in gold. The title would have the word "courtesan" or "dragon" in it. The story would be so far from the truth it would be laughable. *No thanks,* I thought. I had other plans for my writing.

I had been thinking a lot about stories lately, wondering if they could be anything you wanted them to be. Who said there had to be a beginning, a middle, and an end? What if there was a story that was just a series of unconnected moments— moments that left only a vague impression, fleeting and light, of a person or a place?

"Sure," Peter said. "Anything goes in art. You've got to experiment. But whatever you do"— he leaned over and looked me straight in the eye— "don't stop writing."

Zen. For a while that's all we saw. Zen rock gardens. Zen temples. Zen monasteries. There was an American man in my Japanese class (I was taking advanced Japanese three times a week) who used to be a monk. He told me where his "home" temple was, so I decided to visit it with Peter one afternoon. When I told Peter why, he shook his head and said, "Another white guy doing the Zen thing. Probably from California."

It was true. Amos *was* white and from San Francisco.

"They've got this fascination with Buddhism," Peter told me. "But they don't fundamentally understand what it is."

Fundamentally. The way he said the word was emphatic.

I nodded my head sympathetically, but I didn't know a thing about Buddhism either, except for what Amos had told me. My mother was thoroughly Christian. We prayed to the Kami-sama in heaven whose son, Iiyesu Kirisuto, died for our sins. My mother had been converted by American missionaries when she was sixteen.

Peter's family was Buddhist. *Jodo Shinshu* Buddhist, he said, to distinguish it from Zen. Of course, I didn't know the difference, but was too timid to ask.

"A lot of the early Issei immigrants were Jodo Shinshu," Peter told me.

If that were the case, it was likely that my great aunt on my father's side was Jodo Shinshu, too. In her house, she had a little box that looked like an old mandarin crate painted black. It was the family altar. There was a faded gold picture inside of a pencil-thin looking god that looked like a matchstick with its head on fire. In front of the picture was an array of old photos of dead relatives I had never met.

My great aunt never talked about her religion the way a lot of the Christians I knew did. The only thing I remember her telling me about it was when I asked her— I was about eight or nine— why she put a little gold cup with rice in it on the altar shelf every night. She said that it was for her mother and father. "They're watching out for us," she said. "That's why we have to say thank you."

"Zen is not really like that." Peter explained to me. "They don't believe much in venerating their ancestors. In Zen, finding your true self is something you do on your own. No history, no parents, no anything. I think that's why it's appealing to rational-minded Westerners. They don't like to think they can use other people's help, least of all their ancestors'."

We walked the grounds of the temple, our feet crunching noisily on the gravel. It was the first clear day in weeks. June was tsuyu— the start of the rainy season. We both carried umbrellas with us now, just in case. As we rounded the corner to head to the main hall, we saw two bald-headed monks, a younger one and an older one, pass by.

"One good thing about Zen is the master-disciple relationship." Peter nodded at the monks. "It's invaluable."

The main meditation hall was supposed to be the star attraction of this temple. When we got there, no one was there. It was dark and completely empty inside. The air smelled damp. I looked around, curious, trying to find something to focus my eye on. There was no altar or statue anywhere. Peter was standing perfectly still behind me. I did not know how far away he was from me, but I could sense his breathing. It was steady and calm.

"Look up," he said softly.

I turned my head up to the ceiling and was startled to see a massive and spectacular painting of a dragon coiled around and around itself in a big circle.

"Meditate on *that*," he said.

We stood staring at the huge entity. The painted scales and fins shone dully in the dim light. Its belly seemed to expand with each breath now rising and falling in tandem with Peter's and mine. Soon it seemed to swim in the wide circle of the ceiling, a slow aqueous dance, the faraway rhythm of its heart pounding its life through our own silent breathing. For a moment, I glimpsed a monk's pleasure in this hall— this bright circle of entwined life, breathing as surely as we were, in this austere dimness.

August— in Japan, the hottest and most humid month. The air was heavy with thick sunshine that condensed on your skin in beads of sweat. My aunt gave me a handkerchief for my outings, told me to discreetly wipe my brow with it when it got too hot. Peter and I met frequently— sometimes even two or three times a week. I was returning to Canada in early September to start university and time was running out; I still wanted to see as much as possible. We spoke little now on our travels; it was probably the heat, but we had also grown comfortable with one another. In crowded intersections, I would slip my arm into the crook of his bag and he would gently lead me through the swirling melee of people. He was a much better navigator than I was and I trusted his sense of direction.

When we arrived at a site, we would peruse it quietly, Peter only occasionally adding a comment here and there. I no longer felt the need to *blab*, for I'd come to the realization that what I'd been doing earlier was really just blabbing. There was a way of talking now between us where silence was necessary and welcome. Peter once said that in Japanese art, it was the spaces and silences that shaped the form of the object. And *that*, in my mind, had become the art of our communication.

Silence drew out the sounds of nature— buzzing cicadas, chirping birds, croaking frogs. Space heightened the simple object— the vase with the crooked vine, the scroll with the stark black kanji, the ceiling with the coiling dragon. "Everything here is for the pleasure of the eye," Peter said. "Even you." By a circular window in an old imperial villa where the lush green stalks of bamboo were captured perfectly as if in a frame hung in a gallery, he said that to me— "even you"— although I pretended not to hear it.

"I'm going to Korea at the end of the month to renew my visa," he told me then, his eyes drifting towards the window. "So, I guess we won't..." his voice trailed off. The end of the month— how far away was that? I did a quick mental calculation. It was about two weeks from now. I thought of my guidebook; I'd covered a little over half. A strange, almost sickly desperation filled my heart. I wouldn't be able to see everything after all. I wouldn't be able to go with Peter.

We sat in silence. A soft wind rustled through the bamboo, blew gently through the window. A strand of hair fell onto my cheek.

"Your hair," he said softly. "It's gotten longer since I met you."

"I never cut it," I brushed the strand aside. "I wanted it to grow long, you know, like a Heian princess'."

I meant it as a kind of joke, but Peter did not laugh.

"Ah," he said, turning away again to the window. A shaft of sunlight passed through a space in the grove, momentarily bathing his face in light. His glasses started growing darker. By the time we left, I could no longer see his eyes at all.

"It's so hot!" I complained to my aunt. "Everything I wear just sticks."

"Why don't you buy a summer dress?" she suggested. "It'll be cooler."

We went to the department store that afternoon and looked at several light cotton dresses. I finally picked one out— a breezy cream-coloured one-piece that slipped over my body like water.

"You'll have to buy a slip with that or wear some flesh-coloured underwear," my aunt advised.

"Uh-huh," I nodded, looking at myself in the mirror. The dress didn't seem that see-through to me. And besides, I didn't want to wear a slip. That would make it too hot and uncomfortable.

"Iroke ga detteru, neh," my aunt stepped back, looked at me. "It must be your age."

Iro-ke— I'd never heard that word before. When I got home, I looked it up in the dictionary. It meant several things— romantic, naive, coquettish, amorous, to arrive at the age of sensuality.

I wore the new dress the next time I met Peter. It was to be our last time together. We planned to see as many sites as we could in this one picturesque district of Kyoto near the mountains. It was a warm day, sunny and clear, perfect for sightseeing. The district we were going to was only accessible by streetcar, so we boarded one close to where we had met. It was full of people, jostling around to get in and out. Peter quickly motioned me to sit down on an open seat he'd found. I sat down, my dress swooshing at the edges. The old woman beside me frowned disapprovingly. Peter shot me a smile. I remembered his comment: *Nikkei women are more relaxed in their bodies.*

Peter reached with his right hand for one of the hanging hand straps. Then he squarely positioned himself in front of me. I could see his torso— he was wearing a very light checked blue shirt, opened in a vee at the front. His breathing was even and steady. Through the light blue of the cloth, I noticed Peter's stomach and chest. He was not wearing an undershirt as were so many of the Japanese men I saw on the train. I could make out the shape of his nipples, and his firm abdomen. I had not noticed his body before. My eyes flickered away to my hands in my lap. They were curled together on the white plane of my dress as if holding an imaginary bouquet. I didn't know where else to put them. Out of the corner of my eye, I could see a young Japanese woman sitting not far from me. She, too, was wearing a dress and sitting very properly, her knees tightly together, hands clutched firmly in her lap, head slightly lowered, eyes to the ground.

The streetcar lurched to a stop and a crowd of people swarmed in. The force of the incoming passengers pushed Peter closer in to me so that his legs pressed against my knees. His chest bulged into the air in front of me. I could see his left hand clutching the pouch he always carried with him. His hand was small and tanned, the fingers long and sinewy.

We got off at the next stop. There was some distance to walk to get to the place we wanted to see first— an imperial villa. The street leading up to it was completely nondescript, lined with small concrete buildings that looked like apartments. There were no colourful signs or shops to be seen anywhere. I picked up my step, eager to get to the villa.

Peter, however, lingered, scrutinizing the buildings as if he were an architect. A black car that looked like an import pulled out of the garage of one of the buildings. The side windows were tinted so you couldn't see who was inside. The driver was wearing a uniform with a cap and gloves. Must be a rich area, I thought. Then from another building just up ahead of us, a couple emerged onto the street. They blinked at the brightness of the sun. The man was older, a salary-man in a business suit; the woman was young and very prim-looking in a white dress. The only part of her that looked slightly dishevelled was her hair; it looked like it hadn't been combed at all. The man hailed a cab and then assisted the woman into it. He didn't get in himself, but waited for it to drive off before he started to walk away.

Peter stood watching the whole thing.

"It's just a couple," I said, impatient to get on.

"But they came out of *there*." Peter nodded at the building. He walked up ahead to where they had been. The entry was dark and I couldn't see anything.

"So?"

"So what is a businessman doing with a young woman in a building like that at two thirty in the afternoon?"

He looked up at the building again. I followed his eyes.

"Odd, isn't it, that there are no windows?"

He was right. There were no windows in the building at all. Just then a female intercom voice came from the darkened entryway.

"Irrashaimase. Would you like to come in?"

How did it— the voice— know we were standing there? I stepped towards the entrance and caught a glimpse of a woman standing at a glass wicket. Peter suddenly grabbed my elbow and pushed me ahead up the street.

"What are you doing?" I said, indignantly.

"We don't want to go in there," he said. "*It's a love hotel.*"

"What? Oh..." My gaze fluttered to the ground and my cheeks flushed red.

We walked in silence up the road to the villa. I kept thinking of that woman in the white dress, her dishevelled hair, the little nod she gave to the man as he closed the door of the taxi. She did not look any older than me.

Soon we arrived at the villa. It was tucked back into the mountainside in an immaculately kept but lush section of land. My guidebook said that the emperor often came here with his favourite concubine to spend his summer evenings watching the moon rise over the capital. As we padded through the spare hallways and rooms of the villa, I imagined what it would be like to be a woman in that era, my heavy, layered gowns rustling behind me, my hair a shimmering river of black trailing down to the ground.

We stopped to sit in front of a veranda that opened up to the garden. Leafy stalks of bamboo quivered in the distance. To the left and right were shapely pine shrubs and brightly blooming camellia bushes. Cicadas droned languidly in the warm, humid air.

It was getting hot. I pulled out my aunt's handkerchief and patted my brow just as I had seen many Japanese women do. When I was about to put it back into my purse, I noticed Peter staring at me.

"It's funny about that hotel back there, isn't it?" he said softly.

"She was too young for him," I said immediately.

Peter laughed. "I wasn't thinking about *her*."

He stood up awkwardly.

"So, where shall we go next?"

There was a well-known Buddhist temple not far from the villa. It was supposed to have spectacular guardian sculptures encased in a wooden tower gate that one could climb up. According to my guidebook, one of the emperor's wives had come to this temple to "flee the world" and become a nun.

"I can't imagine doing that," I said to Peter as we approached the towering wooden gateway. "There's too much to see and do in the world."

The guardian sculptures in the gates were huge, well over ten feet. They were set in wooden enclaves that formed the pillars of each side of the gate. Both statues looked ferocious, their eyes bulging out of their heads, their muscled arms and thick chests rippling with demonic strength.

"Man in heat," Peter joked.

Looking at the sculptures, I thought of Peter in the streetcar, his taut chest and firm stomach. My gaze fell onto his arm leaning on a post, the thin ribbon of muscle quivering above his wristwatch.

We walked behind one of the sculptures into the tower where there was a steep, narrow staircase that wound upwards. I paused, wondering how I could climb this gracefully.

"You want to go up, don't you?" Peter asked.

I nodded. "The guidebook said the view of the city from the top was spectacular. It's just that—"

"I know, your dress. Don't worry, I'll go first. You follow me."

He climbed up agilely, while I, being very careful, trod slowly on the small wooden steps. When I reached the top, he politely extended his hand to pull me up. It seemed he was being more delicate with me than usual— or was it just me sensing something different in him? We walked down the narrow corridor that formed the bridge part of the gate. It resembled a huge balcony. On one side was a railing with a view open to the city, and on the other side was a wall covered with old paintings. Peter paused to inspect them. They were yellowed and faded, but the solitary male figures in them were clearly discernible.

"These are holy men," Peter said.

Peter pointed to one particular painting. It was of a grizzled old warrior, dressed in rags, carrying a sword. He held the sword up as if he were going to bring it down on something, but the look on his face was calm, placid. Peter bent closer to the picture, squinted at it. Then he muttered something to himself. His body went stiff and his arms tightened as he grasped an imaginary hilt in his fists. He spread his legs a little, mimicking the stance of the ragged warrior.

"What are you doing?" I asked, intrigued.

"Practising his stance," he said. "That's *my* holy man."

I looked again at the painting. The shadowy, smoke-coloured figure, stained and darkened by age, was barely discernible, but now it held the power of some distant vision, some way of discerning who Peter *really* was.

"*Your* holy man?" I said. "But why?"

"Because he is what I came here for," Peter answered cryptically. He smiled, the curve of his lip slightly sardonic. "You didn't really think I was a furyo, did you?"

"What do you mean?" I said, confused.

"You didn't think I came all the way here just to teach English, drink beer, and read books?"

"I-I d-don't know what to think," I stuttered. "I only know what you tell me."

"Ah," he said, turning to the picture.

"I came here for him. A master of the sword. A good sensei to teach me the right way. The true way to do kendo."

Kendo. Suddenly his whole body made sense to me, the hard taut chest, the sinewy arms, the agility, the calmness of his breathing. The whole of his purpose in Japan immediately became real, palpable as it was for me each time I stepped into palaces and temples to find the heart of my imagined place— my kokoro, my Japanese heart. I felt suddenly embarrassed that I had not sensed the similarity of our journeys. I had been too engrossed in myself to know or care that others might trace the same steps in search of themselves.

I turned to the picture. With Peter's revelation, it suddenly came alive. I wanted to know everything I could about that ragged warrior. What was he after? What was *he* trying to kill?

"Probably his desire," Peter muttered rather flippantly. He turned to me and stared. We did not speak for several seconds. His glasses were dark and I could not see through them at all, but I could *feel* his eyes on me.

We moved to the other side, to the railing that overlooked the city. Just as the guidebook had said, the view was spectacular. The day was clear and cloudless. I looked out at the vast splendour of Kyoto— so much of which I had seen with Peter— spread out before me. *So,* this *was the beautiful world,* I thought. What would ever make that nun reject it? A light breeze ruffled my hair. I closed my eyes and let it blow against my face. It felt refreshing. Then I felt something warm against the side of my hand. Peter had inched his hand on the rail so that his little finger had curled over mine.

He was looking straight ahead and not at me. There was a firmness in his jaw, a determination in his face that seemed almost cold, and yet his finger pressed over mine was hot and the rest of his hand curled tightly around the rail as if it were the hilt of a sword.

We stood like that for a long time, neither of us speaking a word. My heart was beating hard and my body throbbed as if all the heat of the sun were pressing down upon me— my face, my neck, my shoulders. Below us was the street we had just walked on, the cool blue tiled roofs of the hotels clearly visible.

When I got home late that evening, I felt exhausted, my body drooping with the wilt of the day's heat and from the nervous, self-conscious tension of being in a dress. As I was about to go upstairs, my uncle called out to me from the kitchen. He had just come home from overtime work and was having a late supper. My aunt and cousins had already gone to bed.

"You're later than me today," he said. "That's unusual. What did you do?"

I told him I had spent the day— the whole glorious day— with Peter.

"That American Nikkei from Seattle?"

I nodded.

"Where did you go?"

"Places," I answered vaguely. I went over to look at myself in the living-room mirror. My dress had gone all wrinkled and my hair flat and limp from the heat.

"It's funny," I said, remembering Peter's body. "He told me today that he did kendo. He never mentioned it before. Not once, the whole time we knew each other."

"Really?" my uncle said. He shook his head. "You Nikkei. You come here to find your roots and you end up being more Japanese than the Japanese."

"You think?" I said rather absently. I looked at the figure in the mirror. She seems so Japanese, I thought, hardly recognizing her— a woman in a white dress. I twisted a loose strand of hair around my finger and then let it drop, watching the reflection to see if it would do the same thing.

I quietly padded upstairs to my room, closed the door, and slid open my drawer. There was my journal. I opened it from the beginning and found the first mention of Peter's name. I traced over the letters of my handwriting carefully. *P - e - t - e - r*. Then I found the next mention and the next, each entry filled with more and more of his presence, until at last I arrived at this day; this day when I could only write down, with bittersweet yearning, his name, over and over again. *Peter, Peter, Peter.*